GARY ARMS

Jack DeWitt is Clueless

 | Books

Published by Advantage, Charleston, South Carolina.
Member of Advantage Media.

ADVANTAGE is a registered trademark, and the Advantage colophon is a trademark of Advantage Media Group, Inc.

Printed in the United States of America.

10 9 8 7 6 5 4 3 2 1

ISBN: 978-1-64225-928-5 (Paperback)
ISBN: 978-1-64225-927-8 (eBook)

Cover artwork and design by Beatrice Schares.

This publication is designed to provide accurate and authoritative information in regard to the subject matter covered. It is sold with the understanding that the publisher is not engaged in rendering legal, accounting, or other professional services. If legal advice or other expert assistance is required, the services of a competent professional person should be sought.

Advantage Media helps busy entrepreneurs, CEOs, and leaders write and publish a book to grow their business and become the authority in their field. Advantage authors comprise an exclusive community of industry professionals, idea-makers, and thought leaders. Do you have a book idea or manuscript for consideration? We would love to hear from you at **AdvantageMedia.com**.

For Susie

Contents

Acknowledgement

A lot of kind people read the early chapters of this book. When I finished writing a chapter, I would ask if anyone wanted to read it. Eventually, I had a crew of loyal readers. It is impossible to exaggerate how much their praise and encouragement helped me to continue. Special thanks to Scott Gurman, who suggested I write this book, Geoff Klein, David Rash, Glenda Nelson, Lenelle Freeman, Robert Cox, Rebecca Hamm, Joe Arms, Darrell Arms, Craig Arms, Carol Ryan Sullivan, Ken Love, Colin Morton, Bob Pelelo, Lisa Steinle, Jenn Sill, Jim Butler, Maureen Butler, and Madison Rhymes. I am grateful to Mary Wente for connecting me to the publisher Megan Drake, to Evan Schnittman for his advice, and to Bea Schares for designing the cover.

1

I Ruin Mother's Day

At an early age, I found out I was traveling down the road to hell.

One Sunday, we were coming home from church when I had a revelation. My dad was driving. It was 1958, and men still did all the driving. Pregnant with my sister Lois, Mom was on the passenger side holding baby Ron in her arms. I (the second oldest kid) was in the back seat with my younger brother Dean and my sister Ellen (the oldest). Gazing out the window at nothing in particular, daydreaming, seven years old, I experienced my revelation.

Earlier that day, when I was in Sunday School, our teacher had told us about Saint Paul. He was riding a donkey to Damascus when he experienced his revelation. It hit him like a ton of bricks and knocked him right off the donkey. That is what a revelation can do to you.

I let out a whoop and announced to my entire family, "Hey, we don't have to go to church anymore!"

My little brother Dean laughed.

My dad, operating the gear shift, said, "What'd that kid say?"

With the utter confidence of someone who has just had the Truth revealed to him, I said, "There's no Santa Claus. People just say that to fool little kids. There's no Tooth Fairy or Easter Bunny neither. And you know what? *There's no God!"*

My dad hit the brakes hard.

The rest of my day did not go well.

I am not sure how the news that the church contained an apostate child leaked out but, from then on, I was considered a dubious character. Certain old ladies took the extreme view that I might be demon-possessed. I had that "look."

Two incidents occurred three years later when I was ten years old that convinced the congregation that Satan had indeed found purchase in my soul.

The first incident occurred in Sunday School class. At our church, kids and adults went to Sunday School first and then proceeded to regular church. Our teacher, an elderly widow named Mrs. Tope, was a sub. Our usual teacher, nice Mrs. Robin was in the hospital having a baby, her tenth. Childless Mrs. Tope had been asked to fill in at the last minute. Mrs. Tope told us that Mrs. Robin had failed to tell her where she kept the plans for our usual assignment, so she was going to have to improvise. We were going to spend the hour reading bible verses and explaining what they meant to us. She said I could start. Many times, she had seen me with my nose in a book, so she had no doubt I could read. She opened her bible, a large one with a leather cover and gilded edges. She found a verse, pointed to it, and told me to go ahead. "Jack DeWitt will read the verse and tell us what it means to him."

I said no thank you. "Since I do not believe in God, I do not care to read the bible. It doesn't mean anything to me." I don't know what possessed me to say such a thing out loud.

The other kids stared at me in wonder.

I helpfully pushed Mrs. Tope's bible over to another kid, Becky Willard, and told her to please read the verse. "You believe in God, don't you? YOU read it."

Mrs. Tope said, "Becky, do not get involved in his nonsense." She raised her chin, gazed at me coolly and said, "Jack DeWitt WILL read the verse."

I looked into the eyes of Mrs. Tope. She looked into mine. Her lips narrowed and her nostrils expanded. I wondered if she was only a moment away from slapping my face.

"No, thank you," I said. I took hold of the bible.

"Jack DeWitt, you will!" cried Mrs. Tope.

I flung the bible.

It bounced off the wall and landed on the floor.

The other kids gasped. I did too. The Word of God! Flung through the air! Sprawling on the floor!

Becky jumped up, retrieved the bible from the floor, opened it at random and read a verse. "It means a lot to me!" she said. "It means we should be Good!"

I felt I was in the midst of a miracle. Mrs. Tope did not slap me. She allowed the Word of God to be passed from kid to kid. Each of them found a verse and read it, and then passed the bible to the next kid.

The whole time, not one person looked at me. It was as if I had become invisible.

As soon as class was over, Mrs. Tope went straight to my mother and told her what had happened.

My mother did not say a word to me during the church service. The whole time the pastor preached, I sat beside her, wondering if, later in the day, perhaps after dinner, I would be executed.

My mother took an entire day to come up with what she hoped would be an appropriate punishment, one that would accomplish two tasks. She wanted to humble me, and she wanted to demonstrate to the entire congregation that, no matter what they had recently heard from Mrs. Tope, I was not completely and irredeemably wicked.

We were on the verge of Mother's Day, one of the most popular days in the entire church calendar, as important almost as Easter Sunday. For that special May morning, the entire congregation assembled in the sanctuary for the Ceremony of Flowers. We would celebrate mothers and then we would go to our various Sunday School classes.

The church was packed. I sat up front with my class and Mrs. Robin, who was holding her brand-new baby, a girl. I located Mrs. Tope; she was sitting safely several pews away from me, on the other side of the church. My mother was seated at the very back in the last pew. She had been required to help with the flowers. By the time she finished her chore, almost all the pews had filled up with people, and so she had been unable to sit in the middle of the church with my father and had to sit in the back with the late comers. My siblings except for baby Ron were sitting behind or in front of me with their Sunday School classes. My father was holding baby Ron.

The railing at the front of the church was lined with pots of flowers: carnations, irises, African violets, and daffodils. Each pot was labeled. The Mom with the Youngest Child (that one would go to Mrs. Robin). The Oldest Mother. The Youngest Mother. The Mother with the Most Children (that one would also go to Mrs. Robin). The Mother of Triplets. The Tallest Mom. The Shortest Mom. The Mom with the Most Girls. The Mom with the Most Boys. The women who organized the ceremony did their best to ensure that every mother got a pot of flowers. That is the chore my mother had been doing, making up labels for mothers that were otherwise hard to categorize. The Mother with Blonde Hair Wearing a Red Hat and a Polka Dot Dress. The Mom who Recently Had Her Appendix Removed. The Mom Whose Middle Name is Ruth.

Before the Awarding could begin, the pastor's wife came to the front and told us the congregation was in for a Special Treat. Young Jack DeWitt was going to recite a Mother's Day poem, "Mother o' Mine"

4

by Rudyard Kipling.

That recitation was to be my punishment. It was designed to humble and redeem me.

This is the entire poem:

Mother o' Mine
If I were hanged on the highest hill,
Mother o' mine, O mother o' mine!
I know whose love would follow me still,
Mother o' mine, O mother o' mine!
If I were drowned in the deepest sea,
Mother o' mine, O mother o' mine!
I know whose tears would come down to me,
Mother o' mine, O mother o' mine!
If I were damned of body and soul,
I know whose prayers would make me whole,
Mother o' mine, O mother o' mine!

It had not taken me five minutes to memorize this poem. In fact, I memorized it so effortlessly I asked my mother if perhaps I could commit to memory a few more poems, longer ones with more difficult words. My mother assured me this would not be necessary. The mere fact that I was not reading the poem from a piece of paper but dramatically reciting it would thrill my listeners right down to their toes.

All week, before I went to school, my mother coached me on my inflections and gestures. My recitation would be a sensation, the highlight of the Mother's Day ceremony. When I uttered the heart-rending phrase "mother o' mine" for the final time, there would not be a dry eye in the sanctuary. When I finished and bowed, the entire congregation would leap to its feet and cheer.

The moment arrived. I made my way to the front of the church and looked out at the congregation. In front of me was a sea of faces.

All the Sunday School classes were there. Grandpas and Grandmas, Moms and Dads. All of them were staring directly at me.

I went blank.

"Go ahead, dear," the pastor's wife said.

I could not remember a single word of the poem. I stammered. I opened my mouth and sounds emerged, but they were not understandable English words.

In the back of the room, my mother saw it happening. She saw I had completely lost my mind and decided to help me. She shouted, "Mother o' Mine."

I shouted back, "Mother o' Mine." And stopped. The congregation moved uneasily in their pews and waited for me to continue.

I could not recall another word of the poem.

From the back, my mother shouted, "If I were hanged!"

Hoping if I got started, I would remember the rest of the poem, I shouted, "If I were hanged!" I looked imploringly at my mother.

"On the highest!" my mom shouted.

"Hill!" I shouted back.

The congregation began to laugh.

That is how my mother and I got through the poem, by shouting at one another.

"Mother o' mine! Mother o' mine!"

"O' mine! O' mine!"

"If I were drowned!"

"In the deepest SEA!"

The congregation seemed to become a single entity, all of them laughing, all of them trying not to. Each time we yelled the hideous phrase "Mother o' mine!" they laughed. They could not help it. It is a wonder they did not shout the phrase with us. It was as if my mother and I were trapped in a nightmarish duet.

At last we arrived at the final line, "Mother o' mine, O Mother o' mine!" Mom and I screamed it in in unison, and I remembered to bow.

I don't know how my mom felt about our performance, but I felt numb. Shell shocked. I wasn't entirely sure I was still alive.

Led by the pastor's wife, the audience clapped. By then, they pitied me. The older ladies wished they could run to the front and hug me.

"Thank you, dear," said the pastor's wife. "Now, we will conduct the Dispensing of the Flowers."

I went back to my seat. My classmates scooted aside so I could sit in the pew. None of them dared to look at me for more than a moment.

For the rest of the ceremony I was in a fog. My ears rang and I breathed through my mouth. My face burned.

When the Dispensing of the Flowers ended, we were sent back to our classrooms for Sunday School. We children were going to get a lesson on how a mother's love for her child is similar to God's love for everyone and then we were going to construct special Mother's Day cards expressing our love for our moms.

I sat down in a chair. No one spoke to me, no one wanted to sit beside me.

A boy in our class, Ricky Fox, was a Scout. To earn a much-prized merit badge, he had constructed a large cross made of matchsticks. The back of the cross was made of cardboard. Each match was lit, quickly blown out, and then carefully glued to the cardboard. I have no idea how many matchsticks this work of art required. Hundreds. Perhaps thousands.

Hoping to calm me, hoping to distract me from my grief, Ricky approached me with the Cross of Jesus. He held it out to me and said, "I made this. You wanna hold it?"

At that moment, I revealed to all that I was a Child of Satan.

I took the Cross from Ricky. I looked at it carefully, appreciating the good job with the gluing. And then I threw the Cross of Jesus as hard as I could. It struck a nearby wall and exploded. Matchsticks flew in every direction.

There was a collective gasp, louder than the earlier one when I threw the bible.

And then there was silence.

I rose and left the classroom. No one dared to say a word to me. I made my way through the church to the entry way and walked out into the sunshine outdoors.

I walked into the street and just kept walking.

I wanted all of them to die. Every single one of them. The Grandpas and Grandmas, the Moms and Dads, the Sunday School children, the pastor's wife. I wanted every single human being who saw my disgrace to fall over dead.

After twenty minutes, I realized I had no idea where I was, no clue what street I was on or where I was going. I did not care. I would keep walking until I arrived at the edge of town. I would keep walking until I found a new town, a town inhabited by people who did not love Jesus or flowers or matchstick crosses or even mothers.

After a while, I noticed a car beside me. A Chevy. It was driving slowly, no faster than I was walking. I glanced to my right and saw it was my dad's car.

My dad rolled down his window and said, "You want a ride, kid?"

"I am not going back to that church," I said. "I will die first."

"I'll take you to Grandpa's," Dad said.

From that moment, everyone in our church knew the truth about me. I was on the highway to hell.

2

Martians

Our family of seven lived on the edge of a factory town in the Midwest. To protect the guilty, I am not going to reveal the name of that town.

In a previous life our neighborhood had been called the town dump but after the war it was taken over by the municipal government and renamed the town landfill. When the landfill got sufficiently full, it was shut down. The mountains of garbage were flattened. Dump trucks rolled in and poured soil all over everything. Underground pipes were installed, and streets were added. Housing contractors came in and built small, three-bedroom, one-bathroom houses on the streets. These houses were sold cheap to war veterans like my dad.

Every house contained children. There were so many kids, our neighborhood was nicknamed Fertility Hill. My dad said if a couple couldn't have kids no matter how hard they tried, all they had to do was purchase a house in our neighborhood, and next spring they'd have triplets.

Downhill from my neighborhood was The Marsh. A creek ran through it. Every few years, the creek flooded the neighborhood, turning the yards into swamps. The houses were built on concrete slabs. What was the point of digging basements? They would just have filled up with muddy water. A lot of the houses were not much more than shacks.

A person could be forgiven for supposing people who lived in houses built on top of a town dump would never look down their noses at people who lived beside a creek that flooded every few years, but that person would be wrong.

According to my mother, the residents of The Marsh were Renters. We, on the other hand, were Homeowners. Children brought up in The Marsh were doomed. She prophesized their futures would include teenage pregnancy, alcoholism, unemployment, and prison.

As a result, I felt a certain connection to the kids who lived in The Marsh. Like me, they were on their way to hell.

Like most of the kids in my neighborhood, I did not dare set foot in The Marsh. I did not even dare to ride my bicycle through it. But I knew the kids who lived there because they attended my school.

There were two categories of Marsh kids, the Marshmallows and the Martians. The Marshmallows were friendly and safe. You could talk to them without getting punched. The Martians were dangerous and glamorous.

I sometimes played with Marshmallows if they visited the school playground, which was considered neutral territory. I liked to pump them for information about their scandalous siblings and parents. It seemed to me Martians lived much more interesting lives than non-Martians. I was especially eager to hear about the two older Grimm sisters and their notorious mother Marge, and Ray Kavanaugh and his terrifying father Red. I was also interested in Tommy White, but for different reasons. So far as I could tell, Tommy was unlikely ever to become a criminal. He was a decent kid — good looking and athletic — but what made him interesting was that he belonged to the only black family who lived in my entire neighborhood; he was the only black kid in my class.

There were three Grimm sisters. They were nicknamed Big Grimm, Middle Grimm, and Little Grimm – like characters in a fairytale. Little Grimm was my age and she was the only Marshmallow in the Grimm family. Big and Middle were Martian right down to their evil bones. According to my mom, each daughter had a different dad. She suspected Little was fathered by a priest.

Big was three years older than me. She could out-fight any boy in her class. Middle was two years older than me; she trailed Big everywhere she went, jumping into the fight if necessary. It was hard to believe Little was related to them because she was petite and girly; she had long dark hair and liked to wear dresses. She was capable of actual kindness. Big and Middle usually wore overalls. They had short hair and were indistinguishable from boys. You didn't want to cross them.

Ray was the son of Red Kavanaugh and a small shy woman named Naomi who was rarely seen. Ray was the same age as Big, but he got "held back." When he was age nine, he caught rheumatic fever and spent the entire school year in bed. The next year, he completely recovered, experienced a series of growth spurts, and was so full of energy he became wild and took to breaking into the neighborhood general store, Bill's Grocery. Eventually Ray got caught stealing beer and cigarettes and at age eleven was sent to reform school. When he came back and joined my class, he was nearly as big as his dad and had homemade tattoos on his hands. Even the toughest kid in our class, a Martian named Nick, did not dare mess with him.

Tommy White was the best athlete in our school by far. He was in my class but was one year older than the rest of us. Kids said this was because Mr. White kept him out of kindergarten until he turned six so he would always be bigger than everyone else. Until Ray joined us, Tommy was the tallest kid in our class. He was fantastic at any game involving a ball. My dad said it was a pleasure to watch him play. For a resident of the Marsh, Tommy was unusual in that he got decent grades and had a paper route. Even the teachers liked him.

Tommy and his older sister Rose were the only black kids in our school. They were the only black kids who lived on our side of town. If you thought about it, it was shocking that they lived among us. One black family in a sea of white people? How did that even happen? Black people in our town lived on the other side of the river in the north end. That is the only place they were allowed to live. It was the early 1960s. White men ran the town, controlled the banks and the jobs. No loan officer was going to give a home loan to a black man unless he wanted to buy a house in the north end. If a black man even bothered to inquire about a house for sale on my side of town, the real estate agent would tell him it had already been sold.

My dad had a theory about why Tommy and his sister lived in the best house in The Marsh and went to our school. He said it was because of Big Bill Ryan. Bill owned a lot of rental houses in the north end which he rented out to black families. He also owned most of the lots in The Marsh and rented all but the best one to poor white families. In our neighborhood, he owned Bill's Grocery, Bill's Footloose Tavern, and Big Bill's Bowling Alley.

If you entered Bill's Footloose Tavern, you saw West Side Sports memorabilia everywhere you looked, baseball bats, footballs, baseballs in glass boxes, autographed photos of star quarterbacks, and framed newspaper stories about the West High 1932 football team that went all the way to the State Championship. They got all the way to the championship game, but they didn't win. They lost by three points in overtime. Ever since, Bill had one dream. He wanted to help put together another team, one that was even better than the glorious 1932 team, one that would WIN the state championship.

My dad said he figured Bill had scouted Tommy White when he was just a little kid and realized he had an unusual degree of athletic talent.

To make Tommy eligible to be on the west side teams, Bill bought the best house in The Marsh and rented it to Tommy's dad. "Where else could old Bill stick a family of coloreds on this side of town and get away with it?"

"But how could he tell Tommy was that good when he was just a kid?"

"Old Bill's got an eye. You don't want to bet with him, not on sports. You wait and see, that colored kid is so good right now he could play on the junior high varsity team. Four years from now, your high school is going to ride on his shoulders all the way to the state championship."

A jock like Tommy White would not normally deign to talk to a scrawny kid like me, but we bonded over the fact we both liked to read books and because of our sisters. Tommy's older sister Rose had had polio and wore braces on both legs. My older sister Ell was born premature with cerebral palsy. Ell was friendly as a puppy, but she never mastered reading or arithmetic. She couldn't count money or write anything except her name. She wore braces too, just like Rose.

Maybe because Ell reminded him of Rose, Tommy White looked after my sister. If any kid on the playground called her a name, Tommy would appear in front of that kid and suggest he apologize. The fact that every offending boy did apologize to my sister will convey how much respect Tommy was accorded by our entire school.

Tommy's sister Rose did not need a defender. She could take care of herself. When outdoors, she spent her time sitting in a wheelchair. When she attempted walking, she moved awkwardly in a way that reminded me of a crab, so you might think she would be picked on, but she had a good brain and a sharp tongue. You did not want to get on her bad side.

Rose White liked to talk. On summer mornings when the weather was good, she would get into her wheelchair and let Tommy push her to the playground across the street from my house. While he played ball with his friends, Rose would sit there in the shade behind the triangle slide. From that position she could survey the entire park. I liked to sit at her feet and get her views on life.

It was Rose who explained love to me.

The summer between sixth grade, the last year of elementary school, and seventh grade when I would enroll at the junior high, I imagined I was in love with a red-haired girl named Mary Margaret O'Hare, a neighbor. Double M got straight As, colored inside the lines, and wore glasses. She aspired to be the first female astronaut and owned the entire collection of Nancy Drew Mysteries. I told her I bet she too could be a girl detective. "Better than Nancy Drew!" And if her detective career did not work out, I had no doubt she would someday walk on the moon. "They will prob'ly name a crater after you!" Despite my love, Mary Margaret never took me seriously as a boyfriend. She preferred the attentions of a boy named Rodney who lived three blocks away and was the son of a TV repairman.

The day after we graduated from the sixth grade, Mary Margaret broke my heart by informing me she and her entire family were moving to Omaha. She told me I probably would never see her again but, if I was lucky, she might send me a postcard. The day her dad loaded her and her mom and sister into the family station wagon and drove away with them, I hid in our basement and wept.

I confided my feelings for Mary Margaret to Rose. Rose straightened her glasses. She wore those cat's- eye frames. She inspected me for a few seconds and then said, "That ain't love. Nothing like. You had a crush. And now you're moping. Get over it."

"Like you know anything about love," I said.

"At least I am not a baby like you. It's a wonder you can feed yourself."

I demanded, "Who have YOU ever been in love with?"

Rose examined a far corner of the park. "I thank the Lord I have never been struck by love."

14

I scoffed.

Rose said real genuine love is far different than a mere crush. Compared to love, a crush is nothing. A crush is like getting a cold. It's like getting an itch. Love is a fatal disease. It strikes hard like the flu. You are perfectly healthy, and then one day you wake up and realize you are sick. You break out in a sweat, see stars, and experience waves of nausea. Then, while you vomit your guts out into the toilet, you realize what has happened. You are in love. Rose said the word as if it was a curse.

All this sounded to me as if it might possibly be true, but I hated the idea of having to submit to the wisdom of Rose, especially since she had never been in love herself.

I said if she knew so much about the topic, maybe she could give me an example of it from our neighborhood, someone who was in love with someone else, sick with the disease. I suggested a few names, and she laughed. She said those were examples of puppy love, but there was one example I should know about, real love in all its hideous glory. "I can't believe you are so dumb you haven't noticed."

"Don't make me guess. Who?"

"Big Grimm is in love. Bad."

The very idea made me shiver. Who with?

"You really are blind as a bat. You need glasses, honey." Hearing the music of the approaching ice cream truck, Rose sat up straight in her wheelchair and fished a coin out of her change purse. "Go on, now. Take this quarter and get me a Fudgsicle. Maybe I'll let you have a lick."

Once Rose planted the idea, it only took me three days to figure out who Big Grimm was in love with.

Although it was dangerous for me to get too close to Big and her friends, I was able to get close enough to hear them talking. Big talked about Tommy White all the time. If he appeared in the park to play ball with his friends or to get Rose and push her back to their house in The Marsh, Big could not take her eyes off him. If Tommy approached Big and her gang, Big went quiet, turned red, and kept her lips pressed together. If Tommy so much as glanced at her, or worse smiled at her, she looked sick as a dog. If any of her girlfriends even mentioned Tommy's name, Big smacked her hard on the shoulder and ordered her to shut the hell up.

Big Grimm was in love with Tommy White. And miraculously, Tommy didn't even notice.

A week later, the attacks on Tommy's house began.

3

Fire

I believed Big Grimm was attacking Tommy's house. What else could she do? She was suffering from wounded love, unrequited love, the worst kind, and could not stand it. She had to do something. It was possible she was assisted by Middle or other girls in her gang but deep down I was certain Big was doing it all by herself. Because a certain kind of job, if you want it done right, you do it by yourself. I believed Big did not enjoy what she was doing. I believed she hated what she was doing but could no more stop doing it than she could stop breathing.

Big Grimm was in love. Rose was right. Big was head-over-heels, hopelessly in love. And it went badly. It went wrong. It went exactly the way it had to go.

Because Tommy was perfect, a head taller than most other boys, faster, quicker. He was popular and easy-going and graceful and kind; of course, she fell for him. But how could she imagine he would ever fall for her? How could Big imagine she was on Tommy's level, worthy of his love?

I knew the answer. It was because Tommy was black, the only black kid in a world of white kids. Real love, requited love, two-way love would have been impossible if he was white. A boy like that, handsome and athletic, could not possibly fall in love with a girl like Big, a girl who looked more like a boy than a girl. But she had something. She was white. She was not beautiful or graceful or athletic but at least she was white.

Big Grimm brooded about it day and night until she concluded it could work. Love could triumph. It had to. Because Tommy was black, and she was white.

According to neighborhood gossip, it happened one warm summer night on Big's front porch. Tommy walked by and noticed Big sitting there on her porch swing in the dark. He made a fateful decision to stop and be nice to her. Pretty soon he was standing on her porch talking to her, and then he sat down on the swing beside her. He talked to her in a gentle, friendly way, lowering his voice as if he was telling her a secret. The source of the neighborhood gossip, two girls – friends of Big – were nearby, hiding in the rose bushes and listening. They said they could not actually hear what Tommy was saying, could not make out the words, but they could hear the tones in his voice. It was like listening to music.

Tommy was so close that night, his voice so low and friendly, how could Big help it? There was a full moon. And there were fireflies in the air. The temperature that night was that perfect temperature when you feel as if you are in a dream. The air smelled of flowers. Big's mother Marge Grimm liked flowers and had roses at both ends of the porch. In that context, the moon and the fireflies and the roses, Tommy so close and his voice so sweet, Big could not concentrate on what Tommy was saying. How could she? Her thoughts whirled. Feelings arose within her until she believed anything could happen, anything was possible.

Big could not help herself. Inspired by the supernatural force of love, Big leaned into Tommy and attempted to kiss him.

Tommy reacted. His head and his entire torso yanked back from Big and simultaneously he pushed her away with his hand as if he had suddenly noticed she had dirt on her mouth, as if her teeth were covered in cooties. Tommy leapt to his feet and looked down at Big as if she was a giant bug, as if for a moment he was looking at a hairy tarantula, and then he recovered himself and said he had to go home, he thought he heard his mother calling him, and he took off, not walking but actually running.

The two girls, friends of Big, members of her gang, who had seen all this reported every detail to their friends, who reported it to theirs. Within 24 hours, everyone in our neighborhood heard the entire story. Even a nobody sixth grader like me heard it.

Two days later, in the morning, Tommy's dad came out of his house to go to work and found all four tires on his car flattened. Someone had taken a key and dragged it from the hood to the trunk, leaving behind an ugly zigzagging scratch across both car doors. The scratch did not merely zigzag. It spelled out a word, a nasty one. The word. The one that, according to my mom, decent white people did not use when talking about colored people. Tommy's sister Rose told me a few days later, "It wasn't even spelled right. Only one G and the last letter a Z!"

One week later, in the morning, Tommy's mother finished pinning the wash to her clothesline and went back inside. Half an hour later, she had a weird feeling, believed she smelled something, looked out her window, and saw the bedsheets and work overalls and towels and underthings on fire. Someone in full daylight had sprinkled them with gasoline and lit them on fire.

Two days later, something completely different happened, something so startling and unusual that it caused all my thoughts about Big and Tommy to vanish as if I had been contemplating an enormous iridescent soap bubble and it popped.

We were coming home from Wednesday night church. The quality of light on summer evenings after sundown but before complete darkness is magical. The first fireflies appear in the air and wink, and then the streetlights flicker on and, if you are a kid, you know the mournful truth: you have to go home now and get ready for bed.

My dad turned into our neighborhood, drove down the street that separated our side of the neighborhood from Tommy and Big's side. People were scattered everywhere we looked. Parents and kids. No one, not even the little kids, seemed to be going to bed. Cop cars were parked on both sides of the road and uniformed cops were out in the street directing traffic. My dad pulled to a stop beside a cop. "Eddie, what's going on?"

"A kid is missing," the cop said and waved us on.

As soon as we got to our house, before the car was even fully stopped, I was out the door and running to ask my friends, "What? Who? Why?"

The weird kid was missing, that was the who and the what. He lived one street over with his older sister and his parents and their cat. My dad said it was a pity they never had a dog. My mom said they couldn't have one because the weird kid was allergic. My dad said how can a kid be allergic to dog but not cat? Mom told him to mind his own business. She heard me talking excitedly to the neighbor kids and demanded I come see her. When I got to her side, she took hold of my shoulder, squeezed it hard until I yelped, and said, "Don't you call him a weird kid. He has a name."

The weird kid's name was Larry. He was in the second grade. At the time, I didn't know why we called him the weird kid. There was something about him that struck us as odd. In the future, kids like him would be labeled autistic, on the spectrum, but in those days no one knew anything about the spectrum. You could talk to him and he would not make eye contact. In the middle of a conversation, he might wander off humming. He was deeply interested in cleaning supplies.

20

If you had him in your house, while his mom was talking to your mom, he would wander into the kitchen, open the doors under the sink and start pulling out plastic bottles of dishwashing soap, glass bottles of cleaning fluids, boxes of powder. He would line them up according to height of container.

The weird kid often wandered off. All of us did. In the summers, we woke up, got out of our pajamas and into our regular clothes, made our beds, and then ran outdoors and looked for someone to play with. We played in the nearby cornfields or on the school playground or in someone's cool dark basement or in the big empty lawn in the middle of our block. We did not come home again until it was lunchtime. Then we abandoned our houses again and did whatever we wanted, whatever we felt we could get away with. We came home for supper, then again escaped our houses and our parents, looking for one another. We did not come home in the evening until the streetlights were turned on.

The weird kid left the house after breakfast and did not come home. He did not come home for lunch. That's when his mother started looking for him. At 3 PM, she called up the place her husband worked and told him he had to leave work immediately, come home, and help her look. The weird kid did not come home for supper. That's when she called the cops and started notifying the neighbors. By the time we got home from Wednesday church, the entire neighborhood was out looking for the weird kid.

"If they had a dog," my dad said, "that dog would sniff him out. But a cat is useless."

"You go help them look," my mom told him.

I was not allowed to join the search. I was forced to get into my pajamas and go to bed. I could not fall asleep. I waited until my brothers were in dreamland (they slept in bunk beds but as the oldest boy I had my own bed), then I got out my flashlight, turned it on and read a book under the covers. Every now and then, I thought I heard noises from outdoors. Yelling, dogs barking. I got up several times and looked out our bedroom window. All I could clearly see was the street, the pool of light cast by our streetlight. Moths flew around the light in circles. I could make out the park across the street, the playground equipment, the merry-go-round and the slides. I could see men out there with flashlights. Men standing together smoking cigarettes and talking in low voices.

They found the weird kid at dawn. Tommy found his body.

"Dad!" he yelled.

"Over here!" Tommy's dad yelled.

Floyd, the weird kid's dad, had been up all night, searching. Tommy's dad and Tommy had stayed with him. Gradually over the course of the night most of the other dads went home to bed. Even the cops gave up, most of them. They said they would return in the morning when it got light.

The weird kid was floating in the creek, in a little pond made by the creek where it ran through a cornfield. By then the two men and Tommy were almost five miles from home. They had followed the creek. At 3 AM they found the weird kid's shoes. He had removed them, probably to keep them clean and dry, and placed them on a flat rock beside the creek. He had folded up his socks and put them inside the shoes. He must have fallen into the creek and drowned. The current had probably pulled him along until his body found that quiet little pool where it stayed until Tommy and Tommy's dad and Floyd found it.

Floyd picked up his kid's body and carried it home. Tommy's dad and Tommy followed him. Floyd carried the body all the way back to his house. Stumbling along in the dark, refusing any help, he carried the body the entire five miles. Floyd's wife was sitting on her porch smoking a cigarette with a neighbor woman on each side of her. A cop car was parked in her driveway. The sun was rising above the horizon and the cops were about ready to start organizing another hunt.

Floyd laid the kid down in the grass of the front yard. He knelt beside it and called his wife's name. More neighbors arrived. The Baptist preacher showed up. The cops called off the search.

People said for five minutes Floyd knelt in the grass saying his wife's name, and his wife just sat there numb and stunned. One of the neighbor ladies had to pull the cigarette out of her hand or it would have burnt her fingers.

"She couldn't cry," my mom told me later. "Sometimes people can't."

I found out what happened an hour later when I ran outside and found the neighbor kids talking excitedly. One of them said she had seen the weird kid's body lying in the grass, had seen the ambulance arrive, had seen the men roll the little body into a white bag and onto a stretcher and put it in the back of the ambulance and drive away with it. She said before the ambulance men closed up the bag, she had seen the weird kid's pale face and closed eyes. "Like he was asleep."

That morning was the first time I realized a little kid, one who was even younger than me, could leave home and not return, could slip away and die just as easily as an old person.

A week later, Tommy's dad herded his family — Tommy and Rose and their mom — into his car and drove them all to Chicago to see the cousins.

While they were away, their house burned down.

4

Crybaby

T he summer before I entered junior high, the summer Tommy and Rose's house burned down in the middle of the night, I had a persistent problem. Crying. Whining. Blubbering.

So far as I could tell, my father and his friends did not cry. They did not whine or blubber. Ever. Their war experiences had cured them of it. Even grown women did not often cry. Little kids cried. Babies did. However, there is a limit. This limit is clearly understood by children. When I was in the last phase of elementary school, fifth and sixth grade, on a regular basis kids informed me that once again I was blubbering. It was disgraceful. I should stop it. Girls could continue to cry all the way into junior high and all through high school. Everyone said it is only natural that girls cry, especially about the cruelty of boys. But boys when they advance toward puberty need to stop it. Stop crying, for god's sake.

When Tommy and his family arrived to look at what was left of their house, I observed them, wondering if they would cry. Rose would, I thought, and her mom. Rose would probably sob like a baby and her mom would wipe away tears.

It took several hours for Tommy, his parents, and his sister Rose

24

to return. They had to drive all the way from Chicago and did not arrive until lunchtime. By then, the fire had been put out. Even the smoldering areas had been subdued. There was not much left. It was what the firemen called a strong, fast fire. For a time, the firemen had been afraid flames were going to leap from Tommy's house to the roof of the house on the east side of it and burn that house down too. They had prevented this from happening, but they had half-destroyed the neighbor's house by pouring water on it. Blown by a snappy breeze, smoke from the fire had poured east and contaminated every house at that end of the block. The firemen had worked on the burning house while cops pounded on doors and evacuated a dozen families in the middle of the night.

Kids I knew – Marsh kids – were still in their pajamas, standing there with everyone else, gawking, whispering. We were all wondering how Tommy and his family were going to react.

"Rose will cry," I told my brother Dean.

"No, she won't," he said.

The firemen said there was no doubt what started the fire.

Gasoline.

The fire had started in the kitchen and spread rapidly in every direction. Fire cannot spread that quickly the firemen said unless someone has splashed gasoline or some similar accelerant on the floors, the furniture, and the walls.

When Tommy and his family arrived to look at what was left of their house, none of them burst into tears. Tommy and his dad didn't, and Rose and her mom didn't either. I was standing not far away watching them. A lot of neighbors were standing there watching them.

White people looking at black people whose house just got burned down.

Another car of black people, the cousins from Chicago, had come down with them, so in all there were nine black people standing there looking at what used to be a house.

Their house.

No one was crying.

A fire marshal and a police detective talked to Tommy's father. The rest of Tommy's family just stood there, not saying anything. I had imagined Rose and her mom would burst into tears. Fall to their knees. Or run hysterically into the wreckage and salvage things that were only partially damaged – toys and family photos and that sort of thing – but in fact the entire family including the cousins just stood there not saying anything.

Neighbors, women like my mom attempted to comfort Tommy's mother. She nodded her head at them. She did not bother to smile or say thank you even when they offered to bring food. The white women did not dare touch her.

Kids like me were mostly interested in Tommy and Rose. They did not speak either. Nor did their cousins. They radiated a feeling, a vibration that scared us. We looked at them but did not approach. I felt as if I no longer knew them, as if Tommy and Rose had transformed into people I had never met.

They had made a mistake, moved into a white neighborhood, fooled themselves into imagining that was acceptable, fooled themselves into believing white people could be decent. Now they had a look. I am not sure how to describe it – as if they could no longer be fooled by the occasional kindnesses of white people. They now knew the truth. White people are evil as poisonous snakes.

After an hour, Tommy's family and his cousins got back into their cars and drove away.

When I got home, I was agitated, and I started to blubber. I knew what was going to happen next. All sorts of feelings and thoughts were going to boil up and swirl inside me until I started sobbing. I was in my bedroom sitting on my bed. I closed the door, hoping no one would come in and bother me until the fit passed. Already I was remembering other times, the way a person might recall other occasions when he had the flu.

My mom's cancer. The death of her twin brother.

It was at my uncle's funeral that it had first happened to me, uncontrollable crying. I had sat in the little country church with one of my cousins because my mom had to sit with her siblings. Mom and I had gone down there to her hometown on the train. My dad had to work and couldn't come. A neighbor lady took care of my two brothers and my sisters, made sure they got breakfast and went to school. I have no idea why my mother thought she should take me with her, why she told my teacher I was going to be gone for four days and miss almost an entire week of school. Maybe she just needed company. It wasn't as if I liked my uncle. He was a war veteran, a car mechanic for god's sake; he smoked cigarettes. If even once he smiled in my general direction, I didn't remember it.

I was fine on the train all the way down there. It was nice to be alone with my mom like that, and not have to share her with my brothers and sisters. She was affected by the death in a deep soulful way, but she didn't talk about it. He was not just her brother. She had three more of those. He was her twin. They were born within five minutes of one another. When they were little kids, they had looked so similar people thought they were identical, little tow-headed barefoot look-alikes growing up side-by-side. My Uncle Billy died abruptly of a massive heart attack. Only in his forties. Lived through the war, saw combat in Europe, had a wife and four kids. He was a strong, taciturn man who usually had dirt under his fingernails, and he dies just like that. Boom, as if a switch was thrown. Or so my cousin told me. This cousin was not the son of my dead uncle; he was another nephew of the deceased, like me. He was three years older than me and had been assigned to get me through the funeral.

I was unaccustomed to death and had only attended one previous funeral: a tedious affair to honor an old maid great-aunt on my dad's side who had died of natural causes at the age of 80. I was determined to soak up all these new experiences in a mature way like a smallish grownup, so I nodded knowingly at my cousin as if he did not have to bother telling me about heart attacks.

When my mother got the phone call with the news about her brother, she showed me the door, opened it for me, in a way. My dad answered the phone and handed it to her. "It's long distance, honey." He hardly ever called her honey.

Long distance calls in those days were a big deal. Long distance was expensive. It was hardly ever good news. She took the phone and listened and then said, "You mean Dad! You mean Dad!" Her father had the same name as her twin brother. "No!" she yelled. "No, it's not true!" She sat down on the floor with the phone still glued to her ear, yelling NO. My dad got the phone out of her hand. He listened to it for a while and said something, hung up. My mother could not stop crying. I had never seen her like that. It must be horrible to lose any brother but this one was her twin. She sat on the floor and wept like the world was on fire.

I was fine all though the funeral, bored the way kids are in church. Eager to be released, eager to get out of my fancy clothes, find other kids and run around outdoors and have fun. When the service concluded, we filed past the casket. My cousin and I waited in line until it was our turn. There he was, my uncle. He looked weird but familiar. His hair combed, reclining on his back but dressed up in a suit and tie, clean fingernails, wearing makeup, his eyes glued shut. Baskets of flowers nearby.

When we got up next to the casket, my cousin said, "Wanna touch him?" He took my hand and touched my fingertips to the cool cheek of my uncle. I was fine for a minute. We moved away from the casket and out into the church lobby. That was when it started.

It came upon me slowly, in waves. Tears welled up in my eyes, blurring my vision. And then the trembling began. My ears began to ring. Whimpering followed by sobs. Loud heart-rending cries of despair.

"Shut up!" my cousin said.

My mother was notified about my meltdown and quickly found me. She put her arm around my shoulders and led me out of the church. I could not stop. She was tender to me, making soft comforting noises, but I could feel her embarrassment. Everyone was looking at her. No other kid was carrying on like that, not even my uncle's actual children. She herded me into somebody's car. We got in the back seat. She kept her arm around me and told me I could take as long as I needed. Occasionally other women came up to the car and asked if they could help.

I sobbed without stop for an hour. At the time I was nine years old.

The same thing happened a year later when we found out my mom had cancer. My dad sat us down in the living room and said it was a family meeting. We kids knew Mom was in the hospital but that had happened before, and each time she had come home with another baby. This time Dad said there would be no baby. In fact, Mom would never again have any more babies. She was having an operation the next morning, a serious operation. He would be with her at the hospital. The pastor's wife was coming over and would take care of us. We would be good kids and not cause her trouble.

"Dad," my brother Dean asked, "is Mom going to die?"

"It is in the hands of God," he said. "We have to be prepared for all eventualities. We are going to pray now."

We kids got out of our chairs and knelt right there in the living room while my dad led us in prayer.

Afterward, I went outdoors and attempted to cry but could not.

Crying is like that; it comes and goes like the weather, does not make a lot of sense, has a mind of its own. I went to the park and sat on top of the big slide. A neighbor lady noticed me out there. She knew what was happening with my mom, so she came out to see how I was doing.

I remained dry-eyed.

I was OK until the next morning when the pastor's wife was there. She had decided there was no point in sending us to school. She sat on the sofa with my little brother Ron and my sister Lois, reading them a story about a talking pig.

I don't know why that set me off, but I did it again. I could not stop. The pastor's wife had no idea what to do. She kept mopping my face with a red rag. "Don't worry," she said. "Everything will be all right."

I kept it up for an hour.

The day after I got home from watching the aftermath of the fire that burned down Tommy's house, I could feel it coming, drifting toward me like fog. It signaled its imminent arrival with tears, just a few of them brimming up in my eyes. Then I felt as if I was the only person left alive on Earth. In due course, I arrived at uncontrollable sobbing.

To this day, I don't know what I was crying about. I was weeping for…everything. For stupidity and loneliness, death and destruction. I was sobbing because I was weak and useless, because my mother no longer had breasts, because the red-haired girl moved away and never even sent a postcard. I wept because white people burn up houses occupied by black people. I wept because we are all so stupid and phony. Because the powerful crush the weak, and the rest of us don't give a shit. Because I was on my way to hell.

Who knows?

At some point, my mom came in and sat on the bed beside me and attempted to comfort me. A while later, when I was maybe forty-five minutes into it, when I had sobbed so many times my stomach hurt, my little brother Dean came into our room. He stood there at the end of the bunkbed he shared with our brother Ron. I looked up at him and saw he had his arms folded and was expressing his contempt for me with his eyes.

"Will you please stop?" he said.

It was as if he had found my emotion button and punched it.

My mom was astonished. She had been trying to get me to calm down for nearly an hour without result. Dean walks in, folds his arms, and says the exact same thing she had said herself who knows how many times. *Will you stop? Can't you stop? Please honey stop.*

Dean says it, and just like that I stop. It was a miracle.

I wiped away the remains of my tears, stood up, and glowered at my brother.

He saw I had returned to my senses, and he went from feeling contempt and superiority to feeling outright fear. I was bigger than him. Dean saw the look in my eyes, turned on his heel, and exited our bedroom on the run.

"So, you're OK now?" my mom said.

"I'm fine," I said.

That was the last time I cried for many years.

Oh, one last weird thing. Big Grimm and her sister Middle did not cause that fire. Just like Tommy's family, they were out of town. Their mom Marge had a new boyfriend. He had arrived in the afternoon and loaded Marge and her daughters into his station wagon. Then he drove them to a lake 200 miles away where he had a cabin.

No way did Big Grimm start that fire.

5

Snakes

We lived close to cornfields, and these fields contained snakes. Lots of them. Lowly garter snakes by the hundreds lived in those fields but also majestic corn snakes and terrifying five-foot-long bull snakes. None of these snakes are poisonous but all of them are impressive creatures, able to panic most humans simply by existing. The kids in my neighborhood, the boys anyway, liked to catch them.

My brother Dean and I developed a fondness for garter snakes. These are slender creatures, black but with yellow racing stripes, easy to catch. When first seized, the snake twists frantically and gums your fingers in hopes you will drop it. If you hold on tight (but not too tight, you don't want to harm it), the snake will eventually quit thrashing and allow you to handle it. Like all snakes, garters are not slimy. They occasionally emit snake poop. Although it gets on your fingers, it is not as putrid as human shit, so I don't know what the fuss is.

Dean and I collected garter snakes one spring. We carried them into the house and hid them in a bucket in the basement. We kept at it until we had 12 of them. We put a loose tile on top of the bucket to keep them from escaping.

My mother hated snakes. On this subject, like so many others, she was irrational. She refused to handle even the tamest and most beautiful snake. She could not be convinced most snakes do not possess fangs and cannot hurt anyone. If she saw a garter, she felt it should be cut in half with a hoe. A man should do it. If no man was nearby, a boy should do it. Dean and I would not do it. It's wrong to kill a snake, especially a harmless garter.

The next morning, we went to school. Before we left, I went downstairs, lifted the tile, and looked at our snakes. They were fine. I went to fourth grade, and Dean went to third. By this time, our handicapped sister Ell went to a special school. A bus came every day and carried her away.

In the middle of the morning, there was a knock on my classroom door. My teacher startled, told us to be good, went to see who it was. It was the principal, an amazingly tall man named Mr. Bosch. He told my teacher that little Jack DeWitt had to go home. Immediately.

Looking at me as if this was a very odd event, my teacher told me, "Your mother needs you." I went out in the hall, where Mr. Bosch was towering over my brother Dean. He told us we should go home, take care of the situation, and then return. He did not seem to know what exactly the situation was.

Our home was nearby, visible from the school. We crossed the little park and ran into our house, yelling for our mother. She appeared at once, looking angry.

Mom led us to the basement door and opened it, pointed down into the gloom. "You will march down there, and you will catch them, every one of them! Get them out of my house! Now!"

On the steps was a laundry basket. The washing machine was in the basement. She had been carrying dirty clothes down there. She had seen a pair of harmless garters at the bottom of the steps, dropped the basket, run back upstairs, and called our school.

Dean and I exchanged glances. Clearly, our mother had lost her mind.

We descended into the basement, stepping over the laundry basket and the dirty clothes that were strewn on the steps. We did not see any snakes. We found the bucket on its side. It still contained one snake. We righted the bucket and put the tile back on top of it.

Dean theorized that all twelve of the snakes must have piled up on one side of the bucket until their combined weight caused it to tip over. They escaped, all but the timid one who was still in the bucket, and crawled in every direction. "They must be down here," he said. "Somewhere."

"They like to hide in dark places," I said.

It was like an Easter egg hunt. "Found one!" "Found two!"

By lunchtime, I had found four garters, and Dean had found six. Four plus six plus the one we found in the bucket totaled 11. One garter was still missing. No matter how carefully we searched, we could not find the last one.

I told Dean, "Maybe we miscounted."

Dean said, "It's hard to count snakes. The way they twist together and all."

We searched the basement one more time. There was a lot of junk down there: old trunks, suitcases, garden tools, discarded furniture, paint buckets, a broken bicycle, stacks of *National Geographics*. The furnace was down there. The washing machine.

We carried the bucket of snakes upstairs and told our mom we had the garters. She could look in the bucket if she wanted.

Before she would feed us lunch, she made us carry the bucket to the nearest cornfield and upend it, freeing the snakes.

11 perfectly good snakes. We felt sad watching them slither away.

We went home, ate our lunchmeat sandwiches, drank our glasses of milk, and went back to school.

One hour later, the principal returned to my classroom. This time, he did not knock, just opened the door and interrupted my teacher in mid-sentence. He strode into our room, all six feet six of him, located me, and yelled, "You! Go home. Immediately."

I entered our house. My mom was waiting for me.

"You told me you got ALL of them! You LIED to me."

"It's hard to count snakes," I said. "Because of the way they—"

"Don't give me your excuses. Go down there and find it!"

While I was at school, my mother had gone down the steps with more dirty laundry and found the last snake waiting for her beside the washing machine. She had screamed and run back up the steps.

The trouble was the snake was no longer where she saw it. I looked everywhere and could not find it. Eventually, school ended for the afternoon and Dean came home. He too was sent to the basement. We would not be allowed to emerge, even to use the bathroom, not until we found the snake. We could forget about supper too until we found that snake, showed it to her, and carried it out of the house.

Dean and I searched until my dad got home from work. My mom informed him until the snake was found he was not going to get any supper either. He came downstairs in his work clothes and helped us look.

Our basement contained a great many places where a snake could hide. We looked in all of them. I looked. Dean looked. My dad looked.

"I don't even think it's down here," Dean said.

"I don't either," I told our dad. "I think she just imagined it."

"Probably saw a shadow," Dean said.

My mother appeared in the open door at the top of the basement steps. "I did NOT imagine it! Don't you DARE call me a liar! You are staying down there until you FIND it!"

At last, my dad found it hiding behind an old license plate. In those days, we got a new license plate every single year and for some reason we kept the old ones. They seemed too valuable to just throw out, I guess. An old license plate was leaning up against the concrete wall of the basement. The garter was curled behind it, sleeping for all we could tell.

My dad seized it and carried it upstairs and showed it to our mom. He carried it out of the house and transferred it to me in the front yard.

"I hope you boys learned your lesson," he said.

"No snakes," I said.

"Not in the house," Dean said.

Dean walked beside me as I carried the snake back to the cornfield and released it.

6

Ricky's Revenge

I t was the custom of the boys in our neighborhood to make use of snakes to initiate new kids. From time to time, a family moved out of our neighborhood. New people arrived. The new people almost always had a few kids. If one of the kids was our age, we would capture him on the playground, probably on a weekend.

The initiation was simple. We would catch a garter snake. When we got hold of the new kid, we would upend him, drop the snake down his pantleg, and tell him, "Don't scream." We would hold him upside down for a minute. "Don't you dare scream." If he managed to keep quiet, we deemed him worthy of our friendship and released him. It was pretty comical watching the new kid jump to his feet and try to get the snake to fall out, lots of leaping up and down and stomping. Sometimes, when the snake was well-lodged, it would not fall out. The new kid would have to de-pants himself right there on the playground in front of everyone.

That was how I met my best friend Michael Taylor. The summer after sixth grade, the summer Tommy's house burned down, I met Michael on the playground carrying a novel borrowed from the library called *Mouse on the Moon*. By that point in my life, I considered any kid who appeared in public carrying a book a potential friend. This was twice as true if he did it in the summertime. I approached the new kid and demanded to see the book. He handed it to me and I read the title. "I know about this book," I said.

I rode my bicycle the three miles to the public library every weekend. My dad had equipped my bike with two big nerd baskets where I put the books I borrowed. I had already read a novel called *The Mouse That Roared*. It was the sort of thing that passed for humorous reading when I was a kid. The check-out lady had recommended it to me.

Americans thought the Marshall Plan designed to repair European countries (including our enemy Germany) after the war was noble, but it was also sort of funny. The Marshall Plan was like welfare but for other countries. The book's premise was that a tiny country (the "mouse") needed money in the worst way after the war and decided the only way it could get any was to con the USA into giving it some. In order to get that Marshall Plan money, the country had to somehow convince the USA that it was dangerous. How was the mouse going to convince the mighty USA it was dangerous? The little country hit upon a great idea. It declared war on the mighty USA! That was the premise of the book. It sold so many copies that a film studio bought it and made the story into a movie starring Peter Sellers. The book and the film portrayed the USA as a sugar daddy and the tiny European country as harmless, just needy. Americans liked that image of themselves, generous to a fault. The novel sold so well the author cashed in by writing a sequel, *Mouse on the Moon*. The tall, good-looking kid was carrying it.

A book worth reading. Outdoors. In the summertime.

I informed him I had not yet read it but had read the previous book and found it hilarious. We bonded in that moment, two bookworms.

I felt a pang of guilt turning a bookworm over to Ray and his gang, but rules are rules. Michael was in our park, on our turf, and he was a new kid. Ray tackled him, held him down, and dispatched a couple of his minions to get a snake.

Pretty soon, they returned with a garter. By that time, Michael was sitting up, perfectly calm. I admired his attitude. He was even chatting to Ray, making him smile. They had love of basketball in common. Tall kids.

Michael was explaining his name was Michael, not Mike. If anyone dared to call him Mike, or even worse Mikey, his mom would explode.

The minions handed the garter to Ray. Michael Not Mike was upended, and the snake was dropped into his pantleg. He did not scream. He was shaken a few times.

The initiation game is less fun when the new kid does not display the least bit of fear.

When the minions released him, Michael jumped up, gave his leg a shake, and the garter fell out and squirmed away. The new kid was no more flustered than if someone had sailed a paper airplane in his direction.

We were friends from that moment. Besides book-reading, Michael and I had one other tendency in common. We were the kind of boys who made snarky, critical remarks about others, especially those we considered to be amusingly ignorant or mentally slow. We mocked them. This habit did not always turn out well for us.

I now come to a sad turn of events in my narrative.

As a boy, I liked to mock the oddity of other people. A decent human being is kind to others, helpful and understanding, but I was not decent. I enjoyed mocking the shortcomings of others. I realize now that this tendency is a character defect, a defense strategy. Children and teenagers are impressed by good looking jocks. In the social pyramid of young people, the athletes are at the top, not the brains. Kids my age were not impressed by bookworms who got good grades. Children who loved books felt slighted. At least I did. A feeling of resentment can build up and vent itself in the form of snark.

Book-readers consider other people, non-readers, to be ignorant. The more we read, the more we know about all sorts of useless topics. We read a novel about horseraces, and we turn into pint-sized lecturers on the topic of Arabian stallions. Acquisition of arcane knowledge transforms us into nerds. Non-readers never know anything about these topics. They have zero desire to learn useless information.

Fine. Good for them. However, their ignorance allows them to be mocked.

In the natural course of things, sometimes people reacted to my mockery. They defended themselves. And not with mere words.

One of my targets at church was Ricky Fox.

Ricky was not a jock, but he thought he was. Compared to me he was. He had no doubt he was higher up the social pyramid than me because he was two years older. Ninth graders do not have to take crap from seventh graders, and I gave him crap. This was an iron law in the world of kids, and I violated it. He was not a bookworm, not by my standards, but he applied himself and got good grades. If he did not maintain a decent grade point average, he would have to face the wrath of his mother: a formidable woman, a female Scout Master. His grade point average was higher than mine. I was the sort of brain who only got high grades in courses that I found interesting. If a course did not interest me, I was perfectly happy to take home a B on my report card, or even a C. Ricky was not like that. Even one B on his report card would cause his mother to go insane.

Not only did Ricky get good grades, but he was also an exemplary Boy Scout, well on his way to becoming an Eagle, the highest possible rank of Scout. I was the sort of loser who did not even manage to stick with the Scout program. I never developed the slightest interest in merit badges. I hated camping. I got lost in the woods. I could not successfully paddle a canoe to save my life. I was a Cub Scout dropout.

In this regard, I was a disappointment to my father. One of my uncles, Uncle Milton, the one who became a pastor and moved to the west coast, told me that in a way my father was an Eagle Scout. They had grown up in tiny towns in South Dakota. The reputation of the great Baden-Powell and the Scouts had reached all the way into that cultural wasteland, but these towns were so unenlightened they did not have Scout Programs.

My dad got his hands on a Boy Scout Manual. He began to earn merit badges. He could not be rewarded with the official cloth badges because in his town there was no such thing as an official Troop. There were no Merit Badge Ceremonies. My father earned imaginary badges by fulfilling every single requirement for them. He was an Eagle Scout who never received a single official badge, an honorary Eagle.

My uncle assured me, "Your dad is an Eagle Scout. For sure. No kidding. Not an official one, but he really, truly is. As God is my witness, he earned every single one of those badges."

I figured my dad's excellence as an honorary Eagle was possible because he had never been a bad boy. No one could expect a kid like me to follow in his footsteps.

I felt that Ricky Fox was fair game because he was a dick. He was older than me, taller than me. He was loathed by several of the girls I knew, church girls my age and older. He would grab them and attempt to kiss them. He was a Georgie Porgie! I was the one who gave him that nickname.

Georgie Porgie, Puddin' and Pie,
Kissed the girls and made them cry,
When the boys came out to play
Georgie Porgie ran away!

Because of me, the girls in our church started calling him Georgie. It drove him crazy. Sometimes his mother would ask him: *Why did that girl just now call you Georgie?*

What could he say? *I have no idea, Mom. Girls are nuts.*

He had long brooded over the harm I had done to his Cross of Jesus, made of matchsticks. I was not even a good Christian. I was a bad influence on the other church kids. I richly deserved punishment.

At the end of the summer of 1963, the week before I started seventh grade, Ricky got his revenge. He did something horrifying. It was supposed to be pretty darn funny, hilarious even. But as it worked out, it was horrifying.

In the aftermath, he blamed the Three Stooges.

Compared to most kids of my generation, I was not terribly influenced by TV because we did not have one in our home. My mother believed TV to be an instrument of the devil. Dean and I did our level best to be corrupted by television anyway. We watched it when we visited my grandparents on Sundays after church. Even if all they ever watched was news programs and Billy Graham Crusades, we watched with them. It was TV, the wonder of the age! Except for our house, every house in our neighborhood had a TV. The most impoverished residents of the Marsh had one. Starved for television, on Saturday mornings and after school, my brother and I would peer into the neighbors' windows at their TV screens — glowing magnets that we could not resist — until they took pity on us and invited us inside and let us watch. Our favorite show, the beloved afterschool show of every kid in our part of the world, was The Doctor Max and Mambo Show. Dr. Max often ran comedy shorts. The slapstick humor of the Three Stooges was a kid-favorite. Who could fail to laugh when Larry, Moe, and Curley did painful things to one another?

On a fateful Sunday, after church when the congregation was filing out of the sanctuary, pausing one by one to shake hands with the preacher and his wife, Ricky got out quick and went straight to the church kitchen, where he found a certain cupboard and a big tin of black pepper.

That Cross of Jesus had been a labor that had taken him weeks to complete. Weeks! All those damn matches carefully glued down until that cross looked like a radiant explosion. His mom told him it was so beautiful it should be hung in a museum, and little Jack DeWitt destroyed it and walked away from the destruction as if it was nothing. Nothing! The destruction of great art! I never was punished, never made to apologize to him or replace his beautiful cross. He had been forced to make a second one, devote another hundred hours of tedious labor to it — all that gluing, people have no idea how HARD it is to make Art —and when he presented it, his second effort, at a Boy Scout Regional Event, it only came in third. Third place is nothing!

Not only had that happened, but every week I mocked him. Ricky was older than me, taller and better looking, had a superior GPA, and was well on his way to being an Eagle! What was little Jack Dewitt, by comparison? A smart mouth, a bad kid who did not even love Jesus. Not to mention, I was the one who got the church girls to call him Georgie Porgy! To his face!

If you thought about it, Ricky Fox was an instrument of the Lord. He was a modern version of an ancient Crusader. All smart-mouth unbelievers should be tied to stakes and stoned. That is what used to happen to people like little Jack Dewitt.

Ricky cupped his hand and poured pepper into it, a healthy dose, and then he added a bit more just to be sure. He hid behind a corner and waited for me, peeked around the corner. I was talking to a girl, walking beside her.

When I got close, Ricky stepped out from behind the corner and flung the pepper directly into my eyes.

A handful of pepper thrown into one's eyes is a reality-altering experience. One moment I was chatting with a girl. The next moment I was blind, and my entire face was on fire. I did not have time to blink. Pepper flew onto the surface of my eyeballs. Pepper landed on the soft skin around my eyes, on my eyelids, got into my eyebrows. Pepper flew up my nose. Pepper flew into my mouth and got stuck to my tongue, to the roof of my mouth, to my lips.

I screamed and clawed at my face.

Reality was transformed in that moment for everyone else too. Kids were yelling. Women were trying to comfort me. Men were barking instructions.

A person who turned out to be my mother dragged me into the women's restroom. She turned on the water, filled the sink, and pushed my head in. Pulled my head out of the water. Used paper towels to wipe off my tongue. Used toilet paper to dab at my eyes.

"Please, God. Please, God. Please."

Someone who turned out to be my dad carried me from the church to the family car. My siblings were left at the church with the pastor's wife. For me, the entire world consisted of my eyes, my nose and mouth, the skin on my face. Even my fingertips burned as if on fire.

My dad drove us away from the church. I rolled down my car window and stuck my head out the way a dog will because the breeze on my face made me feel better. I could not stop shedding tears.

My dad drove while my mother attempted to comfort me. As Dad drove, he and Mom were conducting a yelling argument about money and debt and our lack of eye insurance because the union failed to negotiate it during the last strike at the factory. We were in debt, terrible, crushing medical debt. My mom said I could not be taken to the hospital.

"Do you have any idea how much that will cost?!"

We went to my grandparents' house because it was closer to the church than our house.

My dad carried me into the bathroom upstairs. My mom went to work on me, picking grains of pepper out of my eyes.

"Please, God," she murmured. "Not blind. Please. Not blind."

Gradually, the fire in my eyes died down. Slowly, dab by dab, the fire on my skin, in my mouth and in my nostrils was extinguished.

7

Gum

Apparently, it is a lot cheaper to take a kid to see an eye doctor than it is to take him to a hospital emergency ward because on Monday, as soon as my father got off work, he drove me to an optometrist. My mom gave him a list and said, after we got my eyes examined, he could take me to a discount store and buy me the things I needed for gym class.

My dad found the right office. "This is it right here. 'Optometrist.' That means eye doc."

We went in. Dad talked to the receptionist and we sat down in the waiting room. The skin around my eyes was pink and swollen. My eyes were bloodshot. My lips and the inside of my mouth still felt funny, and I kept touching my face with my fingers to make sure it was intact. I hoped the eye doc wasn't going to tell us both of my eyes would have to be replaced.

I wondered if we could afford new eyeballs. Maybe we could afford just one. A little one.

My dad read a magazine until the doc appeared and led me to his examination room. "Got a little pepper in your eyes, huh?" He gave me what he called a complete exam. This meant after he looked hard at each of my eyeballs through a lens, I had to look at a chart with rows of letters on it. The letters kept getting smaller until it was impossible to see them.

"I don't know what that is. Maybe an O?"

When we were finished, the doc accompanied me to the waiting room where my dad was still reading a magazine. "No permanent damage, but he's gonna need glasses." He handed my dad the prescription and pointed him to the nearby office where we could buy frames and get the lenses made.

"Can we afford them?" I asked when we were in the hallway outside of the eye doc's office.

"You don't need to worry about that," my dad said.

I selected a pair of frames with black rims like the ones my dad wore. The optician told me they made me look like a "real professional." That sounded good. The optician said my glasses would be ready for pick-up the next day.

We stopped at a store and bought the stuff I needed for gym class. My dad explained that in junior high, gym class is taken seriously. "For one thing, there won't be no girls in your class. Your gym teacher is a man, probably a coach. Also, you have to wear special clothes."

"What kind of special?"

"You have to wear a pair of, let me see here," he looked at the list my mom gave him. "Regulation grey shorts with a blue stripe down each leg. Black tennis shoes. White cotton socks and a white tee-shirt. Underpants aren't allowed."

I looked at my dad. *No underwear?*

"You're gonna need a jockstrap," Dad said. "You probably don't even know what that is."

I knew what a jock was, a kid who loves any game involving a ball. A kid like Tommy White, for example. I had no idea why Tommy would need a strap.

"It's for your nuts," my dad said.

I could hardly believe it. My dad said the word "nuts."

The next day, when he got home from work, my dad took me downtown to pick up my new glasses. When we walked out of the optical shop, I could see things clearly. It was amazing! Every single thing I looked at was vivid and in-focus. The people on the sidewalk, the cars on the road, the clouds in the sky.

By the time I got home, I was transformed. The old Jack DeWitt, the one without glasses, was dead to me. The new Jack looked serious and important — like a professional. While my mom yelled at my dad about money, I went into the bathroom and looked at myself. I had been walking around in a blur for who knows how many years. I gazed long and hard at my face in the mirror, trying to determine if I had the mature face of a seventh grader. I had left elementary school far behind. I wondered if my friends would even recognize me.

I noticed I had a pimple.

I walked into Edgar Allen Poe Junior High the next Monday. I carried with me a letter telling me I was now a Raven. The letter also told me my class schedule, the room numbers of my classes, my locker number and the combination, and the names of my teachers. The letter said when I got to school, the first place I should go was the gym where I would meet up with my Student Guide. He would show me where my locker was located and then lead me around the school until I knew where my classrooms were and where the cafeteria was. Then he would take me to my homeroom where I would meet my homeroom teacher and receive my Official Welcome.

The hallways were full of kids and teachers. If we newbies got lost, the teachers looked at our letters and gave us directions. "Go down that hall, past the drinking fountain, turn left. You can't miss it."

The first day of school after summer break, everyone tries to act cool, but I was too scared to be cool. The year before, I was a sixth grader. Sixth graders were the big kids in elementary school. Every kid, every teacher, every room in our school was familiar to us. By then, our school was our second home. Now, we were in a new school – sort of new. New to us. In fact, Poe Junior High was old. Once upon a time decades ago, it had been the town high school. Our elementary school was built right after the war and still looked new by the time I showed up. Poe Junior had been built in the last decade of the previous century, and it looked like a medieval castle. It looked as if it ought to have gargoyles perched on the corners of its roof. We had to climb a flight of stone steps to enter. It had long narrow windows and was three stories high.

Kids from four different elementary schools went to Poe, so the school seemed enormous. It contained four times more students than my elementary school, four times more classrooms, four times more teachers. It had a swimming pool and a cafeteria and a football practice field and a cinder track. There was another huge area – like an enormous outdoor floor made of concrete, with a basketball hoop on each of the four sides. The "net" for each hoop was made of iron chains. The gym had bleachers on both sides.

The rumor was all the good junior high teachers and coaches were clustered on the other end of the west side. They had jobs at James Fenimore Cooper Junior High where the rich kids went. If a teacher couldn't hack it over there, he or she was sent here to Poe.

My guide was a boy named Kevin, two years older than me, a ninth grader.

"We get the reject teachers," Kevin assured me. "The drunks and the screwballs. The old bats. If you ask me, half of 'em should be in prison. Or maybe a mental asylum." Kevin examined my letter. "Look at this. You got Baldy for homeroom. I hope you survive."

"I thought his name was –"

"We call him Baldy. The shop teacher. Because he's bald. Some kids call him The Wart. Because he has a fat red wart right in the middle of his bald forehead. Or some kids call him Old Man Wart. Anything like that means him. But don't YOU call him Baldy or Wart, not to his face. Not if you want to live. He hates kids, especially seventh graders. I recommend you say nothing if possible. Hope he never notices you. Of course, he might like you if you're good with wood. You know how to pound nails, drill, use a bandsaw?"

I had no idea what a bandsaw was. A band was a group of musicians. My mom had signed me up for junior high band. In my last two years of elementary school, I had been taught to play the trombone. But why would a band need a saw? The one time I had tried to hammer a nail into a board was still an unpleasant memory.

"I thought, in homeroom, all you do is just get announcements and stuff. You don't really build things, do you, in homeroom?"

"And you better lose that gum. Baldy hates kids who chew gum." I was chewing a wad of Juicy Fruit. "Jesus, is that Middle Grimm?"

The three Grimm Sisters were approaching us. Middle and Big were side by side, moving through the crowd of kids like two ocean liners through a bevy of smaller boats, and Little trailed a step behind them, looking scared. Like me, Little was a seventh grader. Middle and Big were both in ninth grade. They were in the same class this year because the teachers were making Big take ninth grade over again. Kids were retreating when they saw Big. She didn't look happy to be here. But Middle was drawing a crowd of boys.

The reason Kevin had lost his train of thought was because over the summer Middle's breasts had become enormous.

Suddenly, Kevin noticed something else and whispered, "It's Hamberger! Tuck in your shirt! Hurry!"

I tucked in my shirttail. Other boys around me were doing the same thing. That year, it was fashionable for boys to have their shirttails out.

I saw a tiny woman approaching, obviously a teacher. She wore rimless glasses and had thick iron grey hair pushed back from her forehead as if to make her seem taller. She wore sturdy shoes. She had angry eyes, enlarged by the lenses of her glasses. I noticed she had some muscle definition in her arms and calves. There was something about her that made her seem dangerous even though she was tiny.

"Why do they call her Hamburger? Does she love cheeseburgers or something?"

"That's her name, stupid. She's your band teacher. She hates any boy who has his shirttail out. One of her pet peeves. You want automatic detention, just let her catch you with your tail out."

After we finished my tour of the school, Kevin dropped me off at the wood shop, which would be my homeroom for my three years at Poe Junior.

"If you see me again, don't bug me. Because – you know – I'm a ninth grader, and you're just a seventh grader."

Baldy was just inside the door. He had a clipboard and was checking off students as soon as we entered. "Hello, Mister, um, hello, sir," I said. I was horrified because I could not recall his actual name. I had almost called him Mister Baldy. I dropped my eyes so I wouldn't stare at his wart.

"What's your name, son? Last name."

"DeWitt, sir."

The tables in shop class were made of thick slabs of wood. Students sat on top of stools. Baldy pointed at one of the square tables. "DeWitt, you sit over there." For the rest of my time at Poe, Baldy never called me anything but DeWitt.

I perched on a stool, right beside a vise. I shared my table with three other kids who were already there: a nondescript girl named Amy, a jock named Billy, and Ray Kavanaugh. I could see Ray and Billy did not like one another from the moment they made eye contact. There is a natural enmity between jocks and hoods.

"Hey, Ray," I said.

Ray glanced at me and grunted. That meant he did not intend to let anyone think he and I were good friends. Maybe we had homeroom in common, but that was it. I was a brain, and he would not be in any of my classes. His classes were the ones for the dummies. Ray was not really a dummy; he just didn't give a damn about school. I believed his poor attitude about education developed because he had been held back. He was like a big cuckoo growing up in a nest of little sparrows. Ray was a seventh grader, but he should have been a ninth grader. He had been out for a year due to rheumatic fever, and then he got another year behind when he got sent to reform school.

Ray inspected me for a moment. "Why you wearing glasses? You look like a dork."

My belief that my new glasses made me look professional vanished in that moment. I removed my glasses, folded them up, and put them in my pocket. "I don't really need them," I lied. "Except for reading." The world became a blur.

Baldy started our first homeroom session by reading from a letter called Welcome to Poe. The letter told us we were going to enjoy many stimulating educational opportunities that would help us in our journey toward adulthood. Also, we were going to makes lots of wonderful new friends. We shouldn't worry about anything because our teachers were going to respect us and assist us in every possible way. Unfortunately, the bored and slightly contemptuous tone in Baldy's voice suggested that none of this was true. His voice suggested that, in his opinion, we were going to screw up on a regular basis, flunk most of our classes, lose what few friends we had, and wind up in prison.

While Baldy was reading the letter, I realize something horrifying. I was still chewing gum.

Moving as slowly as I possibly could, I opened the vise. Despite my care, Ray noticed what I was doing and winked at me. The girl Amy also noticed and rolled her eyes. Billy the jock had his attention fixed on Baldy, who was still reading us the welcome letter.

When the two plates of the vise were far enough apart, I removed the Juicy Fruit from my mouth and put my wad of forbidden gum into the vise. Then I silently and slowly spun the handle until the vise was closed tight.

Amy made a snort of disapproval. Ray grinned and shook his head, amused. Billy had no idea anything had happened.

8

Skinny-Dipping

mile from my house was a big farm with a small pond. Kids said the farmer dug the pond himself so, when his field drained, the rainwater would have a place to go. The farmer had poured a load of sand at one end of it, making something resembling a beach. The pond was in a secluded location, surrounded by trees and tall grass. It was impossible to see it until you were right on top of it.

High school kids went skinny-dipping in that pond. When I was in sixth grade, the concept of skinny-dipping had to be explained to me by my friends.

"They swim naked?" I said. "Boys AND girls? Like I believe that. I may be stupid, but I'm not dumb!"

To prove that high school kids really did swim naked in that pond, two of my friends took me there one hot summer afternoon. Even when we were close to the pond, we couldn't see it. I told them I doubted the pond even existed. This was just a wild-goose chase.

"Listen!"

I listened until I heard shrieks of laughter. Girls.

One of my friends crawled forward, disappeared into the tall grass, and then returned a few minutes later, rubbing a mosquito bite.

"They're here all right. Two guys and two girls. No swimsuits."

If there was one thing my mother had made clear to me many times it was that I should never display my private parts to anyone.

"They're wearing underwear, you mean," I said. I was already turning red.

"Go on," my friend urged. "Take a look. But for god's sake, keep quiet!"

I crawled into the tall grass, following the trail forged by my friend until at last I could see it, the pond. Four high school kids. Two guys and two girls. I froze in place, still on my hands and knees. I could see pubic hair. I could see bare breasts.

And then a perfectly dreadful thing happened. One of the girls noticed me, screamed and pointed. "There's someone else here!"

I should have withdrawn instantly into the tall grass, but I was paralyzed.

"Where?" the other girl said. "I don't see anyone."

"Right there!" the first girl said. She was a blond. Her entire upper body, everything from her knees up, was visible above the water. Her long sun-tanned arm was pointing right at me.

The second girl, a brunette, saw me and screamed. The brunette ducked down into the water until only her head was visible.

The blond took a shameless step in my direction and let out a whoop. "Hey, little kid!"

The two boys – big guys – started to move toward me.

I still could not move. Behind me, I felt one of my friends pulling on my ankle. "Come on! We have to go! We have to go NOW!"

And then a perfectly appalling thing happened. The blond waved at me wildly with both arms and yelled, "Come join us, baby!"

That did it.

I unfroze, backed up. My friends and I fled.

I did not dare tell my mother about any of this. With my own eyes, I had seen the rules of civilized behavior violated. I had been invited to participate. By a naked high school girl!

At Poe Junior High School, the rules of civilized behavior were violated on a regular basis. Skinny-dipping was not forbidden. It was mandatory. At least for boys.

My second period class was Swimming. When I arrived in the locker room, I found thirty boys getting naked. Our class was for boys only. Coach Dee was in his office listening to his radio

"I didn't bring my swimming trunks," I said. "No one told me."

"Who cares?" a kid said. He was pulling down his underpants.

"We don't wear 'em," another kid told me. He was sitting on a bench and pulling off his shoes. "The girls get to wear suits in their class, but we don't."

The coach's assistant, a student teacher, was opening the door to the pool.

I yanked off my shirt and tried not to look at anyone. I sat down on the bench and pulled off my shoes. Half the boys were already in the pool area. I could hear splashes and yells.

Never in my life had I been in a locker room. I finished removing my clothes and walked naked with the other stragglers toward the pool. The coach's assistant was taking attendance.

"Is the water cold?"

"Only one way to find out," the assistant said.

In junior high, boys come in every size. Some boys, especially the incoming seventh graders, lack pubic hair. Our voices are just starting to break. Other boys, especially the ninth graders, are hairy as full-grown men.

When Coach Dee walked into the pool area and blew his whistle, all of us were in the water. I felt safer when I was in up to my neck. Most of my fellow seventh graders were splashing around in the shallow end. I was not the only kid who did not know how to swim. We were yelling and splashing when the coach's whistle cut through the din.

The boys began climbing out of the pool and lining up beside it. I climbed out too, dripping, wishing I had a towel.

Coach Dee's white tee-shirt stretched over his big belly and was tucked into the waistband of his gym shorts. "We're doing tests this morning," he said.

I noticed there were four kids who were even shorter and skinnier than me.

Coach Dee told his assistant to take over. He folded his big arms and watched us while the assistant explained that boys who knew how to swim could test out today. If you wanted to get out of swimming class and spend the time in study hall instead, this was your opportunity to demonstrate proper swimming skills. Kids like me, non-swimmers who did not want to be tested, were told to sit cross-legged on the deck and watch.

I counted 11 other boys besides me who were non-swimmers, almost half the class.

The kids who could swim had to swim ten laps. They started at the deep end, swam the entire length of the pool, climbed out, walked past us losers back to the deep end, and dived in again; they did that ten times. If any boy wore out before he finished his ten laps, he had to sit in disgrace with us non-swimmers. Then all the remaining test-takers had to jump into the deep end and float on their backs for ten minutes. It got blessedly quiet. They had to tread water for ten minutes. Occasionally one of them would go underwater, come up spluttering, admit failure, and climb out of the pool.

The biggest boy by far was a full-grown man who appeared to be half-human, half bull. "Who is he?" It was hard to believe he could be a student.

"The Hulk!" the kid beside me whispered.

57

I noticed the Hulk was getting away with murder. When the other boys were swimming ten laps, he swam only two and then stood beside the coach and his assistant, pointing at the swimming boys and making jokes. I guess they were jokes. When the swimmers floated on their backs and treaded water, he got into the water but kept his hand on the gutter that lined the pool.

"He's cheating!" I whispered to the kid beside me.

The kid shot me a nervous glance and shook his head.

The Hulk was cheating right in front of the coach. How could the coach not see it?

When the swimmers had to dive off the diving board, the Hulk just jumped off – a cannonball! No one said a thing about it.

I thought maybe I should stand up, go to the coach, and tell him about the cheating that was going on right under his nose.

The last test for anyone who wanted to pass out of swimming was Retrieving the Brick. The coach had a ten-pound brick covered in black rubber. He tossed it into the deep end. The swimmer had to dive into the pool, swim to the bottom with his eyes open until he located the brick, grab it, bring it to the surface, shove it out onto the deck, and climb out of the water. That was the final task, the one that meant he did not have to take any more swimming classes.

Coach Dee tossed in the brick.

"I'll give it a go," the Hulk said. His voice was an octave deeper than my dad's voice, and my dad sang baritone in the church choir.

The Hulk jumped into the water. He kept his arms at his sides and sank straight to the bottom of the deep end. He stood down there and did not move.

"Maybe he can't see it," the coach's assistant said.

We all looked at the Hulk. Some kids stood up to see him better. Normally, it isn't possible to stand up like that at the bottom of a swimming pool. Your body drifts sideways. If you don't move your arms, you will naturally float back to the surface.

The Hulk just stood down there, not moving.

"Wave your arms!" the coach's assistant yelled. "Swim!"

Kids started yelling too, as if their combined voices might penetrate all the water, arrive at the Hulk's ears, and inspire him to start moving his arms like a normal human being.

"Dammit," the coach said. He motioned at a couple ninth graders, "Henson, Abbot, go get him!"

The boys dived into the water, swam down to the Hulk, got their hands under his armpits, and dragged him up to the surface.

The Hulk did not seem any worse for wear. He did not gasp and cough and splutter like someone who had just survived a near-drowning experience.

"Did I pass, Coach?"

I could hardly believe my ears. *Did he pass?!*

The coach's assistant looked at the coach. Coach Dee shrugged. The brick was still visible at the bottom of the pool.

"Bruiser passes," the assistant said.

Two days later, in home room, I was still talking about what I had witnessed in swimming class. By then I had found out the Hulk was on the football team. He was by far the biggest player on the front line. I did not yet know what exactly a front line was but apparently it was something important. Coach Dee was the football coach. Of course, he was going to pass the Hulk. Just like all the other football players, the Hulk got special treatment. Billy the Jock told me, "His last name is Bruiser. Ben Bruiser! But we call him The Incredible Hulk!"

Ray did not seem terribly interested.

"Oh," I said to Ray, "and get this. You know Middle? Middle Grimm?"

Ray had not been paying attention to my story until I said Middle. "What about her?"

"The Hulk's in love with her. Everyone says so. You don't wanna go near her, not even talk to her, not unless you want to get flattened by the Hulk."

At that moment, Baldy appeared beside us. The whole room got quiet. The bell rang. It was time for Baldy to take attendance. What was he doing standing beside our table, looking at us?

"Kavanaugh," he said softly to Ray. "Why don't you open that vise for us?"

It all came back to me, that thing that had happened my first day of homeroom. Gum!

The gum had been discovered in the vise the same day I put it there but two periods later. A kid spun open the vise just for the fun of it, and there it was, my gum, stretching between the two plates of the vise. Not wanting to be blamed, the kid told Baldy about the situation. Baldy came over and looked.

"You do it?" Baldy asked the kid.

The kid swore on his mother's soul, he had nothing to do with that gum.

Baldy figured it was someone in his first period class, so he waited an entire day to ask the kids at the table if one of them did it.

They all swore up and down they were innocent until Baldy concluded it was someone in his homeroom class.

The vise was bolted to the table, to the corner that was between Ray and me.

Ray looked Baldy right in the eye and grinned a little bit. "This here vise?"

My heart was hammering inside my chest. Amy's face was turning red. Billy looked confused.

Ray spun open the vise. The gum was still there. It stretched between the two plates of the vise like a suspension bridge.

"You did it, Kavanaugh," Baldy said matter-of-factly. "Didn't you?"

"I did it!" I yelled. "It was me! I'm sorry!"

Baldy had assumed it was Ray. Of course, it was him. Ray was a juvenile delinquent. He had homemade tattoos on his hands. He was a ninth grader impersonating a seventh grader.

Baldy's eyes moved from Ray to me. He looked at me as if he had never seen me before, and he wanted to get a good look.

"DeWitt," he said.

"It wasn't me," Billy said. "I had NOTHING to do with it!"

"It was Jack DeWitt," Amy said. "I saw him do it."

Ray was looking at me, smiling a little.

Baldy reached out and took hold of my neck. He had big hard calloused hands. Without a word, he pushed my head into the space between the plates of the vise until the gum stretched across my forehead. "Don't move," he said softly. He began to spin the handle, making the plates close in on my ears. When my head was trapped in the vise, Baldy said, "You gonna do it again, DeWitt?"

"No, sir!" I said. "I will never do it again!"

That is how I got detention the first week of seventh grade.

9

Packers

After I got detention, the hoods gave me a second look when they sauntered past me. Even the girls in my classes noticed me more now that I had taken my first step on the path of crime. Before I was just another scrawny brain, but now I was a notorious gum vandal with a stain on my permanent record.

I also got noticed by a tall, skinny, glasses-wearing boy in my algebra class who was named Calvin. He wanted to know if Baldy had damaged my ears at all. If he had, he thought my dad should sue Baldy. We should sue the school too just for employing Baldy.

"You figure Baldy has much money?" I said. I was pretty sure my dad was about as likely to sue Baldy as he was to grow a second head.

"Maybe not, but it's the principle of the thing," Calvin said.

One thing was for certain, Calvin was never going to get a stain on HIS permanent record. Like most of the kids in my classes, he was incapable of doing anything bad.

At lunch, Calvin sat down beside me and pumped me for information about detention. My new friend, Michael Not Mike also joined us.

Michael was stuck in the dumb kid classes, all because he moved here from Kentucky. How could he take the IQ test? His school in

Kentucky probably didn't even know what an IQ test was. I didn't exactly know what an IQ test was either, but I didn't want my new friends to know there were enormous gaps in my knowledge. I had wondered what IQ meant but was afraid to ask. Idiotic Questions? I vaguely remembered that last year in sixth grade, we were given a test that took three days. It was one of those tests where you use a No. 2 pencil to fill in little dots on the answer sheet. I got the highest score in our class, even higher than the one the red-headed girl got, a fact that made her mad and was probably the main reason she never sent me a postcard. It never occurred to me that that test changed my life and saved me from having to be in the dummy classes.

According to Michael, a high score on that test was the only way the teachers decided who got to be in the good classes. Because he never took the test, he was only thirteen years old and he was already doomed to being bored out of his skull every day. While I ate my chilidog and drank my milk, he told us about how brain-dead the kids in his classes were. "Like in geography, we're doing the Fifty States, right? One kid didn't know Nebraska is a state. Nebraska! He thought it was an island somewhere!"

Calvin thought the Nebraska story was pretty funny. "What other dumb things do dumb kids believe?"

Michael said, "What they don't know would fill an encyclopedia. You realize they are always gonna be like that, and you have to sit in class with them."

Calvin said, "Imagine how bored the teachers must be."

Michael said, "Bored out of their living minds."

Calvin said, "The teachers went to college, right? Worked hard, got good grades, and then what? They wound up here, teaching dummies."

Michael said, "We fill out worksheets and draw pictures. This morning, my English teacher made us read out loud, this story about a kid who gets lost in the woods. It turns out half the kids can barely read. She listened to six kids and then she couldn't take it anymore. She stands up and yells at this one kid to stop reading, 'Did you kids learn ANYTHING in elementary school?' This is her first job, so the stupidity of the kids here is still shocking to her, I guess."

Michael said there was a glimmer of light at the end of his tunnel. His homeroom teacher was a sweet old lady named Mrs. Monroe; she was practically in love with him. "She's gonna go see the guidance counselor and find out if maybe I can take the test by myself on the weekend or something."

Calvin said he had his doubts Michael would be allowed to take the test all by himself. That test could only be given on special days, and everyone had to take it at the same time, or otherwise there might be cheating. He was pretty sure about it.

Michael was so sad about what Calvin said that I didn't tell have the heart to tell him about my classes – which were the same classes that Calvin had, the smart kid classes. They were not what I would call fun, but they weren't outright torture which is what his classes sounded like. The only classes I hated with a passion (besides gym and swimming) were my band class and my trombone sectional class. These classes were run by Hamberger, who seemed to believe she had been put on this Earth to scare the crap out of kids. She certainly scared the crap out of me.

After school, because of detention, I could not walk home with Michael Not Mike, but it turned out I did have a companion – Ray. He also got assigned to detention the first week because he got into a fight with a jock in gym class. The jock didn't get detention because, well, because he was a jock. Ray was a hood so he got two weeks.

On the way home, I tried to impress Ray by telling him about Hamberger, how he was lucky he was not in band because, if he was, he would hate her. Ray had played drums for our elementary school band but had decided not to sign up for junior high band.

Ray knew who Hamberger was because everyone in school did. Between classes, she hung out at the top of one of the main staircases, yelling down at boys who had their shirttails out, and God help you if you tried to go up the down staircase.

Ray said someone should push Hamberger over the bannister when she was leaning over it, yelling at students. He figured one good hard shove would probably do the trick. "That lesbo ain't gonna yell at anyone if her neck is broken."

I thought breaking Hamberger's neck was perhaps going farther than absolutely necessary, and I wondered what a lesbo was. "She shouldn't even be allowed to teach kids," I said.

Ray said he thought the best way to improve Poe Junior would be to set the whole school on fire and watch it burn down.

I had my doubts a school made of bricks would burn that well, but the image of Poe Junior on fire appealed to me.

We spent our hour of detention with an old lady named Mrs. Prohaska. No one knew who she was exactly. She did not seem to be a real teacher. Ray thought she might be a janitor or maybe one of the cooks. She made us sign our names on a piece of paper when we came in and issued each of us a battered dictionary and five sheets of blank paper. Our task was to copy definitions from the dictionary onto the pieces of paper. I had dutifully obeyed her and copied definitions until my hand cramped, but Ray had just drawn pictures.

"Wanna see?" We were on our way home, approaching the Packer Neighborhood.

Ray had created a detailed drawing of a motorcycle that was impressively realistic, but his masterpiece was his second picture. "I made this for the Nazi," he said. "If he approves my design, he's gonna pay me to paint it on the wall of his room."

The Nazi was a weird boy who had sat at the back of the room in sixth grade. He had a real first name, Wolfgang, but except for teachers, none of the kids ever called him that. He was absent a lot and never said much. Ray said the Nazi was a rich kid. He lived in the motel right off the highway. I had seen this motel every time we drove past it on our way to church but never thought much about it. Ray said the Nazi's parents ran the motel. They lived in the two-story house beside it and gave the Nazi every single thing his heart desired because the Nazi was an only child.

"How come you think everyone calls him that?"

"He loves Nazis. That's why. He has a whole bunch of books with pictures of Nazis. Anything about World War II, but it needs to be about Nazis, or he doesn't care. He only comes to school like two or three times a week because his mom writes excuses for him. If he says, 'Oh I can't go today because my little toe hurts,' she writes he's got foot disease or something."

Ray's picture was a large, stylized eagle with its wings outstretched standing on top of a circle that contained a swastika. Ray was totally indifferent to history and politics, but this was a way to make a little money.

I thought maybe it would be boring to stay home with your parents that often. Wouldn't it be more interesting to come to school?

Ray said, "When he's not reading books about Nazis or Hitler, he reads comic books. He has subscriptions! Every week they come in the mail. Spiderman and Fantastic Four and X-Men, Superman, Batman! Whatever comics he wants!"

I loved comic books, but my mom would hardly ever give me money to buy them.

"Plus, you can get pop out of their pop machine."

"They own a pop machine?"

"For the motel guests. In the house, they have this little pottery bowl full of dimes. If you want a pop, all you have to do is take a dime from the bowl and use it in the pop machine. Whatever you want, Coke or root beer or orange or whatever. But you can only drink one bottle. His mom thinks if you drink two, you might get diarrhea."

Ray added, "He has two entire rooms just for him, it's amazing! And he has a lock on the door. If his mom or dad want to come in, they have to knock! I'll take you over there someday."

By then I was losing interest in hearing anything more about the Nazi because we were approaching the Packers Neighborhood. This was a shabby dark neighborhood inhabited mostly by men who worked at the meat pack and their families. The first day of school, Michael Not Mike and I had worked out a route that skirted the edge of it so we could avoid getting attacked by Packer kids. It added four blocks to our walk.

Ray insisted on walking right through the dark heart of Packer Territory. "Guess who lives on this street."

I did not want to guess.

Ray stopped in front of a house with siding made of old-looking brown shingles. "Remember that big guy you were telling me about? The guy in your swimming class? The one who sank to the bottom like a rock and had to be pulled out?"

"The Hulk? The Hulk lives here? We better go. We don't want to linger." I wondered what Ray would think if I just started running as fast as I could to get away from this street.

By then I had learned a few more things about the Hulk and his family, the Bruisers. That was their actual name. The Bruisers. Mr. and Mrs. Bruiser had three sons. All three of them were huge. Ben, aka The Hulk, was the second son. The oldest son Bruce was already in prison because he beat up a cop. An actual cop. The youngest son was still in elementary school, but he was already the size of a gorilla. People called him Baby Huey.

"Let's go," I said.

People said the Hulk was the most dangerous of the Bruisers. If he had not yet murdered somebody, it was only a matter of time until he did.

"Please, can we just go?"

Ray was looking thoughtfully at the house as if he was thinking of breaking into it.

"Ray! Listen to me! What I heard, last year, in a football game, the Hulk broke a guy's leg. But he couldn't be prosecuted because — you know — it was during a game."

"Well, here's what I like about life," Ray said. "Everyone has a weakness."

10

The Fight

Ray went one way and I went the other. He walked toward his house down in the Marsh, and I walked the rest of the way to my house up on the Hill. I had plenty of time to think it through. This thing was about Middle Grimm. Ray wanted her. I would not call it love; love probably had nothing to do with it. I had my doubts a guy like Ray was even capable of love. Hulk had called dibs on Middle. She probably didn't even like him much – as if that mattered. She would have to get used to the idea of being the Hulk's girl because no other guy in his right mind was going to mess with the Hulk.

Ray did not seem to understand these simple facts.

By then I had heard the Hulk liked to hang out in the parking lot of the stadium during high school football games. He would offer to fight anyone. High school hoods. Guys who had already graduated. If they accepted, he would destroy them. Beating guys up was a hobby for The Hulk.

In homeroom, Ray told me he had had a conversation with Weenie. Weenie was a kid in my algebra class. He was so short and immature, he still looked like a fifth grader. He had a brain and was enrolled

JACK DEWITT IS CLUELESS

in the smart classes, not that it mattered to him. What he loved was sports, athletes. He was the assistant manager for the football team. His job was to hand jocks a fresh towel when they came out of the showers after practice. He hung around the locker room basking in their glory until all of them left. Then he locked up the place.

Ray told me he'd had a talk with Weenie and discovered an interesting fact. The Hulk was always the last football player to come out of the showers.

When I got to detention after school, Ray did not appear. By then, I knew how he worked. Mrs. Prohaska was going to mark him absent. Then she would turn in her attendance sheet. The office would find out Ray never showed up for detention. He would have to go see the vice principal tomorrow, but by then he would have a whole excuse worked out. If there was one thing he was good at, it was lying to grown-ups.

I spent my hour copying words from the dictionary. I would never admit it, especially to someone like Ray, but I liked dictionaries. *Aardwolf. A South African carnivorous fox-like quadruped. Abacinate. To blind by putting a red-hot copper basin near the eyes.*

When I got done with detention, I went to my locker and pulled out my trombone case. It was my sectional day, so I had had to lug the thing all the way to school from my house, and now I was going to have to carry it home. According to Hamberger, I needed practice. Lots and lots of practice. Trombone is not an easy instrument. She had six boys in the trombone section. I was the worst trombone. To play trombone properly, a kid needs a decent ear because there are no stops for the slide. You have to develop a feel for how far you should extend your arm. It was obvious I did not have an excellent ear. My ear was a lazy, shiftless kind of ear that did not care if the note I was blowing was correct. Hamberger said she was thinking of switching me to baritone horn. Baritone horns have keys. Even a tone-deaf

70

dummy can play one.

I felt glum about the situation because if Hamberger called up my mom, and my mom said yes to the switch, I would have to lug a baritone in its case all the way to school and back. A baritone is nine feet of brass tube curled up like a snake. It weighs maybe 20 pounds. You hold it in your arms like a giant baby. It comes in a case that weighs – I have no idea how much a baritone case weighs. It's like a big clunky suitcase. Twice a week, I would have to lug it all the way to school and then all the way back home.

Like the other moms in our neighborhood, my mom was taking driving lessons. Maybe if she got her license and my dad let her use the car, I could talk her into driving me back and forth to school at least on days when I had to take my instrument.

The best solution would be to get her to let me quit band, but that was never going to happen. My mother said in our family we are not quitters. In my opinion, this was just one of the many things that was wrong with our family.

I usually exited the school through a door that led out the backside of the school, near the boys' locker room. Carrying my trombone case, I walked down the corridor past the gym, past the door to the locker room. A little kid was up by the door, looking out the window at something.

"Hey, Weenie," I said, when I got close. "What you doing?"

Without turning around to see who I was, Weenie said, "Don't go out there. There's gonna be a fight."

Fights were not uncommon at Poe Junior but usually they did not happen close to the school. Usually the news of an upcoming fight circulated through the school day. As soon as the final bell rang, a crowd of kids would go to the parking lot of the Church of Christ six blocks away. This lot was located behind the church so no grown up driving by could see it. It was surrounded by a wooden fence, so even the neighbors couldn't see what was happening back there. Thirty or forty kids would show up to watch the fight. Sometimes more. At one of these fights, you might see teeth get knocked out. You might see noses get broken. Usually, the fight continued until the kids in the crowd got so wild they could not keep quiet and started screaming encouragement at whichever fighter they liked best. The noise would eventually attract attention and some adult in the neighborhood called the cops. When a patrol car showed up, everyone including the fighters would run like hell. Sometimes one of the fighters would be in such poor shape, he would remain there, lying on the ground, bloody and defeated. It was considered bad form for the loser to tell the cops anything.

"It's the Hulk," Weenie said. "And Ray."

I set down my trombone case and approached the door. It was really two doors, each with a window, the kind reinforced with wires so when you looked through them you looked through a bunch of diamond shapes.

The Hulk was standing, his knees bent and his arms out, and Ray was dancing in front of him, saying stuff. I couldn't hear well enough to know what exactly Ray was saying but I could tell his comments affected the Hulk because his face was red and his eyes were scrunched up and full of hate. He looked as if he wanted to murder Ray. I knew enough about fights to know that if Ray ever got close enough to the Hulk and those big hands caught hold of him, the fight would be over in seconds. The Hulk would bear-hug him, fall on top of him, choke him or start whaling away at him with his fists.

Ray was too quick and smart to get caught. It was wonderful and thrilling to watch him. He kept dancing back and forth just out of reach, saying stuff, needling the Hulk, getting him to think – never one of the Hulk's strong suits.

Then Ray did it, what he must have planned to do ever since he found out the Hulk was always the last person to leave the locker room after a practice. Ray must have waited out there in the parking lot when he was supposed to be in detention, waited for practice to end, and all the other football players to leave, hung around out there until at last the Hulk appeared, still damp from his long shower, surprised to see him.

Ray probably said something right away, something nasty, and it had stopped the Hulk in his tracks. No one ever did that. No one ever gave him crap. Usually it was the other way around. The Hulk was the one who challenged the other guy. He did not bother with mockery. He was not capable of anything like wit or deep insight into the other guy's personality. He just told the other guy he was going to fight unless he was a chickenshit. The guy ran for his life or he stepped up, and if he stepped up, the Hulk would soon catch hold of him and throw him hard to the ground and then hurt him. The Hulk liked to humiliate guys. He liked to make them cry.

For a split-second, Ray got close enough to the Hulk to be grabbed, and in that moment, he kicked the Hulk right in the crotch.

At that time in my life, I was just starting to get hair on my ball sack, long dark hairs, but already I knew what it felt like to be hit in the nuts. It felt like death.

The Hulk did not go down on his knees after Ray kicked him. He staggered backward and his face turned white. He started breathing through his mouth. I could not believe he was still standing. The Hulk was making strange animal noises. He tried to jump forward and get Ray in a bear hug, but Ray danced out of his grasp, whirled and did it again, kicked the Hulk right between the legs.

This time, the Hulk's eyes rolled up so far I could see the whites of his eyes. He staggered backward until he was up against the wall of the school.

The Hulk seemed to have entered a parallel universe. He did not go down. He used the wall to keep himself up.

"Stop this," I said. "Someone stop it."

I could hear Weenie beside me, breathing loudly, panting with excitement.

The Hulk did not stay on the wall but came out a few steps toward Ray with his arms out. But he was slow. It was as if he was trapped in a slow-motion dream.

Ray stepped close to the Hulk and kicked him a third time, right in the crotch. He booted the Hulk as hard as he could, kicked him so hard he lifted the Hulk up off the ground for a moment. This time, the Hulk staggered back to the wall again and slid down it until he was sitting on the ground. His face was green. I don't think he was breathing any more. I thought he was dead, or at least on his way to death. Who could survive three kicks like that?

Ray had an expression on his face. As if he had just drawn a perfect Nazi eagle on a piece of paper. Then he looked up and to his left and grinned at someone.

I followed his look. The doorway where the fight occurred was visible from another wing of the school. There was a window up there on the third floor, and there was a white face in the window. Middle.

Middle Grimm was watching the fight.

He told her, I thought. *He told her to stay up there and wait if she wanted to see something good.*

Ray looked back at the Hulk, maybe to see if he was dead yet.

Something amazing was happening. The Hulk was pulling himself back up, using the wall for support. His face was covered in sweat. He was breathing hoarsely though his mouth and whimpering.

"Don't get up," I said.

Ray said something I couldn't hear and looked disgusted. Then without ever looking up again at the window where Middle was watching, he turned on his heel and left.

The Hulk still seemed trapped in an alternative universe where he could move but only very slowly, as if he was in chest-deep water. He staggered toward Ray, who by then was half-way out of the parking lot, walking away as if nothing of any interest had just happened.

The Hulk bellowed. His arms moved. His fingers clutched at the air. "Come back!" he yelled. "Come back!"

He wants to be kicked again, I thought. *The damn fool wants to be kicked a FOURTH time.*

I looked up at the third-floor window. She was still up there, watching Ray walk away from all of us.

11

Football

The next day was Friday, Game Day.

Ray was in homeroom by the time I got there. For some reason, I was intimidated by him. I sat down on my stool and looked around the room. I was afraid to mention the fight.

Just before attendance, Ray said, "Hey, I know you were there. You and Weenie. No big deal. Hope you got your rocks off."

I looked at him gratefully and would have started talking excitedly, but Ray shushed me by putting his finger to his lips. I was especially curious to know if he had planned ahead. Had he considered the possibility that the Hulk might want revenge? Did he realize the Hulk was on the football team? Was he aware that the Hulk and a dozen of his football player friends might appear one day and kick the crap out of him? Baldy closed the door and started taking attendance so I had to shut up.

Ordinarily, when a big fight occurred, it was the talk of the school the next day. No one seemed aware this one had even happened. All anyone wanted to discuss was the upcoming game.

Normally, we got beat by the Wolves, so we hated them.

In algebra class, I heard that the Hulk was not in school. A boy we called Chubby told me the Hulk was in his homeroom. But the big guy wasn't there. Chubby said he'd heard the Hulk was sick today, which would be a rotten deal if true because it was Game Day. The team needed the Hulk, needed him bad. We were playing the Wolves, for god's sake.

Calvin leaned over and said, "This time, we're gonna beat them!"

Chubby said even if the Hulk showed up by game time, we weren't going to beat the Wolves because they had black guys on the team. He didn't call them "black guys."

Calvin told him he shouldn't use that word. He should say Negroes or Colored People.

Chubby shrugged.

One good thing, at lunch I discovered I did not have detention anymore. No detention on Fridays was the rule. Since I had been assigned only one week of detention for the gum incident, that meant I no longer had to go see Mrs. Prohaska and copy out of the dictionary.

Our last class was cut short because we were released half an hour early so that we could go to the gym for a Pep Rally. I sat in the bleachers with Michael and Calvin. The cheerleaders ran out with their pom-poms and led us in cheers. Michael had opinions about which cheerleaders were cute. All of them. Calvin said he had high standards when it came to cuteness; he said only four of the cheerleaders were truly cute.

After the cheerleaders got us all worked up, the principal ran out onto the gym floor. I noticed he was wearing his leather shoes and wondered if Coach Dee knew it. The coach did not allow anyone to set foot on the precious wooden floor of the gym unless he was wearing rubber-soled shoes. The principal grabbed the microphone and said we Ravens had always been known throughout our town for our amazing school spirit, and he was sure this year would be no exception. He and the cheerleaders led us in another cheer.

I leaned over to Calvin and asked him if he thought the principal was sufficiently cute to be a cheerleader. Maybe it would help if he wore a short skirt.

Calvin did not appreciate my comments.

Then we were introduced to the school mascot, a kid dressed up like a giant Raven in a costume that consisted mostly of large shiny black feathers made of plastic. Calvin leaned toward me and whispered that no one knew the identity of the kid who was inside the Raven costume. It was a closely guarded secret.

"It's Weenie," I said.

Calvin gave me a shocked look.

I pointed out how the lower part of the costume had been pinned up because Weenie was too short for it. You could see Weenie's tennis shoes. He sat beside me in algebra class, and today I had noticed that he wore Converse All-Stars. The round trademarks on the ankles had been replaced by patches. The patches were made of white fabric with a raven head drawn on them with a marker pen. "His mom made 'em," I said.

Weenie ran around the gym floor flapping his wings while we clapped and yelled "Rave-Ins! Rave-Ins!"

The principal yelled, "You're not being loud enough. I can hardly hear you!" Everyone yelled "Rave! Ins!" until the principal was satisfied. Then he handed the microphone to Coach Dee, who introduced the football team. He yelled the name and uniform number and position of each player, and the guy would run out onto the floor wearing his jersey and shoulder pads. I noticed Coach Dee and the players were wearing rubber-soled shoes.

"Do we have to cheer every player?" I said.

"Where's Big Number 66?" Calvin said. "I can't believe it."

I looked at him to indicate I had no idea who Big Number 66 was.

"The Hulk," he said.

By then, I had decided not to tell anyone about the fight. "I heard he's sick."

A girl was sitting behind me. She poked me in the back. "Big #66's not sick," she said. "He's heartbroken." I turned around to look her. "I know it for a fact. Last night, Middle Grimm broke up with him. It's kinda sad really."

I looked around to see if I could locate Ray and Middle, but if they were at the rally, I could not find them. I figured Ray probably walked home already. If there was one thing I was pretty sure about, Ray lacked school spirit.

I walked home with Michael and tried to convince him he should accompany me to the game tonight. "Students can go for free. If you don't go, I won't have anyone to talk to but Calvin."

Michael said he had something else to do and couldn't come to the game. He wanted to talk about a book he was reading. He had discovered the school library had a collection of car books. All the rest of the way home, he told me about a great novel called *Street Rod*, which he said was almost as good as another great novel called *Crash Club*.

That night, I found Calvin at the game. I was wearing my glasses and hoping no one would notice me. I told Calvin the bad news that Michael would not be joining us. He told me he liked Michael, but he was sort of weird.

"Weird how?"

Calvin said, the other day, he was talking to a kid who was in Michael's homeroom. "He won't stand up for the Pledge of Allegiance. He just sits there. And the teacher lets him get away with it."

"Wow," I said. I admired Michael for refusing to stand. I wondered how he got away with it. He had told us his teacher was sort of in love with him. I hated to think what Baldy would do if I refused to stand up for the Pledge.

Calvin said he could not look at our flag, old Red White and Blue, and not feel a lump in his throat. He said, despite his lack of patriotism, Michael did seem to be smart. They had discussed baseball and football and the opinions of Michael were well informed – especially compared to my sports opinions, which were non-existent.

There were not that many people at the game. Calvin said this was because lots of people were at the high school game which was going on the same night at the municipal stadium. He said it was the annual East vs West game. What we had for a crowd consisted mostly of our team's girlfriends and the players' families. Calvin pointed out we did not have a lot of bleachers on either side of the field, so lots of kids were just standing around. He said although anyone can sit in the bleachers, the school tradition is that they are reserved for the families of the players. He pointed out that several adults, especially the old ones who looked like grandparents, were arriving with soft pillows for their butts. "Those bleachers get hard." He said kids like us mostly loitered by the fence.

I looked around and noticed a girl in my history class named Mary Jane was underneath the bleachers, making out with a ninth grader.

Calvin soon figured out that I was woefully ignorant about the game of football. He took it upon himself to be my instructor. I listened as attentively as I could, but my mind drifted. I grasped the basics. Eleven boys – big guys – line up on one side. Eleven more boys – also big – line up on the other side, facing them. A whistle is blown and after a few moments, the two lines of boys crash into one another. The ball is oval-shaped, with points at each end. It doesn't roll very well and is impossible to dribble, so it has to be kicked or flung through the air or carried. If a player can get it past the end of the other team's field, that's a "touchdown," worth six points. Once a team gets a touchdown, they can attempt to kick the ball between two poles called "uprights." A successful kick is worth one more point.

Our team fell behind almost immediately. By the end of the first quarter, the Ravens were down 14-0. Coach Dee was striding up and down the sidelines yelling and waving his arms. I figured if he did not calm down, he might have a heart attack. I sort of hoped he did have a heart attack.

Calvin said that this is what always happens when we played the Wolves. Their school was in the heart of the north end. Seventy percent of the students were black kids. Calvin said black boys turn into men faster than white boys do, and in general they have bigger muscles. He said these were scientific facts.

Across the field from us was another set of bleachers full of black people, the parents, and families of the Wolves.

"Number 23 is their star," Calvin said. "He's only a seventh grader and already he's their best running back." Number 23 was the player who had scored both of their touchdowns. He scored the first one by running through the line, twisting and turning as our team tried unsuccessfully to catch him. The second one he scored by running through the line without the ball, turning around and catching it, and then running the rest of the way to the end of the field. "He's got moves," Calvin said. "They'd be up even more if their stupid quarterback didn't keep throwing the ball over his head."

"Have you got a program?" I asked.

Calvin handed me a mimeographed piece of paper that someone was handing out when we entered.

I looked at the list of Wolf players until I found Number 23.

Calvin said he thought it was pretty funny that the star of the Wolves was a black guy named White. He said most black people are named after the white man who owned their ancestors back in slavery times, so Number 23, Tommy White, was probably the descendant of someone formerly owned by a white guy named Mr. White. "It's pretty hilarious, when you think about it," Calvin said.

I scanned the bleachers where the black families were sitting until I found them, Mr. and Mrs. White, and an old lady I was pretty sure was Tommy's grannie.

I couldn't find Rose until I thought to look at the bench where unoccupied Wolf players were sitting. A girl was sitting in a wheelchair at the end of the bench.

When halftime came, the Ravens were down 24-0.

"This is what always happens," Calvin said.

I told him I was going to the restroom.

I went around the end of the field to the side where the Wolves were. Every step I took, I got more anxious. I was a white kid moving into a crowd of black people. It made me nervous.

The bench was empty by then because all the Wolves players were back in the girls' locker room.

"Hey, Rose," I said. She was reading a book. I thought it was typical that she had brought a book with her to a football game.

To mark her place, she put her finger in the book, and looked up at me. "What you want, white boy?"

I got a lot more nervous. Maybe she did not recognize me. She hadn't seen me since the fire, and I was wearing my glasses.

"Oh, come here, pathetic. I won't bite."

And just like that, it was as if the world righted itself. Rose was Rose, and I was me again. I wondered if Calvin could see me, on the enemy side of the field, talking to a girl who was two years older than me.

"Tommy's having a good night," I said.

"No kidding."

"Well, I just wanted to say hi. I better be going."

A girl walking nearby saw me and yelled, "Hey, Rosie, who's your little boyfriend?!"

"Shut up, fool," Rose yelled back. "How you been?"

Rose and Tommy were now living in the north end, attending

Washington Junior High School. Tommy had grown another inch and was the only seventh grader playing on the varsity team. Rose said she liked her school. "Not so infested with rednecks and crackers, know what I mean?"

I smiled uneasily.

"You got a girl yet?"

I smiled even more uneasily.

"Those glasses make you look more grown-up."

"You are such a liar."

We talked about the fire.

Rose said no one in her family had been back to the Marsh since the fire. She said in the whole time since her family moved, not a single neighbor from the Marsh had called her up or come to visit her.

I said, "Maybe because no one knew where you guys moved to. We thought you guys left town."

"Sure, honey. Keep telling yourself lies." Rose said the fire department officially concluded the fire was caused by faulty electrical wires, which any fool knew was false.

"Who do you think did it?" I asked.

"You don't know?"

"How would I?"

Rose said, the week before the fire, one night her daddy got thirsty and went to Big Bill's Footloose Tavern. He sat at the bar and ordered himself a whiskey. "This fool Red Kavanaugh was in there, already stupid drunk, sitting on a stool. He told the bartender not to serve Daddy because he was not gonna drink in a bar that served black people. The bartender didn't know what to do. Then Mr. Big Bill appeared, the owner of the place, who happened to be our landlord. He tells the bartender to go ahead, serve Mr. White. And Red Kavanaugh says to the bartender, 'You better not pour that drink, my friend.' The bartender is too scared to move, so Mr. Big Bill himself pours my daddy his drink. And then Red stomps out of there. That weekend in the middle of the night when we are six hundred miles away in Chicago, our house burns down. Do the math, honey."

Red Kavanaugh. Ray's daddy. I was so shocked, I could not even reply.

"I hope someday somebody kills Mr. Red Kavanaugh. Every night I pray to God to see to it. Or, if God would just give him cancer of the liver or some such, that would also do just fine. Here come the players. You better go back to your side."

"Nice seeing you, Rose," I said. "Say hi to Tommy for me."

"Call me up sometime. We can talk about books. Run away now, white boy."

12

Native Son

I said, "It says here there were a quarter of a million people there. Maybe more. Look. It's like a sea of people." I was lying on the floor of the living room looking at Life Magazine. When I was young, practically everyone in America subscribed to this magazine. It was full of excellent pictures, often arranged into what the magazine called "photo essays." I was looking at photos of Martin Luther King, Jr. delivering his I Have a Dream speech.

My mom was standing over me, looking down at the magazine. "It's mostly just black faces."

"Here's some white people," I said.

My dad was in his armchair, reading the Sunday paper. He heard us talking and said the funny thing about Martin Luther King was he was so young, but he looked older.

"He's a rabble-rouser," my mother said. "A big mouth."

It took me awhile to call up Rose White. She was older than me. She was a black person. Not to mention, she was a girl. I did not have romantic notions about her, but I missed her. I liked hanging out with her. Rose White was nothing like any of the other girls I knew. Smart, liked books, funny, a bit mean. My kind of person.

I wanted to call her.

I could pump her for more information about Red Kavanaugh. Did she really think he burned down her house? Did she have any actual evidence?

There are some men that just plain scared me. Red was one of those men. He was not a big guy. Ray was already an inch taller than his father. Red was solid though. There was something about him that made me nervous, as if any second he might explode. He had mean eyes. I totally believed Rose's story about how he made a scene at the Footloose Tavern. My dad told me one time that some men, when they came home from the war, "were not right." I believed Red was one of those men.

I wanted to cross-examine Rose about what she knew. My plan was to soften her up first by talking to her about Martin Luther King and his speech. I figured she would have a lot to say on the topic. And then I could gently ease into the topic of Red Kavanaugh.

I called her up on a Saturday afternoon. Her brother Tommy answered the phone. For a moment, I thought I was talking to his father.

"Is Rose there?"

Tommy said, "Yeah, who's this?"

I told him, hoping he would remember me.

I heard him yelling. "Bedbug, it's for you!"

Bedbug?

"It's a white boy!"

Rose answered, saying hello in her suspicious voice, as if she thought I might be someone pulling a prank. When I identified myself, she said, "Oh, it's you. What you want?"

Our phone was in the living room, and my mother had just walked into the room and was looking at me. I wished we lived in a bigger house. I wished I was a rich kid with my own room and my own phone.

"It's Calvin," I lied. "He's helping me with my homework." My mom liked Calvin.

"Don't talk too long." She went back into the kitchen.

"Who's this Calvin?" Rose asked.

"You said I should call. You said we could talk about books."

"What books?"

This conversation was not going as smoothly as I hoped. I tried to introduce the topic of Martin Luther King, but I did it so clumsily that Rose quickly guessed I had no real interest in the Rev. King. It took Rose approximately one minute to figure out what I really wanted to know.

By then I had made the mistake of mentioning that Ray, the son of Red Kavanaugh, was in my homeroom.

"What are you, a junior detective? Am I talking to young Sherlock Holmes?" She laughed. I envied Rose her ability to laugh loudly and easily. I was bad at laughing.

Rose admitted she did not have any proof it was Ray's father who burned down her house. "Even if I did, you think the cops would care? What you been reading?"

I told her science fiction, and she said most sci fi was silly trash for nerds. "I bet the hero is a smart white boy. Reminds you of you?" She recommended I read *Native Son* by Richard Wright and then I should tackle *Nineteen Eighty-Four* by George Orwell. "Since you love science fiction so much."

Then her mom yelled at her and she said, "I gotta go, white boy. You think I want to spend my entire Saturday talking to you? Call me back when you read something good."

Over the course of the next week, I read *Native Son* by Richard Wright. The novel scared me to death. It probably did not help that

I was reading it at night in bed, under the covers, using a flashlight. The story is about a black young man named Bigger, a criminal who is scared to death of white people. He gets involved with a white girl and her friends. The whole time he is with them, he is excited and crazy, feels out of place. The nicer they are to him, the crazier he feels. The girl and her friends get drunk. She makes out with her boyfriend, and that makes him even more crazy. He winds up driving her home. By that point she's drunk as hell and passes out, so what can he do? He carries her into her own house, trying not to wake her parents. The whole time, he's terrified he's going to bump into the furniture and will get caught with a drunk white girl in his arms. When he finally gets in the girl's bedroom ready to put her to bed, her mom comes in. Except it turns out her mom is blind. She's right there, close enough to touch, but doesn't know he's there. He's terrified the white girl will wake up and scream. To keep her quiet, he puts his big hand over her face, and the next thing he knows, the mom is gone and the white girl is dead. Dead! He's accidentally killed her! He's a black guy and has accidentally murdered a pretty white girl!

I called up Rose the next Saturday and told her I had nightmares because of her. I dreamed I was Bigger, the tragic hero of *Native Son*. I told Rose, "In my dream, I'm trapped in a white girl's bedroom and any second her parents are going to catch me in there, so what can I do? I put my hand over her mouth to keep her from screaming. Then I wake up scared, like I just accidentally killed somebody. I have to look over at my brothers to see if I woke them up, yelling in my sleep or something. That book is the most horrible thing I have ever read in my entire life! I hated it!"

Rose laughed out loud and told me I obviously loved it. She said I was funny, dreaming I was a brother. "You're nothing like Bigger. One, he's black. Two, he's dumb or at least uneducated, not to mention strong. You are puny and brainy, sort of brainy, not as smart as you think you are, but still, not like him in the least. And when are YOU ever gonna get caught in a girl's bedroom? In your dreams, that's when!" She laughed really loud.

I got so embarrassed, I told her I had to go, my mom was calling me.

The next day, Sunday, September 15, 1963, four white men put 15 sticks of dynamite under the steps of the 16th Street Baptist Church in Birmingham, Alabama. When their bomb blew up, it killed four little black girls.

I called up Rose that Monday evening to see how she was doing, had she seen all the stories in the paper?

She told me she did not feel like talking and hung up on me.

13

Bald Spot

Mrs. Maple was my English teacher. She was an old bat — not really bad, just tedious. One day, a week after I called Rose, she told us she wanted us to write a short story. She said we should pick a story out of our reader, change a few important details, and make it our story. These transformed stories should be no more than a page long. "This assignment will be fun!"

I decided I did not want to transform a story from our anthology. That sounded boring. Maybe ordinary students would enjoy doing it, but not me. I would invent a new story, a totally original story by Jack DeWitt.

My story was called "Just the Wind."

Once upon a time, a beautiful and kind-hearted Queen ruled over a kingdom, and everyone was happy. Unbeknownst to everyone, the queen had a secret, a twin sister, a monstrous sister. Unless she was chained up, the monstrous sister would run wild and murder people. The queen kept her sister underneath the castle in a dungeon. So long as the monstrous sister was kept in chains in the dark dungeon, the kingdom ran smoothly. All its inhabitants were happy and contented. Everyone pretended they did not know about the evil sister locked up in the dungeon. It was better for everyone if they just acted as if she did not exist. Sometimes, late at night, they heard howls of rage coming from underneath the castle. Whenever that happened, they closed their eyes and said, "Probably just the wind."

The End.

I was proud of this little story. I rewrote it three times, working carefully on my handwriting, which had a tendency to become illegible.

It took Mrs. Maple a week to return our stories. When she handed them back, I was shocked to find out she had given me a B. On the back of my story, she wrote, "Didn't follow instructions."

I did not mind getting Bs in other classes, like Algebra, for example, but this was English class. I was reading way above my grade level and got perfect scores on all the quizzes. Even in our class, the smart kid class, I was one of the best students. I had written a totally original story.

A B!

After class, I carried my story up to Mrs. Maple. I tried hard to keep my voice low, to rid it of anything that might sound like anger. "I think I deserve a better grade."

Mrs. Maple took my story from me and looked at it. She was seated at her desk, so I was able to look down at her and see the crown of her head. She had a bald spot.

Mrs. Maple skimmed my story again, as if she had forgotten which one it was. She handed my story back to me and said, "Don't you think it would be more interesting if you let the evil queen escape?"

She suggested I pick a story from our reader, perhaps one by Edgar Allen Poe since I liked that sort of thing. She told me she would allow me to re-do the assignment for a better grade. "But you will have to follow the instructions."

I was so angry, I could not speak. Old Lady Maple did not understand the whole point of my story: THE QUEEN'S EVIL TWIN MUST NEVER GET LOOSE!

I could not let it go. I kept thinking about it. My story, that B. "Didn't follow instructions." The look in her eyes. Her bald spot.

That night, in my bed, I declared war on Mrs. Maple and began my campaign against her the next day.

At lunch, I told my friends about Mrs. Maple's bald spot. I told them Mrs. Maple combed up the hair all around it, so it was difficult to see. But it was there, a bald spot. Plain as day.

My friend Calvin said, no way. It was impossible. Hair loss is a condition that happens only to men. His dad for example was completely bald on top. Women are immune to that sort of thing.

"Go look for yourself," I said.

In our next class, when the opportunity presented itself, Calvin approached Mrs. Maple when she was seated at her desk and asked her an unnecessary question. He stared down at her bald spot and looked astonished. Several of us were watching, and we did our best to hide our smiles. Well, they did anyway. I smiled from ear to ear.

After that, every day, another one of my friends would go up there, ask her an unnecessary question, and locate her bald spot.

I said we should call her Mrs. Bald Spot.

That was not the worst thing I did to Mrs. Maple.

I made up a story about her nose. One day, when she was telling us we were going to get to read Mark Twain's wonderful and hilarious novel *Huckleberry Finn*, I noticed a spot on her nose. A discolored spot, smaller than a dime.

That day, at lunch I told my friends Mrs. Maple suffered from a nasal catastrophe. This was her secret. A hole was forming on her nose, and every morning before coming to school, she filled it up with putty. If they looked closely, I said, they would see it, the flesh-colored putty filling. I guessed the hole was caused by excessive sniffing. By then, I said, they had surely noticed, when Mrs. Maple talked, she often paused to sniff. Everyone knows sniffing can cause a hole like that to form on a nose. No doubt the putty-filled hole would grow larger. Last year, it had been only half the size it was this year. In a few more years, her entire nose would disappear, and she would have to replace it with putty. Her whole nose!

My story caused the kids in our class to inspect Mrs. Maple's nose with great curiosity. Before long, Mrs. Maple realized she was being stared at by her students but could not figure out why, or whether she should be angry or flattered by the attention.

Then I did the worst thing of all. Like a lot of people, Mrs. Maple had a tendency to use filler expressions. She often made a statement and then added, "You know?" Sometimes she would pause a moment and ask it again, "Do you know what I mean?" She asked this question frequently without realizing she was saying it. She had variations. "Perhaps you understand what I mean?" "I hope you grasp my thought?" "Are you at last beginning to see what I mean?" I started to count the number of times she said it, any variation of it. I told my friends about my discovery and encouraged them to join me in counting her totals. Soon, most of the class was keeping a running tally.

Mrs. Maple didn't understand what was happening. Were we taking notes? She would finish a sentence, unconsciously add a version of the question, and thirty students would make a little mark in their notebooks. Even in her other classes, the students were starting to make those little marks when she was lecturing. What could it mean?

Some of us boys started betting on the daily total. Would she set a new record and say it 20 times in one class period? Could she get up to 30 if we were careful not to interrupt her with questions?

"I do hope you see what I mean?" "You see it now, I hope?" "Are you beginning to understand?"

Then things took a turn. Someone in the class, probably a girl, told

Mrs. Maple what we were doing. One day, she quit saying it, or if she did say it, she caught herself and frowned horribly and then went on. A new tone came into her lectures, one of anger and resentment. She no longer seemed to enjoy teaching us.

This was all my fault.

I am not sure Mrs. Maple knew for certain I was the ringleader, but she had her suspicions. Sometimes I looked up at her and noticed she was staring at me with an expression on her face as if I was something nasty and foul.

Then something happened that I could not have anticipated.

Toward the end of November, there was a knock at the door of our classroom. It was another teacher. He had a strange expression on his face. Mrs. Maple went over to see what he wanted. We all listened in hopes of over-hearing whatever they were talking about. Mrs. Maple closed the door and turned around with a peculiar expression on her face. She said we should close our books. She had something serious to tell us.

"Boys and girls, John F. Kennedy, the president of the United States, has been shot."

Mrs. Maple said we should all bow our heads and pray for the safety of the president.

Then she ordered us to stand up and led us in the Pledge of Allegiance. I think she was about to lead us in the singing of the Star-Spangled Banner, but before she could, the intercom squealed, and the voice of our principal told us he had heavy news. The president was dead.

Mrs. Maple was so shocked she had to sit down. Apparently, she had been clinging to the hope that the president might survive.

The principal said that, under the circumstances, school for the day was dismissed. We should all go home to our families.

I looked around, hardly able to believe it. We were getting out of school? I was startled to see that the girl I had seen making out with a ninth grader underneath the bleachers was weeping. What was wrong with her? Didn't she understand? We were getting out of school! I was 13 years old and had no interest at all in politics. What seventh grader cared about politics? I could understand why adults would care about the president, but we were kids, and we were getting out of school early!

Mrs. Maple told us to bow our heads. She delivered a brief prayer for the soul of John F. Kennedy and then told us we were dismissed.

I did not have the sense to shut up. As soon as I was out of the room, I was telling my friends that this was a great thing. Why the long faces? We were getting out of school! Maybe we wouldn't even have to go tomorrow!

Mrs. Maple grabbed me by the shoulder, spun me around, and shoved me hard into a row of lockers. "What is WRONG with you?"

When she let go of me, I noticed everyone in the hallway was staring at me.

I walked home with Michael but hardly said a word. And then, I exploded. Was it my fault the president got shot? How was I supposed to care if a famous politician got shot, a person I had never even met? She had it in for me! Mrs. Maple was nuts. I should complain about her to the principal. I told Michael about my story, "Just the Wind." It was totally original, and she gave me a B! That started the whole thing! She provoked me. It was unreasonable to think I would love Kennedy. I figured Mrs. Maple was probably a Democrat. My mom and dad were Republicans. They voted for the other guy, Nixon. Why, one time, this was right before the election last year, our pastor preached an entire sermon on the separation of church and state. He said if adults in our church did not vote against Kennedy, the Pope would soon be running our country. Who could blame me for not getting upset just because Kennedy got shot in the head?

"You're hopeless," Michael said. "When the president gets shot, people are going to care."

I made a grumbling sound. "I am not like everyone else!"

Michael rolled his eyes.

After a while, Michael said, "Maybe your story is about your mom."

"What?" I stopped in my tracks.

"Your mom. She's this nice person most of the time, but sometimes she goes nuts. You've told me about it a hundred times. Maybe she's the queen in your story, and that's why you're so mad."

I couldn't believe it. First, I get attacked in school, violently shoved by Old Lady Maple, for no good reason, and now my best friend Michael was out of his mind.

I started yelling and swearing at Michael. I told him to keep his opinions to himself. I told him if he was an Old Lady Maple Lover, I didn't want to be friends with him anymore. "Who are you anyway? A weirdo who is in the dummy classes, who doesn't even stand up for the national anthem! Get lost! From now on, you can walk home by yourself!"

Michael gave me a weird look, turned on his heel, and went in a different direction, leaving me all alone.

That night, in bed, I asked my brother Dean if he thought other people knew.

"How the president got shot? Of course, they know. Everyone knows."

"I don't mean that. I mean how Mom, you know, loses her mind sometimes. You think they know? Maybe the neighbors can hear her?"

By then, I had decided that maybe Michael's interpretation of my story was correct. Maybe it really was about my mom.

Dean said, "Everyone else in the whole country is thinking about how the president got shot, and you're still worrying about what the neighbors hear?"

I thought about telling Dean about my story, about my campaign against Mrs. Maple, but decided it was not worth it. He would never understand.

Dean said, "Mom's not that bad, not usually. She hardly ever uses the belt on you anymore. You need to do what I do. When she gets crazy, leave the house. You always make the mistake of staying here. And then you fight with her."

Dean said if I would get my nose out of a book, I might notice there were always signs. Ever since my mom had all those operations, her arm – the right one – had a tendency to swell. To save her from cancer, the docs scooped out a lot of her muscles in that arm. Every now and then, it would swell up with fluid and turn red. That was the sign to get out of the house.

"She starts ironing," I said. "Like a maniac."

"Exactly," he said.

When my mom was about ready to explode, she started ironing things with her swollen red arm. Not just normal ironing. She ironed bedsheets, blue jeans, underwear, socks, for god's sake. Towels. Her arm swelled up big and turned bright red.

"That's when you should leave the house, but no, you stay in the house until she yells at you about something stupid. Then, you get mad and yell back at her, until she totally loses it." Dean said I took my mom's moods too seriously. "She's not that bad. She's getting healthier. What if our dad was a mean drunk or something, like Ray's dad? I'd rather have a crazy mom than a crazy dad. Count your blessings."

I lay there in the dark, looking up at the ceiling.

Dean said I took everything too seriously. "Not everything is about you." Mom was trying to improve herself. She was taking classes at the college. Before she married our dad, she was a schoolteacher – history and geography. When Dad came home from the war, she quit teaching and started having babies. But now she was going back to college, taking courses, so she could renew her certificate. Neither of us was sure what a certificate was, but once she had it, she could get a job teaching. We would have more money. Dean said I should give Mom a break.

I fell asleep wondering if my story was really about my mom. When she was outside the walls of our house, she always seemed friendly and nice to everyone. But then at home, sometimes she went crazy.

The queen's evil twin got loose.

The next day, at school, I told Mrs. Maple I was sorry I said what I said about the president. I was sorry I got mad at her about the story, about the B. I was sorry about everything.

Mrs. Maple said she was glad I came in and talked to her. I was one of her best students. She said I reminded her of herself, the way she had been when she was my age, always asking questions and getting into trouble.

At lunch, Calvin told me he was proud of me for apologizing to Mrs. Maple.

I made up with Michael. He said not to worry about it. Everyone loses their temper sometimes.

At the end of the semester, Mrs. Maple gave me an A.

14

Room 12

That winter, my grandmother slipped on the ice and broke her hip. In February, the Beatles appeared on The Ed Sullivan Show and changed the world of teenagers forever. And in the spring, Ray decided he needed to further my education.

In my neighborhood, my ignorance about sex was legendary. One day, on the playground, a kid described the mechanics of sex to me. I listened, feeling a bit queasy. Finally, I stopped him and said, "Well, maybe YOUR parents do that. Mine don't!"

"Are you crazy? There are FIVE kids in your family!"

I sniffed. "Maybe they did it ONCE. And it just kept working."

The kid told everyone in our grade what I had said. For months, kids would point at me and yell, "Hey, Jack, tell us about it! How your parents did it JUST ONCE!" The kids would look at one another, their eyes bright, and then in unison they would yell, "AND IT JUST KEPT WORKING!"

That winter, Ray got a job at the motel as a maid. Except he didn't want us to call him a "maid." He said the word was too girly. Except for him, all the maids were female.

"What are we supposed to call you then?"

"A room supervisor."

Ray suggested that I too might be able to get a job at the motel as a room supervisor, but I wasn't interested. "Like I want to empty ashtrays and make beds."

Ray said even if I didn't want a job, I should still go with him to the motel because he wanted me to meet the Nazi. "They have a brand-new color TV! You don't even have a TV at your house. You're always complaining about it."

I shrugged. "The only shows in color are on Sunday night when I have to be in church."

"They have dirty magazines," Ray said.

"What do you mean? They do not!"

Ray said lots of traveling salesmen were regular guests at the motel. The salesmen brought dirty magazines with them and then left them in the rooms. Ray figured this was because they had to go home to their wives and children. I tried to imagine how my mom would react if my dad ever dared to bring home a dirty magazine.

Ray said, when he and the other maids found discarded magazines in the rooms, they saved them. The Nazi's mom put them in a magazine rack in the lobby of the motel, so any guest who wanted a magazine could grab one and take it back to his room.

"Dirty magazines?" I said. "Do you think I'm an idiot?" No matter how often Ray told me about the magazines, I refused to believe him. He described the pictures in vivid detail, but I continued to insist magazines like that could not even exist. They would be illegal.

One day, Ray and the Nazi showed up on the playground when I was hanging out there. Ray brought the Nazi over to me and told him that I dared to doubt there was a rack of dirty magazines in the motel lobby, and that anyone could grab one and look at them.

The Nazi said, "Of course they're there. I look at them whenever I feel like it."

"And your mom doesn't even care?" I found this hard to believe.

The Nazi said he would be glad to show me some dirty magazines, if I ever cared to come visit him.

The next Saturday afternoon, I did it. I walked up the hill to visit the motel. When I got to the parking lot, I almost got scared and left, but the Nazi popped out of the office, delighted to see me. He welcomed me to the motel and gave me a tour. After he showed me the pop machine, he took me into the motel lobby and showed me the magazine rack. "Help yourself."

We carried two Playboys over to his house, plopped the magazines down on the sofa in his living room, and knelt before them. The Nazi turned the pages of his magazine, and I did the same with mine. The girls were beautiful, young, glowing. They were stark naked! Breasts! Legs! More breasts!

"That's nothing! Look at this one!"

We began to giggle, and soon we were laughing helplessly. I felt as if the Ten Commandments had suddenly been suspended and now everything was permitted.

"Boys," someone said.

I stiffened, twisted around. The Nazi's mom was standing right behind us.

I imagined we were going to be killed. She was going to scream at us. She might call my mom!

"If you are going to laugh like a couple hyenas, I'm taking those magazines away from you." She snatched up both magazines. "There is nothing funny about the human body." She carried the magazines out of the house and back to the rack in the motel lobby.

I stared in amazement at the Nazi. Wasn't she going to freak out? Make us burn the magazines? Call my mother?

The Nazi said not to worry. "She just got mad because we were laughing too much."

I thought about it for days. "There is nothing funny about the human body." Those breasts. Those long legs and pretty butts. But especially all those breasts.

Ray said it was time to further my education. I needed to come to the motel on a Friday evening. That was when the Nazi's parents went square dancing. When they left, the Nazi and Ray got to run the motel. If I showed up after 7 PM, I would find them in charge, and I would discover the unspeakable glory known as Room 12.

The motel consisted of a row of rooms, a right angle, and another row of rooms. In the middle of the longer row was a utility closet. If you entered the closet, you would find a wooden ladder built into its wall. The ladder led to a trap door in the ceiling. If you climbed the ladder and pushed open the trapdoor, you found yourself looking at a crawlspace that ran the whole length of the motel.

Each room had a light fixture in the middle of its ceiling. In room 12, the hole cut in the ceiling tiles for the fixture was a bit too big. There was a little space there, a peephole. If you were in the crawlspace, you could peer down into the room. Directly below was a bed.

On Friday evenings, there was always a good chance a young couple would show up. A young good-looking couple with no kids. Ray told me he and the Nazi had a system based on gestures. If the girl was insufficiently good-looking, they would look at one another and briefly close their eyes. That meant, "Nope." If she was attractive, they would rub the tip of their noses. That meant, "Yes! Absolutely! This one!"

I arrived at the motel just before 7 PM. The Nazi's parents were still in the house, getting dressed up for their evening of square dancing. The Nazi's mom stopped by the motel office just before they left. She was a happy, chubby sort of lady, and spun around in the lobby so we could see how her skirt flared out when she twirled. I had never met a mom like her before. A fun mom who loved to laugh and almost never got mad. She said she and her husband would probably not get home before midnight. After their dance, they planned to go out to eat with some of their square dance friends.

When they left, we had the motel to ourselves. Three boys. Unsupervised.

Just before 8 PM, a car pulled into the parking lot and a young couple got out. They came into the lobby and seemed surprised to find three boys running the place.

Ray started rubbing the tip of his nose the moment the girl entered the lobby. She looked like she might be a college girl. The guy was athletic, like maybe he was on the football team. The Nazi rubbed his nose so hard, it was amazing he did not give himself nose-bleed.

I turned bright red.

"We'll put you in Room 12," Ray said. "It's a real sweet room. You'll love it."

"We only need one bed," the football player said gruffly.

"It's got a nice big bed, plenty of room. Don't worry. The ice machine's right there on the sidewalk. There's a pop machine too."

The guy grabbed the key, grinned at his girl, and away they went.

We waited fifteen minutes. Ray could hardly stand to wait. He said if he was with that girl, he would be tearing off her clothes the second they got into the room. The Nazi said, in his experience, it was always smart to wait. For best results, fifteen minutes was better than ten.

We turned on the No Vacancy sign so we wouldn't be interrupted. Ray unlocked the utility closet. All three of us crowded in there. The little room was full of rolls of toilet paper and individually wrapped bars of soap and cleaning supplies. Ray went up the wooden ladder. I followed him, my heart beating erratically. The Nazi followed me, giving me a push when I hesitated.

The crawlspace was dark, but we could see because Ray and the Nazi had flashlights. It was stuffy, as if fresh air never got up there.

There were spider webs everywhere, and I started thinking about brown recluse spiders, said to be the most dangerous spiders in the Midwest. I wanted to suggest we back out while we still could and not return until Ray went up there with a whisk broom and got rid of all the cobwebs, but the Nazi kept prodding me forward. I had been instructed by Ray before we went up the ladder that if I slipped and put my hand on a tile, put my weight on it, I could easily fall right through a ceiling!

When we got a certain distance into the crawlspace, we were there. Directly above Room 12. The young couple was below us. Only one of us could look down through the peephole at a time. Ray went first. He got excited and beckoned me to crawl forward.

My heart was hammering so hard I thought I could hear it. I peered down through the peephole. The football player was lying naked on the bed, grinning at the girl. She was removing her bra, the only item of clothing she still wore. There was a little bit of lint beside the peephole and I accidentally dislodged it with my fingertips. That fluffy curl of dust fell through the peephole and drifted down into Room 12, catching the attention of the girl. She laughed and flung away her bra, but then, instead of jumping into bed with her boyfriend, she looked up at the light fixture. She saw me! Our eyes met! She said something that sounded to me like, "There's someone up there!"

I went into reverse and bumped into the Nazi. It was impossible to turn around. I thought I heard her yell, "There's a BOY up there!" I shoved back against the Nazi. "She saw me! Back up! Back up! She saw me!"

"Jesus Christ," Ray whispered. "Calm down."

The Nazi crawled backward all the way to the trapdoor. "Hurry! Hurry!" He climbed down the ladder, and I climbed down after him. I was certain, if we did not hurry, we would find the outraged football player waiting for us on the sidewalk, stark naked, fists clenched, murder in his eyes.

When we got out on the sidewalk, no one was there. The door to Room 12 remained closed. The curtains were pulled shut. "She saw me," I told the Nazi. "She pointed right at me!"

We hurried back to the office.

"Where's Ray?" the Nazi said.

"He must be trapped up there," I said. "I just hope they don't hear him."

We waited in the office, but Ray did not appear. As the minutes passed, the Nazi became exasperated. "We're missing it," he said. "The whole thing!"

Ray emerged from the utility closet fifteen minutes later. He seemed mightily pleased with himself. "You guys should have stayed," he told the Nazi. "That was the best one ever."

"The best one ever," the Nazi repeated.

That was the last time I was invited to look down into Room 12.

15

The Outhouse

That winter, Grandmother DeWitt slipped on the ice, fell hard, and broke her hip. In those days there was no such thing as a hip replacement. When an elderly woman fell and broke a hip, she became a semi-invalid. When my grandmother was released from the hospital, she needed help with everything. It seemed to the rest of us that my grandmother loved being helpless and giving orders. Her husband, my grandfather, a retired pastor, waited on her hand and foot. He never complained and carried out the most absurd errands.

Grandma DeWitt became a night owl and a TV fanatic. Every night she watched the Tonight Show, starring Jack Paar. She called us the next day to describe in detail what that crazy Jack Paar did the previous evening. She rose at the crack of noon. On a nightstand beside her bed, Grandma had a bell, the kind with a wooden handle. When she awoke from her dreams, she would ring it vigorously until my grandfather appeared with her breakfast on a tray. While she dined in bed, Grandpa fixed her bath. It had to be just the right temperature. When she finished breakfast, she rang the bell again. Grandpa carried away the tray and then returned to help her from her bed to the bathroom.

Like a trained nurse, he helped her to the toilet and then into the tub, washed her back. While soaking, Grandma liked to talk about her dreams, about current events and the weather, about the neighbors, about her grown children and their children, about her favorite soap opera, about birds and bees and tornados. My grandfather scrubbed her back and listened. After her bath, my grandfather helped her downstairs. That was not an easy journey. My grandmother scooted down the steps on her butt while my grandfather waited with her two canes.

We visited my grandparents once a week, after Sunday morning church. Grandma liked to examine her grandchildren and would have us stand before her for inspection. I was too serious in appearance. She felt a boy my age should "radiate happiness and joy in life." I was a failure in this regard and often radiated grim discontent and moodiness. She would question me about my diet and exercise program. My complexion, despite her advice, continued to get worse. "Oh, poor Jack! You have another whitehead." "Oh, my goodness, that red pimple on your chin has been joined by – one, two, three more. Are you squeezing them, dear? You must never squeeze a pimple. It will only get worse! The poison will spread. Are you reading your bible every day?" My grandmother believed that regular bible study is good for the complexion. She had learned, by questioning my brother Dean, that I read a great deal, too much in fact, but the bible was almost never what I read. Instead I read novels about immoral boys who got up to mischief and rarely if ever attended church. She suggested I pray to God about my skin. I had inherited it from my father who, when young, was hideous to behold. Daily bible study had not much helped my father, she admitted. He had been plagued by pimples until he turned 22 and entered the Army. She wondered if the United States Army would accept a 13-year-old boy. Probably not.

By summertime, I could not bear the sight of my face. As much as possible I avoided mirrors. I tried to get as much sun as possible and hoped sunshine is good for pimples.

My brother Dean had clear skin and loved to tease me mercilessly about my pimples. He doubted I would ever be kissed by a girl. I retaliated by telling him if his brain got any stupider, he would never be allowed to go to junior high but would have to remain in elementary school forever. He should not worry because he had not experienced a growth spurt in at least a year. I predicted that very likely for the rest of his life, he would remain the size of a fifth grader. Sometimes I kept this up until tears appeared in his eyes and he threw something at me and ran from the room.

That summer, Ray moved out of his parents' house. He moved into a spare bedroom in the Nazi's house and began to call the Nazi's mother "Ma." I heard a rumor he was driven out of his home by his drunken father. Little Grimm told me Ray beat the crap out of his old man after his father punched Ray's mom in the mouth and knocked her down, just for bringing him a warm beer. She said there were bullet holes in the walls of the Kavanaugh kitchen because, after Ray knocked him down, his father attempted to murder him.

I don't know how it happened, but my brother found out about the Nazi and his motel. He must have followed me up there one day. By the time I found out about it, he was friends with Ray and the Nazi. Dean had in that short time become their pet. Worse, it soon became all too obvious that, so far as they were concerned, Dean was a lot more fun than me. I was uppity and judgmental. And prudish. I would not drink beer or touch cigarettes. I did not appreciate their jokes and did not enjoy setting things on fire, which seemed to be their favorite hobby. Dean showered them with compliments. He was, they said, brave for a little kid. And cool.

Ray taught Dean to smoke. And shoplift. And draw cartoons of large-breasted girls. The Nazi's mom hired Dean to be a maid at the motel. Soon, my little brother had a lot more money than I had. Our parents did not believe in the concept of weekly allowances. I could have had a job too as a maid, but I would not take it. I thought I was too good to clean toilets, make beds, and empty ashtrays. I wanted to spend my long summer mornings lazing in bed, listening to music on my transistor radio (a Christmas present), and reading a book.

That summer, Mom and Dad took us on a 10-day vacation to visit our cousins. I considered my cousins hicks. They considered our town – a smallish factory town – to be a big city. My brother Dean could tell them the most outlandish stories about what went on in our neighborhood and they would believe every word. They were terrified of black people. In their corner of the world, black people did not exist. They assured me no black person would ever stop in their county for gas or at the diner for a burger and a malt. That simply could not happen. When they visited my town, if they saw a black person in a car or walking downtown, they went nuts – as if they had seen a full-grown leopard strolling down the sidewalk.

I brought along plenty of books, so when I got bored at least I would have something to read.

My cousins did their best to get me out of their house and into trouble. Their world was rural: barns, fields, creeks, cows, sheep, ponies. If they said we were going to "the marsh," it turned out to be a real one where we would have to wade through smelly water in order to do horrible things like murder frogs.

My cousins were fond of practical jokes but had little success with me. My brother Dean was a different story; he went along with their most dangerous suggestions. They convinced him to ride a heifer. They got him to pee on an electric fence. They said he was a good sport, while I was a "stiff."

My Oklahoma grandparents, my mother's parents, lived in a tiny house out in the sticks. It did not have running water or electricity.

According to my cousins, my grandparents had never had electricity in their entire lives.

My grandmother was a tiny sun-tanned woman who appeared to me to be about one hundred years old. She rarely said a word, but I often found her little bright eyes trained on me. The second day we were down there, she gave me a present, a pocketknife. I was thrilled for five minutes, but soon realized I had no idea what to do with a knife. I wandered outside, looking for something to stab, and finally carved my initials on one of their trees.

The next day, my grandmother found out what I had done to one of her fruit trees and made me return the knife. She said I was too young and stupid to possess such a thing. I suspected Dean had taken my grandmother to the tree and showed her what I had done.

Behind my grandparents' house was a wooden barrel, full of water. When I peered into it, I noticed a raft of mosquito larvae. By that time, I had collected a dozen mosquito bites; one of them so itchy, I had bloodied myself scratching it. In hopes of winning back my grandmother's regard, I emptied the larvae-infested barrel, dumped all the water it contained onto the ground. Afterward, I ran straight to my grandmother and told her about my good deed in hopes she would realize I was much more intelligent and mature than she realized and give me back my knife. Instead, she went straight to my mother and told her I had emptied out her barrel of rainwater, precious water that she used to wash her hair. She told my mother that she had long suspected there was something wrong with me and now she was sure of it.

Dean and I had to spend the night with my grandparents. This was considered a special treat, but when my parents drove away in their car, I wasn't thrilled. They did not have any extra bedrooms, so Dean and I would have to sleep on the floor of the living room on top of blankets.

After Grannie made us say our prayers, Dean told her he had a little bit of a stomachache. Could he possibly sleep on Grannie's sofa? She said he could. I thought this was a dirty trick. As the older brother, I should be the one who got to sleep on the sofa.

I lay on my back and tried to sleep. It was impossible. I wished I was home in my bed. When I closed my eyes, I heard odd, mysterious noises that made me nervous. I decided I needed to pee. I should not have drunk that extra glass of my grandmother's room-temperature lemonade. I got up and tiptoed out of the dark house. There was no bathroom. I would have to use the outhouse.

I hated the outhouse, a smelly little building the size of a closet. Inside on a big nail was a roll of toilet paper. There was a bench that contained two holes, a big one for big people and a little one for kids. Dean and I had been instructed to use the little one, but I always used the big one, even though it was scary to sit on the big hole. Underneath the outhouse was a deep pit full of horribleness.

Wasps loved the outhouse. They were forever building nests up in the corner behind the door. My grandfather would knock down the nests but soon there would be another one in progress.

It was dark outside, so I decided to use my grandfather's new flashlight. I had been shown this flashlight and told to use it when it was dark but to be very careful with it because it was expensive. It was an unusually long flashlight that required three batteries.

I stepped out the back door of my grandfather's house and switched on the flashlight. A powerful ray of light illuminated the path to the outhouse. I could hear sounds coming from the trees, locusts. An owl hooted. The sky was full of stars, a million stars – the Milky Way.

I entered the outhouse very carefully, slowly opening the door and using the flashlight to inspect every inch of the little room to make sure no wasps were anywhere in sight. When I was certain everything looked safe, I entered, pulled down my pants, got comfortable perched on the big hole. I carefully set Grandpa's flashlight on its side between me and the smaller hole. I thought about stars and space travel and pocketknives.

I accidentally brushed the flashlight with my fingertips. As if it had a mind of its own, it rolled into the small hole and vanished. I heard a splash.

I crept back into my grandparents' house. I lay down on the floor and closed my eyes. I prayed to God to make my grandparents forget about the flashlight.

In the morning, my grandmother shook me awake and demanded to know where the flashlight was.

I thought about lying but realized I had no choice. I had to show her. The light was still on, pointing upward.

Everyone in the family found out about what I had done to Grandpa's flashlight. All day, family members arrived, all my cousins, and heard the story of my disgrace. They went into the outhouse and looked down through the small hole at the flashlight, sunk up to its neck in poop and pee. They made hilarious suggestions about how I should be lowered down head-first and made to rescue the flashlight.

For the rest of the week, those batteries did their job. A powerful beam of light illuminated the bottom of each and every family member who used the outhouse. After a week, the light grew a little weaker, and a little weaker. The day before we drove back home, it finally went out.

"He's not right," my grannie told my mother. "He's not right in the HEAD!"

When we finally got home, a neighbor came over when we were still pulling our suitcases out of the trunk. While we were gone, she told my mom, something amazing had happened. Something terrible.

In the middle of the night, someone had entered Red Kavanaugh's garage. Red was sleeping in there, passed out drunk. Someone – no one knew who – killed him. The murder weapon, a hammer, was still lying there on the floor of the garage.

16

Wipeout

I went to Red's funeral with the Nazi and his parents. Ray sat near the front with his sister, his mom, and his old aunts. The Nazi pointed at a large man sitting close to the family and said, "Big Bill's here." He said Bill paid for Red's casket, a nice one, hand-carved and lined with satin. Bill paid for all the funeral expenses.

"How come?" I asked.

The Nazi shrugged.

His dad heard us talking, leaned over to me and whispered, "Customer service."

It took me a minute to work out the joke. Red was a regular at Bill's tavern, The Footloose. Over the years, Red must have spent a small fortune in there.

Mama Grimm, Big, Middle, and Little were on the other side of the church. Big was sitting beside her new boyfriend, a husky guy named Micky who had just graduated from high school. He had what Big expected in a boyfriend: biceps and a hot car.

The funeral was held in a Catholic cathedral, which my mom told me in advance I would not like because it would be overly fancy and contain statues. She warned me that, when the sermon ended, the priest would consecrate the Eucharist, which is what Catholics called communion. All the Catholics would file up to the front to get their wafers, but Protestants like me would have to remain in our pews because only true Catholics are allowed up there. "The Catholics will get those little dry crackers. That's all. Only the priest gets to drink the wine. And you better believe it's real wine too." She made a look of disgust. At our church, when the pastor offered communion, everyone got to eat a cube of Wonder Bread and drink a tiny glass of grape juice.

There were more people in the church than I had expected. All the Kavanaughs within driving range were there.

The priest told us Red was in paradise already – as if anyone who knew Red could possibly believe it. I wondered if Red ever attended this church. Sure, Mrs. Kavanaugh came here on the regular, but Red?

Red's body was at the back of the cathedral in a closed casket, but I had seen it on display at the funeral parlor the day before. I went there to look at it with the Brooms. As we approached the casket, we had to go past a line of Kavanaughs: the old aunts, Red's three brothers and their wives, Ray and his sister, and finally Naomi. I shook hands with all of them. Ray's face was pale and sweaty; I figured he was hung-over. When he saw it was me waiting to shake his hand, he grinned and did his best to break all the bones in my fingers.

At the visitation at the funeral home, there was a lot of interest in Red Kavanaugh's head. The undertaker had turned it into a work of art, and you could hardly tell it had ever been damaged.

The night before, the Nazi and I went to the wake, which was held at Ray's house. Ray was already drunk by the time we got there, wearing a dress shirt and a black tie. Middle was with him; she kept hugging his arm and kissing him on the cheek.

The house was overflowing with people. The kitchen table was covered with plates of food donated by women from the neighborhood.

On the counter beside the fridge there was a row of liquor bottles and clean glasses. You could help yourself to the liquor. The fridge was full of cold beer. People said the Footloose Tavern donated all the booze.

Soon, dozens of people spilled out of the house because it was so hot and stuffy in there no one could breathe. I was eager to look at the garage where it happened, but the Nazi wanted to get himself a beer.

Ray's mom, Naomi, was sitting on the davenport with a nun on one side of her and a priest on the other. People kept kneeling down in front of her to offer their condolences. She never said a word except thank you for coming. The Nazi said she was probably on tranquilizers.

We went out to see the garage. Men were standing in front of it, peering in but not actually entering. The Nazi said after Ray moved out, Red started coming out here to the garage at night to do his drinking. Red said he couldn't stand to drink in a house full of nagging women, meaning his wife and daughter. He dragged a chair in here and then added an old sofa. When he was too drunk to walk, he would sleep it off on the sofa. He had a radio so he could listen to the ball game.

There were stains on the sofa and the Nazi told me they were blood. After the cops got done investigating everything in the garage, the site of the murder, the old aunts wanted to haul the sofa away to the dump, but Naomi wouldn't let them because it was Red's final resting place.

The Nazi said the mysterious attacker hammered Red's head over and over, seventeen times at least; broke his nose, his jaw, his eye sockets, broke out his front teeth.

There were plenty of rumors about who killed Red. He got into bar fights, so there were many possibilities. It was more or less impossible to find anyone who liked him.

The hammer was wiped clean, the Nazi said, no fingerprints. Ray's little sister and his mom were asleep in the house the whole time. The attack probably happened around 2 AM.

While the Nazi was getting a beer out of the fridge, I leaned against a wall near an open window and listened to the conversation of two men who were standing in the side yard. One of them wiped his mouth and said, "I figure it was a husband."

The other man said, "Wouldn't surprise me."

Before I could hear any more, Ray appeared, put his arm around my shoulders and dragged me over to where Middle was with Big's new boyfriend, Micky. They were drinking rum and Cokes. "Where'd Little go?" Ray said.

Middle gave him an annoyed look and said, "To the bathroom if it's any of your business."

Ray squeezed my shoulders and said, "She's got a crush on you, kid."

"Who does?"

Middle said, "Did you invite him yet? She says we have to invite him."

Ray said, "There's gonna be a party this weekend, Saturday afternoon. We want you to come."

Middle said, "You mean Fancy Nancy does."

Nancy was Little's real name.

"Just a sweet little record party," Ray said. "So wear your dancing shoes."

Middle said, "Does he even know how?"

I couldn't get my bearings. They were inviting me to a dance? Little had a crush on me? I was supposed to arrive wearing special shoes?

"She wants to play Seven Minutes in Heaven," Middle said. "That should be interesting."

Ray whispered into my ear, "Somebody's gonna get laid!"

* * *

After lunch the next day, I walked over to the Grimms' house in the Marsh. When I arrived, Ray and Middle, Micky and Big, and Little were already there. Everyone except me brought records. Ray brought "Wipeout" by the Surfaris. The name of the group had the word "surf" in it because the previous summer, all the kids were listening to surf music even when they lived in the Midwest like us and were a thousand miles from the nearest ocean. Ray fancied himself a drummer, so he arranged pots and pans on the kitchen table and drummed along with the record using wooden spoons for drumsticks. The song starts out with a stuttering scream, like the mating cry of an insane bird, and then a person who sounds intoxicated says, "Wipeout!" From then on, the song is two and a half minutes of wild incessant drumming and surf guitar music. Ray made us listen to it three times and would have made us listen a fourth time except that Middle said, if he did, she was going to murder him.

"Besides, you're getting all sweaty."

Ray said it was impossible to drum along with "Wipeout" and not get sweaty. "Besides, you like it when I get sweaty."

Middle made a face and said, "You wish."

All of them except Little were a bit drunk by the time I arrived. It seemed amazing but the people at Red's wake had not managed to drink up all the booze. At least that is what I thought until Little explained that Ray stole a bottle of Irish whiskey and two bottles of vodka when no one was watching and hid them under a bed. "The whiskey is for him and Micky, but we can drink all the vodka we want."

By 2 PM, Micky was working on his third glass of whiskey, explaining why he figured no one would ever be arrested for the murder of Red Kavanaugh. "Because the cops don't give a shit. If we kill each other, do they care? They don't. They only care about rich people."

Little poured me my first drink. "I'll fix you just a little one, OK?"

She poured a finger of vodka into a tumbler and then topped the drink off with a couple inches of Coke. "You want any ice? We have plenty."

I felt all of them were watching me, and I became possessed by the Spirit of Recklessness. I picked up the open bottle of vodka and said, "Hey, if we're gonna drink, let's drink!" I poured in enough vodka to fill up the tumbler.

"Jesus Christ," Ray said.

"No way he can drink that," Micky said.

Middle put on a record called "The Shoop Shoop Song" by Betty Everett, which she said was appropriate if we were going to play Seven Minutes in Heaven. The subtitle of this song is: It's in His Kiss. According to the song, there is only one sure way a girl can tell if a boy is truly in love with her. How good is he at kissing?

While I was drinking the entire contents of the tumbler, Middle played "The Shoop Shoop Song" twice in a row.

"You shouldn't let him drink that much," Big said.

To play Seven Minutes in Heaven, two kids, a boy and a girl, go into a dark closet. The door is shut on them, and they have to stay in there in complete darkness for seven minutes. They do whatever they want but they are not allowed to emerge from the closet until their time is up.

By the time Little and I entered the closet, it seemed to me I was living underwater.

"Are you OK?" Little said.

Big pushed shut the door, and we were in darkness.

I felt as if I was a deep-sea creature living at the bottom of the ocean, one of those monstrous creatures with big glowing blind eyes.

"Do you wanna kiss?" Little said. She felt for my hand in the darkness.

We kissed. We kissed seven times. I remember thinking her mouth was strangely rubbery and moist.

"Wanna French?" she said. "It's OK."

I seemed unable to speak.

Her tongue entered my mouth.

That is the last thing I remember.

According to Ray, who told me the story the next day, Little screamed and tried to get out of the closet, but Big was on the other side and would not let her out, not until the entire seven minutes had elapsed.

Finally, Big opened the door and let Little escape, but by then it was too late.

"You threw up!" Ray said. "Mama Grimm's fur coat was in there! You threw up all over it!"

When I woke up two hours later, I was lying on my back in the grass of the Grimm family backyard. Ants were crawling on me. I felt odd, as if — like Red Kavanaugh — I was no longer among the living.

The Grimm house was empty. Micky had taken them all out for a drive in his car.

I walked home, feeling very sorry for myself. My head throbbed, as if it was a drum and Ray was banging on it with wooden utensils.

17

Tarzan the Magnificent

That was the summer of the Beatles, the *first* Beatles summer, the summer of the movie *A Hard Day's Night* starring John, Paul, George, and Ringo, which every kid in America saw except me. My mom believed movies were sinful, so I was not allowed to go to them. Besides I didn't have any money. I didn't get any allowance and didn't have a job, so I couldn't even sneak off, take a bus downtown, and see the greatest film ever made.

My friends went to see the movie. Some of them saw it six times. Some of them saw it four times. Some of them couldn't even remember how many times they saw it. They could quote all the funny lines and sing the songs. I heard about *A Hard Day's Night* so many times, and heard the songs on the radio so frequently, that I got where I almost imagined I had seen the movie. The weird old crook, Paulie's uncle. "He's very clean." The snooty lady who thought she recognized John, and then he convinces her he is not "him" and she winds up saying he looks nothing like "him." George and the shirt guy. Ringo wandering around by himself. All of them acting like happy kids, running around and having fun. The Beatles were about fun. We all wanted to have fun.

I wondered if I had to be Little's boyfriend now. If you make out with a girl, is that a commitment? I wondered if I should go see her. I wondered if they got the vomit out of Mama Grimm's fur coat. And how could someone like Mama Grimm even own a fur coat? Aren't they crazy expensive? I thought only stinking rich people own them. And why would anyone keep a fur coat in a closet in the hot summertime, a closet used for kissing?

I was afraid to go over there. What if Mama Grimm answered the doorbell and presented me with the cleaning bill for her coat? Was it even possible to clean puke out of a fur coat? What if she brought the vomit-ruined coat to our house and ordered my mom to clean it? Or else she would sue us? I thought if my mom ever found out I got drunk and played Seven Minutes in Heaven with Little Grimm, I might as well just kill myself.

Every day for a week, I hoped Little would call me. I felt I should call her. I didn't call her though. I told myself no doubt she was mad at me. Probably I wasn't that good at kissing. Probably if you make out with a boy, and the boy vomits on you, that's a deal breaker. If Little still cared about me, wouldn't she call me? She never did.

I didn't go to the Nazi's either because I didn't want to be teased any more. I went up there the day after the catastrophe, and Ray and the Nazi took turns teasing me. "Seven Minutes in Heaven? It sounds like Seven Minutes in HELL!" I could take it from Ray, but the Nazi had never kissed a girl in his life. "Hey, you want us to fix you a tall glass of vodka and Coke?" Probably I would never hear the end of it. Probably Ray told everyone he knew, and the Grimm Sisters told everyone they knew. By now, our entire town knew the story. When I was an old man in my sixties, I would still have to hear about it, how I kissed a girl and threw up on her mom's fur coat.

People should not even have fur coats. In a decent world, they would leave the little furry animals alone. There should be a law against mixing vodka and Coke.

I became a lonely, isolated bookworm, hiding in my house.

After another week, I did get a phone call, but it was not from Little. It was from Little's best friend, Noreen. Noreen said I had broken Little's heart. She said she hated me. She said all Little's friends hated me. I ought to be ashamed of myself because Little was a wonderful person. A kind loving girl with a good heart. I did not deserve a girl like Little or any girl. But Little was not crushed. I should not even dream I had hurt Little's spirit. She was made of strong stuff like iron. Maybe Little was now on the rebound. Maybe I wanted her back, of course I did, but I could forget about it, because even if I crawled on my knees and begged, Little would never take me back. Why? Because Little had already found a new boyfriend. A much, much better boyfriend.

Ricky Fox.

"What?" I said. Just like that, I snapped out of my mental fog. "Who?"

"Ricky Fox is her new boyfriend. And he is so much better than you. Taller, stronger. So much better looking! A tenth grader! Ricky knows how to take care of a girl!"

Ricky Fox? The kid who threw pepper in my eyes? The Eagle Scout? How did she even meet him?

She met him at the swimming pool. After I broke her heart, Little started going to the Riverside Park Public Swimming Pool every single afternoon, and there she met Ricky the Fox. Slowly, over the course of one week, she fell in love.

"Ricky the Fox? That doesn't even make sense."

"That is what EVERYONE calls him. He's so popular and good looking! Especially compared to you!"

The next day, I rode my bike to the Riverside Park Public Swimming Pool. Because I was agitated and unhappy, I forgot my shoes and rode barefoot.

I did not have a quarter, so I could not pay the admission fee to get into the pool. Instead, I wandered around the fence that surrounded the pool until I found them. There they were, Little Grimm and Ricky Fox. In their swimming suits, practically naked. The sight sickened me. They were in the four-feet deep area, and Ricky the Fox was carrying Little in his arms. She had her arms around his neck and was staring right into his eyes.

I wanted to scream something. I wanted to climb over the fence and run to the edge of the pool and throw insults at them. Or rocks. If I had a handful of pepper, oh, what damage I could do to the self-satisfied smirk on the face of my nemesis, Ricky Fox!

After a few minutes of it, I could no longer bear to look at them. I returned sadly to the bike rack, where I left my bicycle, only to discover, while I was hanging on the fence staring at Ricky and Little, eating my heart out, someone stole my bicycle. The lock I used to keep it safe was lying on the ground, its u-shaped bar cut apart with a bolt cutter.

I had to walk home. Barefoot. It was over ninety degrees. The sun was beating down and the sidewalks were so hot, after a while, I realized the soles of my feet were getting burnt. The last mile, I had to walk in the grass of people's front yards. By the time I got home, the blisters had arrived. For two days, I couldn't even walk except on my heels.

My brother Dean thought this was pretty funny.

When he heard about my troubles, the Nazi came to visit me and lent me a Tarzan novel I hadn't read yet. "Read this one. It'll make you feel better." That summer, I was working my way through his complete collection of Tarzans, and then I was going to start on his complete collection of John Carter of Mars books. I believed Edgar Rice Burroughs, the author of these books, was a literary genius.

That night, I called up Rose White because I wanted sympathy. I could have called Calvin or Michael, but I was pretty sure Calvin had never kissed a girl in his life. Michael probably had kissed plenty of girls, but he wasn't telling. He was too cool to kiss and tell.

I didn't want to plunge right into my troubles, so I told Rose what I was reading: a Tarzan novel.

I have no idea why I was stupid enough to imagine Rose White, a tenth grader, would share my enthusiasm for Tarzan, the Ape Man, but I did imagine that. I blabbed away about how fun Tarzans are to read, how well written and exciting, until she got mad and interrupted me. She said she could not bear to listen to another word about Tarzan. I was a disgrace to bookworms. Did I ever manage to get through George Orwell's *Nineteen Eighty-Four*, the book she assigned me to read months ago?

I lied and said I very much wanted to read *Nineteen Eighty-Four*, but it was always checked out at the library. Rose snorted in disbelief, so I confessed. I had started that novel but only got through the first fifty pages. It was too grim, and I was not in the mood. My plan was to try it again when I was older and more in the mood for that sort of thing. "Maybe I'll wait until 1984 and then read it."

Rose said I was hopeless and threatened to hang up on me. She said Tarzan novels are written for idiots. She denounced Edgar Rice Burroughs as a white fool who probably never set foot on Africa in his entire life. And Tarzan! "What a stupid name by the way, what does it even mean, is he made out of tar? Like a naked white man is going to be able to beat the crap out of lions and tigers with his bare hands. Plus, doesn't he beat up black people, warriors? And Muslims?"

Obviously, Tarzan was a racist.

I said well, no matter what she thought, Tarzan novels were popular and sold millions of copies.

When she got tired of denouncing Edgar Rice Burroughs, I wrenched the topic around to what I really wanted to talk about, the sad story of my kissing misadventure.

Rose told me she could not give me kissing advice because she had never been kissed, thank God. She had witnessed kissing and it was not for her. *Yuck.* Her brother got a new girlfriend about every six weeks. The girls who fell in love with her brother were idiots. The white girls were even stupider than the black ones. She thanked the Lord she was an untouchable because of her lame legs, and believed I should be one too, because like her I was basically a nerd, plus there was my skin condition problem, which was the Lord telling me to forget about kissing.

While she was blabbing away like this, I studied the cover of *Tarzan the Magnificent.* The subtitle read: *Tarzan's most fantastic adventure – in the Land of the Warrior Women.* On the cover he was mostly naked as usual, huge chest and biceps, long black hair. He was holding the limp body of a beautiful blond, possibly Jane, who was wearing nothing from the waist up except a pointy-tipped bra. The woman was unconscious, but it seemed to me, if the Ape Man tried to kiss her, the sharp tips of that brassiere would probably drill holes in his chest. Not that Tarzan would mind, because he was indifferent to pain. Also, a dead lion was lying at Tarzan's feet with its paws up.

By then, Rose was telling me that three civil rights workers were murdered last month, was I even aware? Not to mention our stupid president Lyndon Baines Johnson was sending more troops to Vietnam. Why? So they could kill poor Asian people. While I was reading Tarzan novels, the world was on fire. Did I even care?

By then I had started reading the exciting first page of *Tarzan the Magnificent.*

Then I heard Rose say the words "murder" and "Red Kavanaugh" and I put down the book and listened.

Rose said the day after they discovered Red's body in the garage, two detectives came to her house to visit them. "Because if there is any possible way to blame black people for a crime, the cops are going to jump on it."

"The cops came to your house?"

Fortunately, the weekend of the murder, her entire family was in Cleveland with their mom's sister and her husband and their cousins. The very night it happened, Rose and Tommy were at a James Brown concert. Tommy loved to take her to concerts. Because Rose was in a wheelchair, Tommy could push her right up to the edge of the stage.

"James Brown?" I had no idea who that was. I wondered where Rose and Tommy got the money to go to concerts.

James Brown and his Fabulous Flames. Mr. Dynamite! The hardest working man in showbiz. Rose incorrectly imagined I had heard his records. She told me records are great but to truly experience the genius of James Brown, you have to go see him. You need to experience soul-power in all its magnificent sweaty glory.

"Soul-power?"

She and Tommy were so close to the hardest working man in show biz, they got drops of his sweat on them.

"Yuck," I said.

"The man can levitate. The man has moves inspired by God." She said I needed to understand soul. She felt I was lacking in the soul department. James Brown possessed a power given him by God to make the crowd go insane. "I was dancing in my chair. His total control over his band, the rhythm, the horns and drums. Never in my life outside of church have I heard music more soulful."

She said, in a way, James Brown was better than church because he was church plus sex.

"Church?" I said. By then, I was completely lost in this conversation. Soul? Sex?

The church my parents made me attend had music, what they called music. They had something called congregational singing which was horrible. They had this one woman named Angela Hoover who often stood in front of the choir and sang solos. She was heavily into vibrato and shook the life out of every note. Rose actually LIKED church music? Obviously, she did not attend the same church I did. Church music has NOTHING to do with sex.

In any case, what did Rose know about sex? She had never even been kissed. I at least had been kissed.

I said my idea of a really great group was the Beatles. I didn't really know what soul was, but the Beatles must have it, a lot of it. They were the greatest group in the entire history of the world. I didn't know who James Brown was, but he could not possibly be better than the Beatles.

Rose said I should be listening to the black station, not the Top 40 station. She said even on the Top 40 station, I could hear a little bit of soul. Every now and then they played Mary Wells singing "My Guy" or Miss Dionne Warwick singing "Walk on By."

I told her the Beatles produced a brand-new hit record... like *every single week*. "Have you even seen *A Hard Day's Night?*"

She said the Beatles were over-rated. The station she listened to did not even play them because they lacked soul. I needed to expand my horizons, quit reading racist Tarzan novels and listening to stupid Beatles records, quit getting drunk and kissing stupid white girls. I needed to open my eyes and realize what was really going on in the world.

I told her if she did not love the Beatles, she must be deaf.

She said obviously I was still a child and had no soul, none, not a single drop, and then she hung up on me – which was all too often the conclusion of our phone calls.

For some reason, talking to Rose always made me feel better.

18

Square Dancing

The only thing about eighth grade gym class I still recall, the one event that in fact I can never forget, is square dancing class. That is because of the horrible thing that happened to Fatty Patty Dyson and Paul the Wall McCord.

When summer concluded, and we returned to Poe Junior High and began the eighth grade, we learned that changes had been instituted. In gym classes, the grades would be segregated. Ninth graders would exercise only with other ninth graders; eighth graders would do jumping jacks only with other eighth graders. Also, football players and cheerleaders were exempt. They no longer had to take gym class because they got enough exercise practicing for their sport.

Also, for the first time ever, eighth grade gym class would include a dance class. For the four-week duration of dance instruction, the girls' swimming classes would be merged with the boys' gym classes. These temporary mergers were possible because the two classes met at the same time. Instead of leaping into the pool in their swimsuits, the girls would don their shorts and white blouses, and their teacher Miss Greene would lead them into the gym, which would be occupied by the boys.

Boys and Girls together! Dancing! The very idea drove the boys wild with excitement.

It soon became apparent that dancing class would be run by Miss Greene, a tall flat-chested pony-tailed woman who wore a zippered sweat suit. Coach Dee was there in a merely supervisory capacity. In his usual shorts and white tee shirt, he stood on the sidelines with his arms folded, ready to intervene if there was any trouble.

We were not taught ballroom dancing (too dangerously sexy); we were taught good wholesome square dancing. The music was provided by a record player in the corner of the gym, operated by a student. Miss Greene explained that after we had formed into pairs, we would form into squares, and she would function as our "caller." She said we must always pay extreme attention to her calls.

As she spoke, Miss Greene paced back and forth and played with her silver whistle. She informed us that Square Dancing is a thinking person's activity. The interaction of the caller and the dancers to complete a movement keeps minds sharp and bodies flexible. We would soon discover that square dancing is a healthy escape from stress and an intellectual form of exercise, much less boring to the young mind than calisthenics.

She had four couples come to the front of the gym and used them to demonstrate a square. Each couple stood together on one side of the square, facing the middle. Miss Greene signaled the record player operator to start the music and began issuing "calls."

Allemande Left! Circle Left! Circle Right! Do-Si-Do!

The couples performed these interactions so beautifully I realized they must have practiced them. When they returned to their home positions, panting slightly, Miss Greene encouraged us to applaud the dancers. She said these maneuvers might seem complex at first, but soon we would all be doing them as if by second nature.

"We will now create The Pairs! Line up, please. Will you please assist, Coach Dee?"

While Miss Greene ordered her girls to line up on one side of the gym, Coach Dee stepped forward and told us boys to line up on the other side of the gym.

Miss Greene and Coach Dee could have saved everyone a lot of anxiety and grief if they had arranged us alphabetically, but for whatever reason they let us line up as we pleased. I blame this mistake in planning for the tragedy that ensued. It need never have happened.

The absence of cheerleaders and football players brought confusion and excitement because now the status arrangements that had been firmly settled in seventh grade were in disarray. There was a vacuum at the top of the social ladder. Second-tier boys and girls were free to advance to the first position.

Before we ever arrived in the gym, some of the eighth-grade girls had decided that the front of each line should be reserved for students who were in love. The pretty girls should go right to the front of the girls' line. The boys who loved them should go to the front of the boys' line. Lovey-dovey couples to the front. That much, they felt, was only common sense. But what about the remainder of each line?

For a minute, chaos prevailed. Then, by a mysterious but natural process, the middle of each line filled with wannabe couples. Girls who liked certain boys. Boys who liked specific girls. In order to pair up with the appropriate girl, all a boy had to do was count back to where the girl was in her line, and make sure he was in the same position in his line. When the two lines united, he would be able to take the girl's hand. She would be his designated partner for the entire four weeks of dancing class.

Unfortunately, girls kept changing positions with one another, hoping to escape having to be paired with a boy they did not like. Also, sometimes two boys desired the same girl; both boys would then begin pushing one another. Coach Dee had to get involved.

The end of each line, again according to the natural order of things, belonged to the Untouchables. I of course went straight to the end of the line. It turned out there were more boys in my gym class than there were girls in Miss Greene's swimming class. This meant that the final square would consist entirely of boys. That sounded fun to me. Other boys had the same idea, so it turned out there was competition, even for the end of the line. I wound up not at the very end of the line, but near it.

Right in front of me was Paul the Wall. Like me, he wanted to be at the end of the line. As our lines marched toward one another, Paul again counted the girls and realized he needed to get farther back or he was going to wind up dancing with Fatty Patty, the girl at the very end of the girls' line. He turned around, grabbed me, and forced me to change places with him.

Unfortunately, by doing this, he caught the eye of Coach Dee, who strode toward us and ordered Paul back where he had been. Then the coach stood there glaring at us as the two lines advanced, so it was no longer possible for anyone to change his position in the line.

Eventually, despite his effort, Paul the Wall ended up holding hands with Fatty Patty, a perfectly harmless and friendly girl who happened to be quite large. I wound up in the square of Untouchable Boys.

What exactly is an untouchable? It is a loose category, well understood by eighth graders, but not entirely determined by appearance. It may be that untouchable teenagers have simply given up on romance. It may be that they are not ready for it yet. They will be ready in a few more years perhaps, but not yet.

Calvin and I felt that although we were untouchables, our friend Michael was not. Girls liked him; they pursued him, handing him notes that included their phone numbers. That sort of thing never happened to Calvin and me. If girls liked us at all, they assured us they liked us only as "friends." They would never dream of kissing us. Yuck.

It would be like kissing a brother.

Calvin believed that he was untouchable because he was a brain. For some reason, junior high girls do not lust after brainy boys unless the boys are also athletic and good looking. He observed that no overweight brain had a girlfriend. Calvin was the opposite of overweight; he was tall, skinny, uncoordinated, and wore glasses – a classic nerd. I was an untouchable because not only was I a puny brain; I had pimples. I should wear glasses but refused to because of vanity. As a result, I walked around in a fog, and everyone thought I was a snob. I was a snobby, semi-blind, brainy weakling with pimples. Obviously, that combination of defects placed me firmly in the untouchable category.

I felt that while Calvin's conclusions were reasonable, I was not totally and completely untouchable. There had been the incident with Little Grimm. Also, a girl in history class named Cathy once slipped me a folded-up note. She did this in the middle of class, and I did not want to get caught by our teacher, so I put the note in the back of my history book, intending to read it later. Regrettably, I forgot to read it. Every day, for a week, Cathy became more irritated with me and finally she told me, "You are so rude, Jack DeWitt! I hate you!" A week later, I discovered her note at the back of my textbook. It included her phone number. I felt that these two events suggested that even though I walked around in a fog and had pimples, I was not entirely untouchable. I felt my problem was that I was only attracted to cool good-looking girls who were far out of my league.

In any case, I wound up in the Untouchable Boys Square, and Paul the Wall ended up partnered with Fatty Patty.

Nothing too dreadful happened that first day. We learned to obey the basic calls. Grab your partner! Allemande Left! Allemande Right! Do-Si-Do!

On those occasions when I glimpsed them, I noticed Fatty Patty was attempting to be gracious and helpful to Paul the Wall, while he was clearly angry and resentful.

I am not sure how Paul the Wall earned that nickname. He was not unusually wide. Over the summer, he had a growth spurt and became rather tall and gangly for an eighth grader. One got the impression that his reflexes were a bit sluggish when it came to adjusting to his new height and his changed center of gravity. As a result, he tended to trip over his own feet.

The terrible thing occurred the third day of square dance class, when we all believed we understood the basic moves, and when Miss Greene felt she could shout calls at us without causing every square to collapse into total confusion.

As the class proceeded and the music played, we all got better and better. We began to have fun. Miss Greene was right. Square dancing does in fact sharpen the mind. It really is an excellent form of exercise and a stress reliever. Faces were flushed. Kids were smiling, hooking elbows, spinning, returning to Home Position. It was wonderful.

What is art? What is civilization? It is the triumph of order over chaos.

Grab your partners! Allemande Left! Allemande Right! Do-Si-Do!

And then it happened. A horrifying scream pierced through the music and the dancing and the general happiness. All of the squares stopped; dancers stumbled, bumped into one another. What was happening? The record player operator abruptly stopped the music.

Fatty Patty had fallen on top of Paul the Wall. He was lying underneath her, screaming, his leg twisted in a strange position.

Coach and Miss Greene ran to help. A circle of boys and girls formed around the stricken pair of dancers. Fatty Patty was lifted back to her feet; she was unharmed.

Paul the Wall's right leg was broken in three places. An ambulance was summoned. The rest of us were sent back to our respective locker rooms.

By three o'clock, the entire school learned what the term "compound fracture" meant.

To this day, I do not know what exactly happened. Did Patty miss a step and accidentally take Paul down with her? Did Paul the Wall trip over his own feet and pull down Fatty Patty? None of us who were in the gym that day will ever forget the sound of his screams.

I lost track of Patty Dyson for decades. I saw her again many years later at a high school reunion. By then, she weighed 300 pounds and was married to a little bitty man, no taller than five feet four. They were dancing together, dancing slowly, Patty and her husband, holding one another and dancing with surprising grace all by themselves in the middle of the dance floor to "Never My Love" by the Association.

I am sorry to report that Paul the Wall McCord walked with a limp for the rest of his life.

19

The Bowling Alley

The night Ray asked me to help him break into the bowling alley; I was already in a bad mood because of the paperboy thing. It was December and we were in the middle of a cold snap. Several waves of snow passed through town. Every day my dad and I had to shovel. My brother Dean was exempt from this chore because even though he was now in seventh grade, my dad felt he was still too short to operate a shovel. The good aspect of this job was, after we got done clearing the driveway and sidewalks and came inside, my mom would hand us mugs of steaming hot chocolate. My mug always had marshmallows floating in it. They would melt into a layer of sticky deliciousness.

This kid I knew, Brody Majors, who lived a block away had a paper route. Every day in the early morning when it was still dark, Brody delivered papers to his customers. In the evenings after supper, he would go door to door with his book of tickets and collect the money the customers owed. It was a simple job and brought in what he considered a decent amount of money. Brody and his paper route were matters of zero concern to me until the moms got involved.

Mrs. Majors called up my mom and said Brody had an earache

problem. There was a foot of snow everywhere you looked. An icy wind blew through our neighborhood every morning. The snow and wind were having a terrible effect on Brody's ears.

Mrs. Majors suggested a simple solution. Brody would stay home and sleep in. Jack DeWitt, who had healthy ears, would deliver the papers until the weather improved. By doing this little task, Jack would earn decent money and learn the value of hard work.

My mom told me I was taking over the paper route.

I didn't particularly like Brody, but I said OK. We were approaching Christmas. There were presents under the tree in our living room, and I could see I was going to get my usual items of clothing and maybe a board game. I wanted a record player. I had my heart set on one. If I agreed to the paper route thing, I would make enough to buy my own Christmas present. I started looking at pictures in the Sears catalog of affordable monaural high-fidelity record players with spindle arms so you can stack your rock and roll singles and listen to a stream of hits in uninterrupted comfort.

Brody screwed me. It was possible that he did not mean to do it. Like most kids, he was just sloppy and forgetful, more interested in himself than in my problems. This is what happened. Brody never took proper care of his book of tickets. Every newspaper subscriber had a separate page in the book. The page assigned to a customer was divided into little squares, one for each week. When the customer paid for a week's worth of papers, Brody tore off the square with the appropriate date printed on it and gave it to the customer. If the customer failed to pay up, then the little square remained in the book. That was how Brody could tell he had a deadbeat; those extra squares were still on the page. When he had a page like that, he could ring the guy's doorbell and explain, "Hey, mister, looks like you owe for three weeks."

This was a fine system, but Brody messed it up. Occasionally, a customer would call the paper and cancel his subscription. When that happened, the paper told Brody about it. He was supposed to yank out the customer's page and throw it away. Brody failed to do that six times. He left those pages in the book. Since he knew not to deliver a paper to those houses anymore, what difference did it make?

It made a difference to me because I had no idea those customers had canceled their subscriptions. Every morning, I delivered a paper to their door. That meant I ran out of papers. The last six houses on my route did not get one. I imagined the stupid guys at the paper were shorting me, not giving me enough papers. I called the dispatcher and told him they were going to have to take care of those customers. "Give me the right number of papers, for Christ's sake." An old guy from the paper had to make a special trip to the end of my route and deliver the missing papers. That happened every morning.

Worse, I tried to collect from the former customers, who I thought were deadbeats. I showed up at their doors and showed them the ticket in my book. "Looks like you haven't paid, sir, in four, five, six weeks." Some of these idiots actually paid me. Others swore at me and called me a crook. Some of them called the paper and said I was trying to cheat them.

Eventually, the weather got warmer, Brody's ears miraculously improved, and he said he wanted his route back. We settled up in his kitchen, with the two moms right there watching. I pushed over all the money I had collected and returned his collection book.

Brody explained that I had screwed up. He said I had delivered papers to the wrong houses and failed to deliver papers to some of the right houses. As a result, the paper was docking us, charging us for all those extra papers. It was newspaper company policy. He couldn't do a thing about it.

When it sunk in what Brody was saying to me, I wanted to hit him, but how could I with the moms right there staring at us? My mom said, "These things happen." She said she had known me for my entire life and boy she knew I could screw up. She looked at me and said, "I hope you learned a valuable lesson."

Brody subtracted the money we owed the paper and he pulled out his share. Even though he had been sleeping in for all those mornings, the agreement was he would get to keep a share of the profits. With all these subtractions, I wound up with almost nothing.

Christmas came and went, and I did not get a record player. My dark mood deepened.

The Nazi invited me to spend the night at his house. At our school, Christmas break consisted of the week between Christmas and New Year's. I was invited to spend the night of December 27th with the Nazi and Ray. The Nazi's mom called my mom to make sure it was all right. My mom felt maybe it was the sort of diversion that would get me to snap out of my foul mood. She agreed I could go, but I should wear clean underwear and be on my best behavior. I promised I would. But I still wanted to kill someone.

By then, Ray was living with the Nazi and his parents. He was calling the Nazi's mom "Ma." It was as if he had turned into the Nazi's brother.

It is possible I would never have taken another step down the path of crime if Ray had just asked me if I wanted to help him break into the bowling alley. I would have laughed and said no way, do I look like a fool? But that was not how he approached me. Instead of telling me his plan, he told me the Nazi was a chicken, and he could prove it. He said he would casually suggest something just a little bit dangerous and ask the Nazi if he wanted to participate. The Nazi would say no and come up with a ridiculous excuse as to why not.

Ray and I cornered the Nazi in his room, where he was watching TV. Not only did the Nazi have his own room, his own record player—a console stereo in a wooden cabinet, he also had his own TV set.

Ray waited until Mr. and Mrs. Broom went to bed, and then he stood between the Nazi and his TV show and said, "So… me and Jack are going to the bowling alley. You wanna come with?" Ray had a part-time job at the bowling alley. He cleaned up the place and sometimes stood behind the counter and handed out shoes to the bowlers.

The Nazi said, "It's closed." It was after 10 PM. "Get out of the way. I'm watching a show."

"It's a commercial. Come on. It'll be fun."

The Nazi gave him a look. "You plan to break in? The cops will be there in five minutes. There's probably an alarm right on the door."

Ray took a pair of keys out of his pocket and dangled them.

"If they find out you stole those, you're gonna be in so much trouble!"

Ray said, "We're gonna get something from the bar. And then we're gonna bowl a few frames. It'll be fun. You in?"

The Nazi said he would love to help with this project. It sounded like good fun. Unfortunately, he had a stomachache. "I don't feel good, or I would. I think I might even throw up." He put his hand on his tummy. "I think I ate too much."

Ray gave me a look, poked me in the ribs. His look said, "What'd I tell you? He's chicken!"

I did not want to help Ray rob the bowling alley. Despite my bad mood and my desire to murder a certain paperboy, I did not really want to walk voluntarily into a situation where I could wind up in jail. But how could I say no and not seem like a chicken? The Nazi and his stomach issue reminded me of Brady and his ear problem.

I told Ray I would participate.

As Ray and I trudged through the snow toward the bowling alley, my ears rang and my stomach churned. I felt like I needed to pee. Ray on the other hand was happy and alert. He said the cold night air wakes a guy up and makes him feel as if he can do anything. Anything!

Ray had a job at the bowling alley because he was a good bowler. Big Bill Ryan, who owned the place, was the patron of two junior teams of bowlers, one for girls and one for boys, and Ray was the best bowler on the boys' team. On weekends, Big Bill loaded them up in a van and drove them to tournaments. Because he was on the team, Ray got to bowl for free and he got to earn a little money working behind the counter, which was how he managed to steal the keys.

Walking down the sidewalk as the snow fell, I kept fearing a cop car was going to come along. I figured we looked guilty. Teenage boys out wandering around on a cold dark street after midnight? Obviously, we were up to no good.

The parking lot of the bowling alley was lit up. No cars. I was terrified someone passing by would notice us crossing the lot, going around to the back. Ray was having fun, seemed unaware of any danger, eager to get inside out of the cold. He wanted to bowl a few frames, show off his skills. We went around to the back. There was a door in the middle of the long wall and there was a little light perched right above that door, so the door was in a pool of yellow light. It seemed impossible for anyone to see us back there, but I was still scared until at last Ray got the door unlocked and we went through and were inside the bowling alley.

The place was empty and dark and silent. Big public places are creepy when they are empty of people. The silence is ominous as if the place might be full of ghosts. Ray went straight to the bar area and stole a full bottle of whiskey. He was completely relaxed and at-home, as if he was taking a can of pop from his mom's refrigerator. He went to the counter up front and turned on a bunch of lights. The whole place lit up. He flipped a switch and made the lanes come to life. The noise scared me, but Ray said not to worry. The bowling alley was a giant box without windows. "No one can see us!"

Ray had his own dark blue ball with a swirly design on it. It had his name engraved on it. "Big Bill bought it for me special. These holes are drilled to fit my fingers." I admired his ball. "It's perfect for me but probably too heavy for you." He took me to a rack of balls and picked out one not too heavy that I could use. I stuck my fingers into the holes. Ray said, "Comfy?"

I had never bowled in my life.

We went to a lane, Ray's favorite. We took off our parkas. Ray opened the bottle of whiskey and took a pull, wiped his mouth. "Want to bowl a practice frame? Get loosened up?"

I rolled a gutter ball.

Ray showed me the little triangles painted on the lane and told me if I aimed at one of them, I would have a better chance of keeping my ball in the middle of the lane.

He rolled a practice frame and knocked down every single pin. "That's what we call a strike."

Ray explained the difference between strikes and spares and started a score sheet for us. "I won't even count my first one because it was just for practice. But I'm gonna take a pull anyway." Ray said the game was, if he rolled a strike, he got to take a pull. If I knocked over five or more pins, I got to take a pull.

I rolled another gutter ball but this time, because I had aimed at an arrow, the ball stayed in the lane until it was almost all the way to the pins. Ray suggested I select a different arrow. "Don't even look at the pins, just hit your arrow." He said I could take a pull anyway since it was my first time bowling.

Once we got started bowling officially, Ray rolled a spare in his first frame and then got four strikes in a row. I rolled gutter balls but occasionally knocked down a few pins. One time my ball rolled right down the middle of the lane and took out seven pins.

"Take a pull!" Ray said.

A while later, I had no idea what was happening, but I was happy. Most of the time my ball was taking out a few pins. One time I even rolled a spare. Ray was rolling spares and strikes and telling me about a girl on Big Bill's girls' team. He was pursuing this girl day and night for weeks, but so far she was resisting his charms. I wondered if Middle Grimm knew Ray was chasing other girls.

One weird thing that happened that winter. In November, Middle Grimm disappeared. I heard first that she was no longer going to high school. She and Big were now in the tenth grade – in theory. People said they showed up only when it pleased them. Now, Middle wasn't showing up at all. Then I heard she was no longer in town. She was helping out her aunt who lived in St. Louis. It seemed weird. Ray seemed to know more than he was telling. When I asked him about Middle, he grinned but wouldn't say anything.

By then we were taking pulls whenever the mood struck us and no longer keeping score. Ray was doing funny things like bowling backwards with his eyes closed.

"Ray?" someone said. "Ray Kavanaugh? What are you doing here?"

We spun around and saw a lady. Ray got scared the moment he saw her and started lying. "Mrs. Ryan!" He grinned and talked fast. "Didn't Bill tell you? He wants me to get in some more practice. Bill knows we're here! Don't worry!"

"Darn it, Ray," the lady said. "I'm afraid I've called the police."

When Mrs. Ryan was driving past the bowling alley, she noticed someone had forgotten to turn off the lights on the sign. She had a key to the front door, so she came in to take care of it and noticed all the inside lights were on. Then she heard our voices, thought we were burglars, went into the office, and called the cops.

Ray kept talking and grinning. He wanted her to call the cops again and tell them false alarm, but she wasn't going for it. I could see nothing he said fooled her, but she found him amusing. I saw her notice the half-empty bottle of whiskey.

"Did you boys steal any money?"

"No!" I said and turned bright red. It was the first sound I had made since she appeared. She looked at me for a moment, and then the cops walked in. Four of them. First two, and then two more. She smiled at them and called them "officers."

They relaxed the moment they saw her, then tightened up when they saw me and Ray.

"You OK, Mrs. Ryan?" They knew her name. "What's going on?"

She laughed, this wonderful cool laugh that made you feel good inside, and said she was embarrassed. "I thought it was a burglary, but it's only Ray and his little friend. Ray is one of our best bowlers."

The cops said they knew all about Ray, and I noticed they were looking at him the way dogs look at a rat. Did she want to press charges?

Mrs. Ryan said that would not be necessary; she hoped she did not cause them too much trouble.

Oh no, certainly not.

While this chitchat was going on, I was so terrified I was on the verge of throwing up. Ray was trying to act cool but obviously, he was scared too. I had never seen him afraid before.

Mrs. Ryan said Ray was a good boy, mostly. The way she said the word "mostly" made the cops smile. She said it was a tough time for Ray and his entire family, which made us all think for a moment about Red Kavanaugh with his head hammered in.

The cops pretended they were capable of feeling sorry for Ray, and he did his best to look pitiful.

I saw one cop poke another cop and nod his head at the open bottle of whiskey.

Mrs. Ryan saw the same thing and laughed and said, "Where are my manners? Are you officers thirsty? Can I offer you a drink?"

The cops thought that was funny. I could see they thought every single thing about Mrs. Ryan was wonderful. I felt the same way.

Pretty soon, the cops left. She walked them to the door. I think that was to make sure they were absolutely certain Ray and I were not holding her hostage or anything. She came back and said, "Ray, I'm a little disappointed in you."

Ray hung his head and said he was sorry.

"You boys better go home now. Do you need a ride?"

Ray got serious for a moment and asked her, "You gonna tell him?"

"He's my husband, Ray. You know that. I tell him everything."

She turned to me, asked me my name and where I lived.

I wanted to lie but I told her my name, my real name and my real address. Something about her eyes and the way she was looking at me convinced me lying was pointless.

"You boys go home now. I'll lock up. Oh wait. Ray, do you have a key? I'll take that. And I want you to take that bottle back to the bar. Would you, please?"

When Ray and I were leaving the bowling alley, we didn't get far before Mrs. Ryan opened the front door and yelled at us, "Jack, you forgot your hat!" She had my hat in her hand. Ray called it my nerd-hat because it had ear flaps.

I ran back to her and got my hat. "Thanks!" I told Mrs. Ryan. I pulled on my hat.

"You be good," she said. "Stay warm, honey."

"I will," I said. I loved it that she knew my name and called me honey.

Five minutes later, Ray and I were walking back to the motel through the falling snow. Ray was acting cocky as if nothing had happened, as if he had planned the whole thing. He was talking a mile a minute, but I was not listening to him. I was thinking about how she did it, how Mrs. Ryan handled the cops, with laughter. Confidence. The laughter of women is amazing. Women like her. I had never met a woman like her before. I thought of my female teachers, my mom and her friends, the women in my neighborhood, the ladies at our church. None of them seemed the least bit like Mrs. Ryan.

I wondered how she learned to laugh like that. My mom almost never laughed except to make a loud barking sound. My mom's teeth went rotten when she was right out of high school; she had to have them extracted. Now, she wore dentures. She hardly ever laughed – probably she feared she might jar her dentures loose with too much laughing. If she got too stressed, my mom often sounded like a Southern hick. Mrs. Ryan sounded like a movie star, or like Jackie Kennedy, the most glamorous woman in the world. She wore cool pink lipstick and her fingernails were painted the same shade. She had a suntan. There was a foot of snow on the ground, and she looked as if she had just stepped off a plane from Miami. When Mrs. Ryan looked at me, there was something in her eyes that made me feel good.

Ray was saying he knew Mrs. Ryan wouldn't let the cops arrest him. He was the best bowler on the team, the high scorer. Bill loved him. She wasn't going to tell anyone because Mrs. Ryan was cool.

Cool.

I realized cool was the word. Mrs. Ryan was the first truly cool adult I ever met. She was cool like Marilyn Monroe and Cary Grant, like Jackie Kennedy and Frank Sinatra and the Beatles. Cool people own the world and make it seem easy. The rest of us love them for it.

Ray wished we still had the whiskey. He said he was sure Mrs. Ryan wasn't going to tell. Even if Ten Dollar Bill asked her why she was late coming home, she wouldn't say. Because she was cool.

"Ten Dollar Bill?" I said.

Ray wouldn't tell me what it meant, why he called Big Bill Ryan that, but later that night the Nazi did. When we got back to the motel, he was still up, watching a Japanese monster movie. His stomachache had disappeared.

Ray said he was tired and went to bed, but I stayed up to watch the movie with the Nazi. The voices in the movie were dubbed, and every now and then one of the actors would say "damn." It was strange because the lips of the actors said something in Japanese and another voice would come out, this weird American voice. Damn. Dammit. I had never watched a movie in which anyone used the word damn. It was shocking, but I liked it. I approved. The world was changing.

Kids like us could break into a bowling alley and get caught and yet not be arrested. Monster movies could use the word damn. Life was wonderful. Wonderful and cool.

Before we fell sleep that night, I told the Nazi that Ray had been scared. When the cops were there, I could hear it in his voice. "He was afraid. He didn't want her to tell her husband. Ray was scared she was going to tell."

The Nazi said if Mrs. Ryan had decided to charge him, Ray could get sent back to reform school. He said, "Bill got him out, and Bill can send him back."

"Got him out?"

The Nazi reminded me that the reason Ray had to go to reform school in the first place was he broke into Bill's Grocery.

"Bill got him out? Why?"

"When he found out Ray can bowl, he got him out."

I said, "Ray called him Ten Dollar Bill."

The Nazi snorted.

"What's it mean?"

"When Ray mows his yard, he gets five bucks, but he gets ten bucks if he mows it with his shirt off."

"I don't get it."

"Big Bill likes to sit on his porch and drink beer and watch Ray mow. With his shirt off. That's what I mean. Jesus, how dumb are you?"

20

Earflaps

I got a shirt for Christmas, a long-sleeved dress shirt my mom said I could wear to school. There was a pleat on the back of the shirt and an ornamental cloth loop at the top of the pleat. The girl sitting behind me in English class popped the loop off my shirt with her pencil. That was a trick girls were playing on boys that year. Some of the girls had whole collections of those little loops. Unfortunately, it left a hole in my shirt, just a little one, which my mom found that weekend when she did the wash. Apparently, she examined every item of my clothing with a microscope. She ran upstairs with the shirt and waved it in my face and blamed me for ruining my brand-new Christmas shirt. "Your grandfather gave you this shirt!"

At least I did not get a maroon sweater, even though I begged for it and put it on my list of Stuff I Want for Christmas. That first day back at school after the break, practically every boy in my grade except me (and hoods like Ray) was wearing one of those maroon sweaters. It was as if we'd suddenly turned into a Catholic school and had to wear uniforms. Before the break, a popular jock on the basketball team showed up one day wearing a maroon V-neck sweater and just like that every boy in my grade wanted one exactly like it because junior high boys are herd animals. Looking around at the sea of identical maroon sweaters, I thanked my lucky stars I did not get one. The girl who popped off my loop with her pencil told me, "At least you're not wearing one of those ugly sweaters like all the other boys." As a result, I felt special, distinguished. I march to my own drummer, I told myself.

I noticed at lunch that both Michael and Calvin were wearing maroon sweaters.

I managed to lose my ride home by the second day of the first week.

That year, all the women in my neighborhood including my mom learned how to drive. And most of them got jobs. My mom got her teaching certificate renewed and obtained a job teaching World Geography and American History in a little Catholic high school located twenty miles out of town. She couldn't give us a ride because she had to leave too early in the morning.

To solve the problem of how to get Dean and me to school, Mom called up Mrs. Albertson, a lady who lived a block behind us. Mrs. A had two sons, one of them my age and one of them Dean's age. Mrs. A gave her kids a ride to school and picked them up in the afternoon. She could take Dean and me too if we got to her house on time in the morning. She could give me a ride home in the afternoon. Dean wouldn't be able to go with us after school because he had just gotten a job as the assistant manager of the basketball team and had to stay late. This job was a big deal to Dean; he loved hanging around with jocks. Basketball practice ran for two hours after school every day except Friday. That was going to work out great because my mom could pick up Dean on her way home from her job. She liked to stay late at her school after the kids left and grade papers. She could pick up Dean, no problem, and I could catch a ride home with Mrs. A and her boys. In theory, these arrangements were going to work perfectly but, because of Hamberger, everything went to hell.

Miss Hamberger the band director had decided the semester before that she had too many trombones. What our band needed was more baritone horns. She called me in one day and told me she was switching me. I was one of her worst trombone players, so it was not going to be a problem to the section to lose me. She said I would have an easier time playing baritone than trombone because a trombone has a slide. To play it properly, you need a good ear, so you know exactly how far to extend the slide. I did not have a good ear and was always extending my slide a millimeter too far or too near. Hamberger said she would not go so far as to say I was tone-deaf, but …. She did not finish her sentence. The baritone, she explained, is an instrument with three keys. Keys are much easier to operate than a slide. Even an idiot like me could learn how to play a baritone. So that was that. I was no longer playing trombone.

I thought I could describe the situation to my mom and get out of band. "If I can't play the trombone, I don't want to be in band at all!" If my mom would just let me quit, this was going to turn out great. I hated band. Unfortunately, my mom said I could not quit band because DeWitts are not quitters. She called up Hamberger. The two of them had a long talk, teacher to teacher, and they decided no way was I going to quit. Participation in music is the cornerstone of a well-rounded education. According to Hamberger, the sky is the limit for any boy able to play the baritone. Why, someday he might wind up becoming President of the United States.

Twice a week, on band practice day and on baritone sectional day, I had to haul my baritone and its black case to school and back. On Tuesday morning of that first week, when I showed up at Mrs. A's house with my baritone, Mrs. A did not like it. "Your mother never mentioned any horn. That big ugly case is too big to go into the back seat. You three boys AND that thing? There's not enough room!" She said my baritone would have to go into the trunk. It fit but just barely. "That thing better not leave scratches on my trunk!"

After school let out on Tuesday, I had to get my coat and school stuff from my locker and then run up to the band room closet to get my baritone and then lug it out to the parking lot where Mrs. A and her kids were waiting for me. Mrs. A was mad that they had had to wait. She opened her trunk and stood there watching while I got my baritone in it. I was very careful not to leave scratches, but she made a sniffing noise and said I was the sort of boy who only thought of himself. "You had better not make me wait again, not even one minute, or you can just walk home!"

I lost my temper and said I would rather walk home than sit in a car with an old (bad word) like her and her stupid brats. Mrs. A got so angry, her face turned red. She pulled my baritone out of her trunk, set it down in the snow, slammed shut the trunk, got back into her car, and drove off without me.

I had to lug my baritone all the way home, three miles. It was cold and a wind was blowing in my face.

That evening, Mrs. A called my mom and told her about the bad word I had called her. She said I was rude and ungrateful, and she was no longer willing to give me a ride. She would still give my little brother Dean a ride to school in the morning because he was a nice boy, but not me. So that was how I wound up having to walk back and forth to school every day in the coldest part of the winter.

That Thursday (sectional day), I was walking home after school lugging my baritone. The wind was so bad I was walking backwards. I was telling myself I was stupid. Mrs. A was right. I was ungrateful and rude. Would it have killed me to swallow my pride and be nice to her? No, I had to smart off. Now I was in hell. People are wrong to think hell is fire. Hell is icy cold wind and snow. Hell is cold that bites right into you, freezes the hair in your nostrils, and makes your lungs ache. While I was walking backwards and mentally berating myself, a long white car approached. The driver saw me and pulled over to the side of the road. The window rolled down and a voice I recognized said, "You need a ride?"

It was Mrs. Ryan. Driving down the street, she noticed a weird kid with a huge black case walking backward. She recognized my earflaps and pulled over.

I put my baritone into the back seat of her Cadillac. There was plenty of room. I went around to the passenger side of the car and got into the front seat. It was like entering heaven.

In the afternoons, it turned out, Mrs. Ryan liked to go to the bowling alley bar, which was almost always deserted at that time of day. She told me she liked to sit in there and read. She pointed at a book lying on the seat between us, *The Agony and the Ecstasy.*

"Oh, I know that one," I said. I had checked it out from the library the previous summer. "It's about Michelangelo, the artist." That was the best possible thing I could have said because it turned out Mrs. Ryan was a bookworm. I was a bookworm and she was too.

She said, "I think people who read books are spiritually related. What do you think? Is that silly?"

By the time, Mrs. Ryan dropped me off at my house, I felt my luck had turned. She said she drove by my school at about that same time every afternoon. "I could stop at the school and pick you up. Don't you get out every day at 3 o'clock? That's perfect for me. I have to drive right past your neighborhood, so why not give you a ride? We can talk about books."

When my mom got home that afternoon and hung up her coat in the front closet, she sniffed and snorted and said she smelled cigarette smoke. Oh, for God's sake, I said under my breath. She pulled out my dad's coat, sniffed, then Dean's coat, and then mine. She said my coat smelled of cigarette smoke, a smell she found putrid.

"What are you, a bloodhound?" I said.

She was obviously right on the verge of accusing me of smoking cigarettes on my way home from school, so I told her what happened. "A nice lady stopped and gave me a ride. She smokes. So what? People smoke, Mom."

My mother sniffed my parka again and said she could detect the smell of cheap perfume.

"I doubt it's cheap," I said.

That night, Mrs. Ryan called my mom and introduced herself. She explained our arrangement and asked my mom for permission to drive me home from school. To my amazement, when that phone call ended, my mom was smiling. She told me I was lucky to know someone like Mrs. Ryan. My mom said she had heard the Ryans sometimes gave promising boys from our town scholarships. In a few years when I went to college, I was going to need financial assistance.

By the second week, Mrs. Ryan and I were good friends. In her company, I was not an idiot. I was funny and intelligent and loveable. Despite my earflaps, my bad eyes, and my pimples, I was charming. I made her laugh.

Mrs. Ryan's car was a Cadillac Coupe DeVille, a white one with creamy white leather interior. Her husband Bill had a black one with a black leather interior. She said that was Bill for you. Every year, he had to have a new Cadillac, and his wife had to have a new one too, even if she didn't need it. She said Bill preferred the Coupe DeVilles to the Eldorados. Some people prefer the Fleetwoods, especially the convertible. But what good is a convertible in the winter? She said there was a DeVille convertible, if you like that sort of thing, but the sedan was just fine as far as she was concerned.

I had no idea what any of this meant but, if Mrs. Ryan said it, I believed it. Every day as she drove me home, we would talk about books and everything else. She encouraged me to talk. She said she liked to listen to me. Soon, I was telling her about my mom's operations, about her temper and mood swings and uncanny ability to smell smoke, and about my idiotic teachers. I told her about the time, when I was only nine years old, I was sitting on the front porch railing when my little brother Dean gave me a poke, and I fell over backward, landed on my head on the sidewalk, got a skull fracture, and had to spend an entire week lying on my back in the hospital. "Ever since, my whole family says, no wonder I'm cracked."

Mrs. Ryan found this story hilarious.

In my English class that year, we read *Romeo and Juliet, A Tale of Two Cities, Lord of the Flies*, and a novel called *A Separate Peace*, which was about rich, spoiled, private school boys. I told her all these books were so boring that the kids hated them. So far as I could tell, the whole point of English class was to get kids to hate books. What I really liked to read, I told her, was H. G. Wells. I told her all about *The Invisible Man, The War of the Worlds, The Island of Dr. Moreau*, and *The Time Machine*. I told her even though the author H. G. Wells was dead, I considered him a genius and a prophet. I said the only possible way to improve a book like *A Separate Peace* would be to have the private school invaded by blood-thirsty creatures from Mars.

Mrs. Ryan said I was a wonderful storyteller. She would almost rather hear me talk about a book than actually read it. She said I could call her Catherine, but I kept calling her Mrs. Ryan. I thought everything about her was beautiful and classy: her fingernails and her hair and her lipstick, her filter-tipped cigarettes, her perfume. It turned out I was right about that perfume; it came from France and it was not cheap.

She said her husband Bill sort of adopted boys if they were athletes, including a boy like Ray who was a talented bowler. She said I was not really the sort of boy Bill liked, but I was exactly the sort of boy she liked, a smart one who read books and saw the humor in life.

I wanted Mrs. Ryan to adopt me.

She said she had a daughter the same age as me, and boy was Cathy a handful. She would have to introduce us sometime. Mrs. Ryan's name was Catherine and her daughter was named Cathy. I thought this was wonderful. I thought probably every female person on earth named Catherine or Cathy is wonderful.

To this day, I remember what she said about the books she was reading that year. "I read all the best sellers. I probably should read, you know, the classics, what's his name Tolstoy and … have you ever heard of Faulkner? Or Marcel Proust, the French writer? But I am just not up to the task. I'm an ordinary woman, and I like to read the sort of things ordinary people are reading."

I was certain that Mrs. Ryan did not have an ordinary bone in her entire body.

The Agony and the Ecstasy by Irving Stone. "Do you suppose all artists are as tormented as Michelangelo? I suppose this world, the ordinary world is just not interesting enough for them, do you think? That is why they make such beautiful things, to improve the world. Next summer, Bill is taking me to Florence, Italy. He says they have the most wonderful art there. Well, you read the book, so you know. All those gorgeous statues that almost seem alive, and of course truly amazing buildings. Michelangelo reminds me of my husband in some ways. I know that sounds silly, but I think some men, they just seem superior to other men, larger and braver, don't they? Artists have a certain confidence. They think bigger, don't they? Bill likes to tell people business is an art, buying and selling things. Everything is an art if you are an artist. Don't you think?"

Fail-Safe by Eugene Burdick and Harvey Wheeler. "It is about how a bunch of stupid men almost start World War 3 – I couldn't finish it. Do you want it? I think you may like it more than I do. Bill liked it."

Hawaii by James Michener. "This one, it is LONG. It is very informative, but it never rises above a certain level, does it? You certainly do learn a great deal about Hawaii, about volcanoes and missionaries and indigenous people. The really good thing is, after Bill read it, we went there!"

The Feminine Mystique by Betty Friedan. "I'm not sure I understood all of it. I may have to read it again. I doubt you would like it, Jack. It's nonfiction. It's all about how unhappy women are, how we need more in our lives, much much much more, do you know what I mean?"

The Chapman Report by Irving Wallace. "I don't think you should read this one. We should not even be discussing it. Your mother would never approve. It's based on the Kinsey Report, have you ever heard of that? Well, never mind. A bunch of rich society women in California are being interviewed about their…histories, I guess you would say. I will just observe that women in California seem to have a LOT more adventures than some of us do here in the Midwest."

By spring, I was completely and totally in love with Mrs. Ryan, a woman old enough to be my mother.

21

Soul Power

Our history teacher Mrs. Rabbit liked to spend five minutes at the start of every class talking about current events. She showed us a film of the black ooze of communism covering North Vietnam and then dripping down into South Vietnam. "Communism is just like cancer." She pointed at the screen, "This is what will happen if we do nothing." The cancerous ooze spilled over Thailand and Cambodia and then hopped over the ocean and engulfed Australia and New Zealand. Mrs. Rabbit said, "This is why we are in Vietnam, a country I'm sure most of you have never heard of. Any questions?"

A boy in the front of the room said, "We should just nuke 'em!"

A girl in the back of the room said primly, "But that would be wrong."

Everyone laughed.

"But that would be wrong" immediately became our catch phrase. Whenever anyone said anything ridiculous, someone else would say, "But that would be wrong." Everyone would laugh. It didn't even have to make sense. Someone could say, "I heard it's gonna snow tomorrow." Someone else would answer, "But that would be wrong." Laughter. Calvin liked to say it when I was ranting about something or other.

He would let me talk, wait for my voice to get overly loud, and then he would raise his hand and stop me in mid-rant by saying, "But that would be wrong." And everyone would laugh at me. I would turn red and fall into confusion and get mad and have to shut my mouth.

The year before, over in Vietnam, a bunch of Buddhist monks, bald guys in sheets, self-immolated. That is what the newspaper called it. They sat cross-legged in a public place like a town square, poured gasoline over themselves, and protested the war by setting themselves on fire. I found myself talking about it at lunch sometimes. "Imagine caring about something so much that you would do that. Kill yourself. That's true religion for you. Try to imagine a pastor doing anything like that. Come to think of it, I wish they would. I would absolutely love it if Pastor Anderson at my church set himself on fire. In fact, if he ever pours gas all over himself, I will light the fire myself."

"But that would be wrong," Calvin said.

In math class, Michael told me I needed to lighten up. By then, he had been liberated from the dumb kid classes and he was in almost all of my classes. "You take yourself too seriously sometimes. No offense. We all know you have a wild imagination but, sometimes, you know, THINK before you speak."

That was one of the many wonderful things about Mrs. Ryan. She never made me shut up. It was a whole lot more fun to talk to her about current events than to listen to Mrs. Rabbit lecture about them. For one thing, Mrs. Ryan never pretended she had any idea what was really going on. I found that refreshing. She never contradicted me or told me I was an idiot. She never said, "But that would be wrong."

In February, a famous black preacher with the weird name of Malcolm X was assassinated. It was on the front page of the paper. I thought I should call Rose White and get her angle on the murder but most likely, if I did, she would just tell me I was an idiot. I told Mrs. Ryan I found the story pretty confusing.

She said she did too. "I guess he was a Muslim?"

I said, "He was a Black Muslim."

"Do Muslims come in colors? Are there Green and Blue and Red Muslims?"

"Don't ask me. Maybe Black Muslims wear black robes."

"Oh no, well, not the men at least. I've seen pictures. They wear bow ties. I think their women may wear robes though. Or is it veils?"

I told her what I had learned from Calvin, that black people have slave names, the names of their former masters. "They don't even know what their real names are, I mean the old African names. So that's why he called himself Malcolm X. X means he didn't know his real name."

"Bill says he was a radical."

I said, "That's my favorite thing about him. That and the bowtie."

Mrs. Ryan laughed. I loved to make her laugh.

Neither of us understood why Malcolm X was assassinated not by cops or racist white men, but by members of his own church.

My friend Calvin read news magazines and considered himself an expert on the Black Muslims. At lunch, he said their religion was basically a religion for criminals, but you have to be black, or you can't even go to their church. "They believe us white people are evil clear through because of the big-headed scientist." According to Calvin, the founder of the Black Muslim religion, a former convict named Elijah Muhammad, taught his followers that originally all human beings lived in Africa and had black skin. There was no such thing as a white person. Then this one guy with a big head became a scientist, sort of like Dr. Frankenstein. He started kidnapping people so he could do experiments on them in his secret laboratory, trying to bleach their skins white. He finally succeeded but, to do it, to bleach out all their skin color, the big-headed scientist had to remove their souls.

"You're making this up," I said.

Calvin swore it was true. He said he read it in a reliable news magazine. "They believe whites don't have souls. None of us do."

I wondered if this could possibly be true. James Brown had soul. He was the undisputed King of Soul. According to Rose, Ray Charles aka The Genius more or less invented soul. The Temptations had soul; probably the Supremes did, but did any of the white groups? Even the Beatles? As a matter of principle, I didn't believe in souls. The soul is just an imaginary thing invented by priests and pastors so they can pretend no one ever dies.

At some point, I quit thinking these thoughts and started stating them out loud. I ended my rant by saying, "All churches should be closed by law." I took a swig from my carton of milk.

Calvin said, "But that would be wrong."

Everyone at our lunch table laughed at me.

Calvin said the reason Black Muslims shot Malcolm X was because he split with their church and took a bunch of his followers with him. He went around preaching it was possible for white people to be Muslims. We too have souls. "So, they killed him."

That spring, Middle Grimm returned to town, and the Gospel Brothers came to my church for an extended stay.

I saw Middle and Big at the playground. Middle was telling anyone who asked she had a wonderful and relaxing time helping her aunt in St. Louis, and Big was giving anyone who kept asking questions the Death Glare.

Every time I saw Big Grimm, I wondered about her boyfriend, Micky. He had enlisted in the Marines, and I wondered if he was now in Vietnam, killing communists.

When the Gospel Brothers came to our church, it was billed as Four Days of Jesus. They were not your common garden variety of travelling preachers. They were a music group. The kids at my church got excited just looking at the poster that announced their imminent arrival. They were young. They had sort of long hair, and they plugged in their instruments. The girls decided they were cute, especially the lead singer. They were like a religious version of the Beatles, which made them in the minds of some people better than the Beatles. I sneered of course – as if anyone could be better than the Beatles.

The Gospel Brothers were going to play electric guitars in our church. They were going to play drums – in the sanctuary. It was almost impossible to imagine electric guitars in our church – not to mention drums. Normally speaking, so far as I could tell, the good Christians of our church hated drums. They didn't even like bongos. What the pastor and the adults liked was organ music. The only other time they brought in a musician for our religious entertainment, it was a tall blonde lady who played an enormous harp. People said she was an angel in human form. Maybe so, but a lot of people including my dad fell asleep listening to her.

Wednesday night, the first big night of the show, there was a lot of concern whether the Gospel Brothers were even going to show up. Their bus had broken down in Pennsylvania. The pastor's wife was so nervous she looked as if she was running a fever. She kept sneaking looks at her watch and saying, "Don't worry. They're on their way!"

Five minutes before show time, with the church maybe 70% full, the bus rolled into the parking lot. The four Gospel Brothers did their own set up but the pastor and men from the church helped them. The Brothers did in fact bring an entire drum kit that looked like something Ringo might play. Amplifiers were hauled in. Wires were run. Microphones. The electric guitars arrived and an electric bass. Just watching the set-up was entertaining because the Gospel Brothers kept making jokes. None of the jokes were especially funny but no one seemed to mind.

I started to wonder if the Gospel Brothers always arrived late just so they could tell their corny jokes and get people to help them. Maybe it was part of their act.

When they were set up, the singer led us in prayer. By then people were so hopped up with anticipation, they were sweating. The church did not have air conditioning.

The Gospel Brothers leaned more toward country music than rock and roll, but man their guitars got loud. Their music reminded me of early rockabilly, like Jerry Lee Lewis. The drummer was so good at his job, it was nearly impossible for the kids to stay in their seats. Our church taught that dancing was wicked, so it was impossible for the kids to take to the aisles and dance their hearts out; they had to content themselves with wiggling and swaying in the pews. All the songs were about Jesus and the joy of the Lord. Sometimes the singer got the crowd to clap. Sometimes he taught them the chorus and got everyone (except me) to sing along.

When the concert portion of the show concluded, the singer conducted an altar call. The bass player abandoned his instrument and sat down at our church organ. He played an old gospel song called "Just as I Am" over and over, while the singer begged everyone who was in a condition of sin to give his or her heart to Jesus. All over the church people started swaying and weeping. My brother Dean ran straight to the front of the church, knelt in front of the altar, and began sobbing. Soon he was surrounded by ladies including my mom. I wondered if he was confessing. My little brother was one of the most talented shoplifters in our neighborhood. He never walked into a store without walking out with stolen stuff in his pockets. He was so little and cute, the store clerks found him adorable. One time, I watched him steal a bottle of pop. He paid a nickel for a pack of gum, but he had the bottle of pop hidden behind his back. No way was he going to pay for it. Five adults were standing in the line behind him. Every one of them could see he was stealing the bottle of pop. They were smiling and shaking their heads. Not a single adult said a word.

That was how good Dean was at stealing stuff in plain sight. He had a gift. I figured he was up there telling the church ladies and our mom about his many sins. I found the sight depressing.

Half a dozen people besides Dean were saved that night. One of the other people who got saved was my nemesis Ricky Fox. After Jesus saved him, Ricky stood up and testified that he had sinned, not just once, many times, but now he was saved and probably sanctified too. "Praise Jesus." Church ladies took turns hugging him.

The second night, Thursday, Ricky Fox arrived with Little Grimm at his side. That night, the lead singer would preach for a while and then lead the band in a song, then more preaching, then more singing. Even when he preached, the rest of the band would hum and play quietly in the background.

The climax every night was the altar call. By then, everyone would be on their feet, swaying to the music. "Just as I am. Without one plea." The singer would implore people to come forward, lay down their bags of sin, let Jesus set them free. It was almost impossible to resist. As the organ played the same riff over and over, your head began to fill up with images of all the bad stuff you had done. In my case, it was telling lies, saying mean stuff about people, looking at Playboy pictures of naked women, and sassing my mother.

Just as I am, without one plea
But that Thy blood was shed for me
And that Thou bid'st me come to Thee
O Lamb of God, I come! I come!

The more times people would sing that last line, *I come I come*, the harder it was to resist. The altar call had physical force; it was like standing in a tide. When I looked around the church, I could see people "under conviction." This meant they were full of guilt and shame. They would want to run up to the altar and fall to their knees, but they would be resisting. They would grip the back of the pew in front of them so tightly their knuckles turned white.

"Oh, Lamb of God, I come! I come!"

At last, they could not hold out another second. They sobbed and let go, stumbled forward, staggered toward the altar. It was as they had been lassoed by an invisible rope, as if Jesus himself was up there yanking on the rope, dragging them – poor lost sheep! — all the way to the altar, where they could collapse to their knees and be washed clean of all sin. Ricky Fox and Little Grimm were saved that night. So were two dozen other people. Dean was saved for a second time.

Friday night, Little Grimm returned and brought her family with her. I would never have believed it except I saw it with my own eyes: Mama Grimm, Middle and Big – in a church.

On the way home, my dad said he and the other members of the church board had had serious reservations about the Gospel Brothers. Amplified music in the church? Drums? Some of the board members argued that drums are African in nature; they are pagan tools often used by Satan to arouse the basest feelings and create the atmosphere of sensuality. The board members had expressed doubts, but the enthusiasm of the pastor had carried the day. The Gospel Brothers were hired. My dad said he no longer had any doubts. None. God himself had sent them to us.

"Bless the Lord," my mom said. "Praise Jesus." She glanced at me in the back seat of the car, smiled sadly at me, and then closed her eyes to indicate she was praying for me.

At the Friday night altar call, the entire Grimm family had run up to the altar. Apparently, their sins were numerous and extreme because, after kneeling beside them for a minute, the pastor found it necessary to shepherd them out of the sanctuary and back into his office, where they were treated to a special private prayer session. While that was going on, my brother Dean got saved again and so did all my other siblings. I was the only member of the DeWitt family to remain unsaved.

Several people of the church told me they were praying for me. "Praying hard."

Saturday night was the Special Healing Service. It was standing room only. By then I had had all I could stomach of the Gospel Brothers so, half-way through, I snuck out of the church and wandered around outside. To my surprise I found the drummer outside too, leaning against the back wall of the Sunday School Wing, smoking a cigarette. He seemed happy to see me and offered me a Marlboro.

"No thanks," I said.

He said since he had seen the healing service about a million times, he hoped God would forgive him for sneaking out.

"Right."

He confided that he was not really related to the other three Gospel Brothers. They were true brothers, but he was just hired help. He figured this was why their voices harmonized together so well. "They've been singing together since they was babies."

"Sure," I said.

He said drumming for the Gospel Brothers was a pretty good gig, but his real ambition was to be a session drummer in Nashville or maybe tour with someone like Johnny Cash.

I had no idea what a session drummer was.

"That would be seriously cool," I said.

"I better go back in," he said.

"Hey," I said. "Can I ask a question?"

He lingered. "Lay it on me, kid."

I asked him about soul. Did he think only black people have soul? Did the Gospel Brothers have it?

He said, "Well, gospel is black, mostly. It comes out of the black churches. You can't have any more soul than that. Do the Brothers have soul? Hell, yes!" He winked at me. "See you down the road, kid."

I stayed outside and looked up at the night sky and the stars and wondered what the big-headed scientist did with all those souls he stole from the white people.

22

Bloody Sunday

A t Sunday church, everyone was still buzzing about the Gospel Brothers. They had loaded up their bus and departed Saturday night after their final show. We had pretty good church attendance, including several new couples and their kids. Ricky Fox was up near the front with Little Grimm sitting beside him, but I noticed the other Grimms were not attending. My mom reminded me they were Catholics, as if that explained anything.

The service felt anticlimactic. Instead of the music and excitement of the Gospel Brothers, we got Pastor Anderson in the pulpit talking about the Gospel of Mark. And this Sunday, he was not at his best. He had a bad cold. Possibly the stress and excitement of the Four Days of Jesus had been too much for him. He told us his wife was home in bed; she too had succumbed to a cold. Halfway through his sermon, his voice faded to a whisper and then completely disappeared. He had to signal to one of the deacons to come up and lead us in prayer. The deacon said, all things considered, maybe we could send the pastor home to his sick wife, and not expect him to come back this evening for the Sunday night service. "He deserves a night off, don't you think? Can I get an Amen?" Everyone yelled Amen. The deacon said he figured Jesus would forgive us if we went ahead and canceled the evening service, just this one time, unless someone else wants to lead it. Anyone on the Board feel the need? No one raised his hand. So that was how I happened to watch Bloody Sunday on TV.

My dad drove us to my grandparents' house, where my grandfather prepared fried chicken for us to eat. Since there wasn't going to be any evening church, we stayed at their house and played board games with my grandmother with the TV on in the background.

The reporters kept saying it was history. The event that had transpired in Selma, Alabama, was history exploding right before our eyes. Yes, it was. They seemed unsure how they should talk about whatever had happe6+ned. How serious was the event? Pretty darn serious, but as serious as the assassination of JFK? What should it be called? A fight? A battle? What would happen next?

A bunch of black people had attempted to march somewhere for some reason, and a bunch of cops stopped them. And the result was pretty serious. The TV network had footage of the whole thing, so don't turn the channel! The TV network did not yet have the footage, but it was on its way. They were going to tell us what happened, but pretty soon they were going to be able to show it to us.

What happened? The details were still coming in. White cops beat up black people. State troopers and sheriff's deputies, some of them on horses, armed with billy clubs and rifles, engaged in full-out armed combat against non-violent protestors. The footage was on its way. Cameras had captured everything.

The TV news guy said it could be called crowd control. The event, the occurrence, whatever it should be called. The intervention. The crowd had been warned. They had been told to desist. Their leaders had failed to retreat. They had been informed they did not have permission. A man who failed to obey official instructions was possibly shot. A Negro man.

That man was killed. Wait! Hold on! Yes, he was dead. That was now confirmed. Officially? Yes, officially confirmed! Lots of other people were hurt, men women and children too, even old ladies. Grandmothers. Wounded marchers were still lying in the road. No, they were recovering in a hospital. They were being attended to, but this one man got shot in the back, a Negro man, and now he was dead. That was definitely confirmed. Is that footage here yet? It's on its way!

He had been trying to help his mother when he got shot. Did he get shot in the back or the front? It was probably a law officer who shot him. It may have been. The law officers were heavily armed. There was a lot of confusion. No, the identity of the officer had not yet been announced. It may have been an accident. It is normal procedure to protect the identities of law officers. It may have been an inexperienced volunteer who shot the Negro man, a temporary deputy who was not well trained. It could have been an accidental discharge.

My mom said maybe we should turn off the TV. It didn't seem the sort of thing children should watch. My grandmother agreed. What we should do instead was play a board game. But by then it was obvious my dad and grandpa were fascinated by the news. No way were they going to quit watching.

"The footage of the entire event will be here in one hour! Exclusive footage! Don't turn the channel!"

My grandmother suggested I take all my siblings out to the backyard. We could play a fun game out there. We could set up the croquet hoops under the apple tree. We could play marbles.

As soon as I heard I should not watch, I concluded it was super important that I watch. I argued that I should be able to watch because I was 14 and no longer a little kid. Dean caught my excitement and said he was 13, not a kid either. I suggested Ellen and Lois and Ron should play marbles in the backyard for the duration. Or they could sit in the dining room and occupy themselves with gospel coloring books.

Without ever taking his eyes from the TV screen, my dad said, "These kids, all of them, even the little ones, can watch because this is history."

When the footage of the event finally aired on the screen, we were sitting at our TV trays, eating our chicken sandwiches and drinking our glasses of milk.

Black marchers, men wearing hats and overcoats with their hands stuffed in their pockets, women and children behind them, were trying to cross a bridge. They were on their way to Birmingham, the state capital of Alabama, to demand voting rights. Pretty soon, the whole sidewalk of the bridge was full of marchers, hundreds of people. At the other end of the bridge, right in their way, was an unorganized mob of law enforcement. Patrol cars, uniformed cops, and civilians. State troopers and deputy sheriffs. Most of the cops were wearing helmets, big men with serious faces. The deputies were mounted on horses. The troopers put on gas masks. As the marchers filed toward them, the cops pulled out their clubs and formed a line at the end of the bridge. Their belts were adorned with I don't know what: gas canisters, extra ammo? Grenades?

"This is an unlawful assembly. You have to disperse. You are ordered to disperse. Go home or go to your church. This march will not continue. It would be detrimental to your safety to continue this march."

"Mr. Major, I would like to have a word, can we have a word?"

Once the troopers got themselves arranged in a line, they advanced on the marchers, who just stood there on the bridge, waiting. The troopers held their batons horizontally and advanced in a line until they were right on top of the marchers who were still standing there with their hands in their pockets.

It was eerily quiet for a moment, and then the cops lurched forward, using their clubs to push the marchers back, no resistance. The marchers in the front were shoved into the people behind them. Some people fell. People started screaming. The cops kept pushing forward. The marchers tried to escape but there was no room. They were too bunched up to retreat.

And then, the deputy sheriffs on horseback charged.

Pretty soon, I couldn't tell what exactly was happening. Too many people were in motion at the same time. Fallen marchers were lying face down on the ground with cops standing above them. Some of the cops were swinging their clubs. I heard a man's voice say, "You're nothing but a bunch of bullies."

Then there were pops like firecrackers going off. Grey-white clouds of gas enveloped everything. People were stepping over the fallen marchers. Small groups of people were attempting to pick up the people who had fallen or were trying to protect them from getting stepped on.

These scenes went on and on until my dad said he had seen enough. He looked at my grandfather and then he switched off the TV.

Grandma asked if any of us kids wanted to play a board game with her.

Grandpa told us to kneel. "I will lead us in prayer."

Grandma stayed in her recliner because of her broken hip, but the rest of us got out of our chairs, knelt, and shut our eyes, while Grandpa prayed for the United States of America.

Three nights later, I figured enough time had gone by that I could call up Rose White and get her angle on what had happened. My idea was to approach the topic of the events of Bloody Sunday indirectly. I would ask her about the black writer James Baldwin and his book *The Fire Next Time*. I would get her to talk about the book, had she read it yet, did she think I should read it, and then when I felt the moment was right, I would ask her about Bloody Sunday. Or I could ask her about the Rev. Martin Luther King, Jr. He had not been at the march; he had been elsewhere raising money. What did she think of that? Would the situation have gone better if he had been there?

She answered the phone, "Who is it?" I told her it was me, but already I could tell I should have waited at least another day. "What you want?" I could hear in her voice that she was not thrilled it was me. I forgot all about James Baldwin and Martin Luther King, Jr., and plunged right into what I really wanted to know.

Bloody Sunday, did she watch it on TV?

She said, "Did I watch it? You're askin' me did I watch it?"

"I just want to understand," I said.

She made a weird noise and said, "Like it's my job to help you UNDERSTAND!"

"I'm sorry," I said. "I shouldn't have called."

"If you don't understand today, you aren't gonna understand tomorrow. You hear me? This ain't about you!"

"Sorry! I'm awful sorry!"

"And don't call here anymore."

I started to apologize some more and then I realized she had hung up.

23

Ticket to Ride

The best unintended consequence of the Gospel Brothers: the DeWitt family finally got a record player. We got a record album before we actually got a record player. The record was the Gospel Brothers' album *What a Friend We Have in Jesus* (*15 Huge Sacred Hits*). After the healing service on Saturday night, my mother felt led by God Himself to buy the album, which all four of the Brothers autographed. My dad was dispatched the following Monday afternoon to buy a record player so my mom could play her record. I will not say he purchased the cheapest one in the store; it may have been only the second cheapest. A houseplant was removed from its stand in the corner of the living room to make room for it.

After listening to the 15 sacred hits four days in a row, my mother began to miss her houseplant. Dean and I were finally allowed to carry the record player out of the living room and install it in our bedroom with the understanding if either of my parents should suddenly decide to buy a supply of Billy Graham records featuring the great singers Mahalia Jackson and George Beverly Shea, the machine would be returned without argument to the living room for their listening pleasure.

When summer returned, I sometimes had money and could buy records. Michael worked in the summers for his older brother Thomas who had his own lawn care service. I was not normally a member of the lawn care team—Thomas had a policy of only employing members of their church—but occasionally someone would get sick or they would need an extra mower.

Michael loved lawn care. So far as he was concerned, it was the perfect summer job. This is what usually happened on the days I assisted. Thomas drove us to a neighborhood inhabited by the kind of people who live in large houses surrounded by enormous lawns. We jumped out of Thomas's pick-up, removed two mowers from the back end, made sure they had plenty of gas, fired up those bad boys, removed our shirts, and started mowing grass as fast as we could, being careful not to run over any flowers or pets. The sun would strike Michael's torso and make him as sun-tanned as a young Greek god.

In my case, that sort of transformation was not possible. But Michael was of the opinion that the sunshine was good for my pimples.

Sometime later, when we were nearly done, a pretty girl would emerge from the house with a glass of lemonade, which she would offer to Michael. He would turn off his mower, accept the lemonade, and talk to the girl. I would continue to mow the grass. So far as the girl was concerned, I did not in fact exist.

Michael called these girls *princesses*. So far as he was concerned, each and every princess was beautiful, but his absolute favorites were the blondes. They did not attend our school, Edgar Allen Poe Junior High. Some went to Catholic school and others to our Westside rival junior high or even West High School.

Even high school girls one or two years older than us were not immune to Michael's charm. During the last year it had multiplied geometrically. The sun caused blonde streaks to appear in his light brown hair. His dark suntan made his smile dazzling, irresistible. All he had to do was drink the lemonade, gulp it down, letting some of it run off his chin, look at the girl, wipe off his chin with the back of his hand, grin, and she was smitten.

By contrast, I had a sunken chest, narrow shoulders, and even the sunshine did not help my pimple situation all that much. As my mom liked to tell me, I looked better with my tee-shirt on than off.

But what the heck? Thanks to lawn care, I made a little money and could spend it as I pleased.

The first singles I bought were "She Loves You (Yeah, Yeah, Yeah)" by the Beatles, "I Want to Hold Your Hand" by the Beatles, "Can't Buy Me Love" by the Beatles, and "Eight Days a Week" by the Beatles.

The first album I bought was *Help!* by the Beatles which includes, besides the title song, "You've Got to Hide Your Love Away," "The Night Before," "You're Going to Lose That Girl," "I've Just Seen a Face," "Ticket to Ride," and – take a deep breath – "Yesterday." So far as I was concerned, "Yesterday" was the greatest musical composition in all of history, a song superior in value to the entire collected works of Mozart and Beethoven. If you dared to say otherwise, I would fight you.

One warm evening in July, I was sitting on my parents' porch doing nothing, thinking nothing, enjoying the appearance of the very first fireflies, when something amazing happened. Ray arrived in my driveway in a long red convertible with the top down. I stood up, stared at the car in shocked astonishment, ran to the convertible, looked at it from one end to the other, and cried, "Whose is this?!"

Ray said, "Hop in, baby!"

The moment my butt hit the seat, I got scared I was in a stolen car.

Did Ray even have a driver's license?

Ray assured me the car, a Lincoln Continental for the love of God, belonged to his uncle who was letting him borrow it for the evening. While we sat there in my driveway, he removed a bottle in a paper sack from underneath the front seat and told me there were cups in the glove box.

I found two coffee cups.

"Aren't these from the motel? Does Mrs. Broom know you took her coffee cups? Is that Mr. Broom's whiskey?"

Ray splashed whiskey into the coffee cups and gave me one, put the car in reverse and backed out into the street. I wondered if my mom was looking out the window and seeing all this. Was my brother Dean watching? If he was, he was going to be so jealous.

As we drove away from my house, Ray said we were going for a drive in the country and then we were going to the Bel-Air Ballroom. He knew the band and the drummer gave him two passes.

I wondered if the neighbors were watching. Did any of my friends see me riding in this huge red boat? The convertible is a car for show-offs, exhibitionists. I felt I should wave at everyone we passed.

Ray said if cops see you drinking alcohol while driving in a car, they object. But if you are only drinking coffee, what do they care? He said if we happened by any cops, we should smile, wave at them, and toast them with our coffee cups.

I started getting anxious again.

Ray said he was friends with the band that was playing tonight at the Bel-Air, The Rock and Roll Cannibals, and we were going to get in for free. A certain girl he was chasing was going to be there. Even if she wasn't, there would be a hundred other girls, many of them without boyfriends. He said loud music and dancing make girls crazy for sex. Even a loser like me should have no trouble finding someone. We were going to pick up two girls and drive in the magnificent Red Beast to some secluded location, and then my sexual education was going to take a Giant Leap Forward.

Ray drove us out of town and into the country, driving too fast and too crazy, scaring me to death. When he was making a turn, some of the whiskey leapt out of my coffee cup and landed on my shirt. The Beatles' song "Ticket to Ride" was playing on the radio. I told Ray I knew a secret about that song, something I had learned from the Jewish kid who worked at the record store, Jimmy Levine. Ride is a real place in England, a place where knocked-up girls go to get abortions. "She's got a ticket to Ride, and she don't care!" That meant....

Ray told me to shut up and let him listen to the song. He said talking about songs while they were playing on the radio wrecked them. Songs don't have any "meaning." They just are. He was drumming along to the song on the steering wheel. Ray said he loved Ringo Starr, who was left-handed. Ray was also left-handed. He said, "Ringo's not a fancy drummer, not a show-off. He's the best because he always knows exactly what the song needs." Ray ran right through a stop sign without even pausing. By then we were way out in the country on a gravel road. The Red Beast was throwing up a huge plume of dust.

Ray said someone like me, a word guy, a bookworm cannot possibly understand a song anyway. Only a music person like him could really understand Ringo and his simple but tricky drum patterns. He said I was smart but also dumb, wicked smart about books and so on, school, but stupid about important stuff like life. Plus, I was a chicken shit. If I did not look out, I was in danger of becoming a chickenshit AND an asshole. "Is that what you want? To be an asshole?"

I said I did not want to be an asshole.

Ray pulled over to the side of the road and refilled our coffee cups. He said, when I talked, sometimes I made a weird clicking noise with my tongue. He said that click was very irritating. He said an overly large brain like mine can make a person stupid. In fact, when he thought about it, almost all Brains are stupid. "Think about it."

He floored the accelerator, and away we went.

Ray said we might as well finish off the bottle because once we got to the Bel-Air Ballroom, we were not going to be able to carry alcohol in with us. If the bouncers saw our whiskey, they would bar the door. "Showing up lit will a good thing because it'll give us confidence when we ask chicks to dance."

I said, "But I don't know how to dance!"

Ray said being lit would give me dance-confidence. "If there's one thing chicks love, it's confidence. They can't resist it."

"I don't even know how to do the Twist!"

"When a chick realizes you're lacking in confidence, she'll cut you dead. But if you're lit, what do you care? You don't care! That's when you're irresistible baby." Ray said confidence is what the Beatles meant when they sang, "She has a ticket to ride/ and she don't care!"

"When you're lit, you have that Ticket to Ride, that magic ticket that means you can do anything. You can grab the hand of the prettiest girl and drag her out onto the dance floor. You can dance with freedom and style, man!"

By the time we arrived at the Bel-Air Ballroom, the bottle was nearly empty, and it was getting dark. I realized if I got home at all tonight it was going to be after midnight. My mom would probably be waiting up, in her bathrobe, furious, but I was lit and I had a ticket to ride, and I didn't care.

On the way into the ballroom, we ran into a kid that Ray knew. He told us the Dancing Queen was inside, conducting a Dance Off.

Ray said, "Is she here? Is Middle here?"

It turned out the Dancing Queen was not Middle.

We pushed through the crowd of onlookers that surrounded the dance floor and found the Dancing Queen dancing with three guys at once.

They were having the kind of Dance Off that depends more on stamina than on artistic excellence. The band would play faster and faster, and the dancers would dance ever more wildly until they began to flag and drop out until only one was left.

"It's Big," I said happily to no one. Big Grimm was the Dancing Queen. She was dancing with three boys and, so far as I could tell, all of them had a Ticket to Ride.

Ray watched for a minute, and then he could not stand it, could not bear to be a mere bystander another moment. He leapt out onto the floor, and just like that, Big found herself dancing not with three boys, but four.

On the other side of the dance floor, in the midst of the crowd, I saw a familiar face: Ricky Fox. Was Little here? I heard they had broken up. He looked pale and sad. Poor Ricky. People said Little had broken his heart. People said he had actually asked Little to marry him. He was only 16 years old but that was how hopelessly in love with Little he was.

One of the four dancing boys gave up the attempt to dance Big off the floor. The guy retreated to the sidelines panting. He bent over and put his hands on his knees, attempting to catch his breath.

A tall girl appeared beside me, touched me with her index finger to get my attention. She looked familiar. She said, "Aren't you a friend of Michael, Michael Taylor?" I stared at her until I remembered who she was, or at least what she was. A blonde princess. The daughter of a doctor. "Is he here?"

I said, "Nope."

"So... do you know where he is?"

I shook my head, more interested in the dancers than in her.

The second dancing boy dropped out of the contest. Now it was just Big Grimm and two guys, one of whom was Ray.

The princess leaned close to me and talked into my ear. She wanted to know more about Michael. "Where does he hang out, what's his phone number? You can tell me that at least. Does he ever go to the country club pool or the golf course?"

"Don't know, don't know, nope, don't think so."

She said, "When you see him next, tell him Candace Johnson said hi. OK?"

"Sure," I said.

"My number's in the book. I have my own phone. He can call any time. Even late at night."

"You bet," I said.

The third guy dropped out, and now it was just Big and Ray.

The crowd by then was rapt, hypnotized, swaying to the music, which kept getting faster and faster until it was a tornado of sound whipping around the two dancers.

Ray's face was bright red. His long dirty blonde hair was pushed back out of his eyes. His eyes were glowing, and he was breathing through his mouth. Big's hair was flipping through the air like a flag. Both of them were connected directly to the music, to the drummer and the guitar player, to the hurricane of sound.

Big was staring hard at Ray as she danced. I thought there was something evil in her look, something malevolent and dangerous. Ray was in his own world, caught in the spell of the music. I noticed he was wearing his Beatle boots, ankle-high boots with zippers. He called them his dancing shoes. There was nothing in his eyes but freedom.

I remembered something the Nazi once told me. When we were kids, Ray had to drop out of school one year because he had rheumatic fever. It just about killed him. The Nazi said the fever went on for weeks and months and weakened his heart. He said Ray was too wild and crazy. Someone with a damaged heart like that should take better care of himself, but he never did.

For just a moment, I thought Big knew about it, knew about Ray's wounded heart. She was trying to kill him. She was attempting to dance him to death.

Ray gave up the attempt. He stumbled to a stop while the music was still blaring. He held up his hands in glorious defeat and bowed to the Dancing Queen, and then he fell backwards theatrically and hilariously into the crowd. Guys had to catch him and hold him up.

I thought he was for a moment a kind of god, even in defeat.

The Queen danced all alone in triumph for a moment, and then two drunken boys jumped in, but the crowd booed them. The band had had enough. The Queen stopped, stood immobile for a moment, and then nodded regally at the guitar player, and smiled – a cool icy sort of smile as if once again she had proved she was true royalty.

The singer said the band was going to take a fifteen-minute break.

Five minutes later, I found Ray. He had gone to the concession window and got himself a cup of 7-Up. He was still covered in sweat, panting, happy.

"You danced great," I said.

He had his eyes elsewhere. "Here she comes," he said.

It was Big herself. She too had a tall cup of something. She looked great. Magnificent. It was hard to believe she had just danced four guys including Ray off the dance floor because she was not even sweaty. She stood directly in front of Ray, and I think, for a moment, he imagined she was going to congratulate him, compliment him for his dancing, something like that. Instead, she doused him with the entire contents of the cup she was holding.

She didn't say a word, just stared at Ray as if she wanted to murder him. Then she turned on her heel and left him, standing there with a stupid grin still on his face, dripping.

"What the hell?" I said.

Before Ray could tell me what was eating Big, a guy ran up to us and yelled the cops were outside. "Aren't you the ones who came in that big red convertible? The cops are towing it away!"

Ray sprinted for the exit, and I trotted along behind him.

When we got outside, a tow truck guy was hooking the Red Beast to his rig. Two cops were working the crowd, asking questions.

I told Ray, "You gotta stop them, tell 'em who you are, that you got permission from your uncle!" And then I stopped. Ray was right about how a brain like mine can make you stupid. I said, "Your uncle doesn't own that car, does he?"

Ray grinned.

"And you never got permission to borrow it. I bet you don't even have a driver's license."

And then both of us started laughing.

We had to walk home that night. Ray kept sticking out his thumb and trying to get a ride, but no one would stop for us.

Ray said his one regret was the whiskey under the seat. He thought there was at least an inch left.

When we finally got back into our neighborhood, it was after two in the morning. Ray went toward the motel and I walked toward my house. Maybe my mom would be asleep.

Before I finally got home, I figured it out, why Middle Grimm took a vacation in the middle of her tenth-grade year, why she went to St. Louis, why she broke up with Ray, and why Big Grimm wanted him dead.

24

Forgiveness is a Virtue

After my night out with Ray, I was grounded for a week, not even allowed to make phone calls. Nothing much happened during that week except one afternoon I was sitting on the front porch reading a science fiction book *Stranger in a Strange Land* by Robert Heinlein, when two little kids rode by on their bicycles. They were talking and must have been oblivious to the fact I could hear every word they said. One of them nodded at my house and said, "That's where the retard lives." Meaning my sister Ellen. The other little kid noticed me on the porch and said, "Is that him?" "Yup," said the first kid.

Great, I thought, now all the little kids in this neighborhood think I'm a retard. I wanted to stand up and yell at those kids as they rode away, *I am NOT a retard! I am SMART!*

In fact, I often felt I was not smart. People were always telling me I was intelligent, but then they would immediately qualify the compliment. I was bright IN A WAY. In all the other ways, I was an idiot. I wondered glumly if there was any difference, any *substantial* difference between a brain-damaged person like Ell and me, a person who had a seemingly good brain but constantly used it unwisely. I was not even sure I had a good brain. The evidence was mixed. As Ray said, I was book smart and life stupid. Probably portions of my brain were well above average but they were attached to other portions that were inferior grade.

I had many dismal thoughts of this type about myself that week. When my release date came, I walked up to the motel and found out what happened that night after Ray and I went in different directions.

Mr. Broom woke up from a sound sleep when Ray tried to sneak back into the house in the middle of the night. He jumped out of bed and confronted Ray. He told him to pack up his things and go.

The Nazi and Mrs. Broom woke up when Ray was leaving. They came out of their bedrooms still wearing their pajamas and were shocked to hear what Mr. Broom had done.

It turned out Ray had indeed stolen the Lincoln convertible; he had stolen it from the motel parking lot. A rich kid 17-years-old, the son of a dentist, had arrived in the convertible, which belonged to his father. He had been allowed to borrow it. The rich kid rented a room. With him was his 16-year-old girlfriend, the offspring of a different dentist. She was hiding in the back of the convertible.

Mr. Broom had looked at the phony ID of the rich kid and pretended he believed it was genuine. He had also pretended he had not seen the underage girlfriend who was crouching down in the back seat of the convertible but kept poking up her head to see what was going on.

The rich kid parked the convertible in front of the room he had rented, Room 23. He very likely had his mind on other things than the safety of his dad's car because he neglected to remove the keys from the car's ignition. He and the girl disappeared into Room 23.

While these events were occurring, Ray had been loading bottles into the pop machine wishing he had something fun to do on a Friday night, something more enjoyable than hanging out with the Nazi watching TV. When he finished his chore, Ray had walked by the convertible and noticed the keys in the ignition. So far as Ray was concerned, the beautiful Red Beast was a gift from God. He walked over to the Brooms' house and stole a fifth of whiskey from Mr. Broom's private stock. He put the bottle in a sack, returned to the parking lot, jumped into the Lincoln as if he owned it, hid the bottle under the seat, switched on the car, and drove to my house.

Listening to this story, I was very glad Ray had never told any member of the Broom family, including the Nazi, that I was with him that night.

Some while later, when the sky started to grow darker, the happy and satisfied son of the dentist had opened the curtains to Room 23, looked out at the parking lot, and noticed that his father's Lincoln was missing.

After that, all hell broke loose.

The cops were called. The dentist was called. The other dentist was called. The rich kid said the motel and its management were crooks and car thieves. He said the motel was a notorious love nest. He had been lured here.

The girl emerged from Room 23 fully dressed and started to weep. She said she did not know anything about anything. Her weeping continued until her parents arrived and then got worse. Her father had brought a blanket and wrapped his weeping daughter up in it and drove off with her. Before he drove away, the girl's father told the police he was considering filing charges against Mr. Broom and the motel for contributing to the delinquency of a minor. He shook hands with the other dentist and left.

The dentist who owned the Lincoln told his son not to speak without a lawyer present and that he was grounded for the rest of his life. Then he grinned at the cops and told them he was a life-long supporter of law enforcement. He said he had no doubt the cops would locate the convertible, which he described as his "fun car." The cops said they would do their best.

Mr. Broom was a level-headed man who had run a motel for many years. He did not believe anyone was going to charge him with anything. He did not believe either of the dentists wanted the names of their beloved children to appear in the newspaper.

"Is Ray here?" he asked his wife after the cops left. "He's not here, is he?" He went back into his house and discovered he was missing a bottle of whiskey.

Mr. Broom was a kind man, a generous man, but no matter how you looked at the thing, Ray — this kid he had taken into his home out of the goodness of his heart — had abused his privileges. Ray had put the motel in jeopardy. He had spit in the face of his benefactors. He had to be punished.

When Mr. Broom confronted him that night, Ray had not attempted to lie. He told Mr. Broom not to worry about the car. The cops had the car. There wasn't going to be any more trouble about that car.

Mr. Broom said, "I'm sorry, but you can't live here with us, not no more."

Ray went home to his mother and sister. So far as I know, they were happy to see him.

Mrs. Broom was wise enough to wait until the next day to begin her campaign to reinstate Ray. It troubled her mightily that Ray had not taken any clothes with him or even a toothbrush. Not even a change of underwear. She made the Nazi load up a suitcase with Ray's clothes and take them to Mrs. Kavanaugh's house. "You tell Ray we miss him very much."

Mrs. Broom loved Ray. She was a soft-hearted woman, a natural mom to anyone who needed love, and boy oh boy did Ray need love. Her blue eyes teared up every time she thought of Ray. That poor boy. The way he had grown up sickly with the rheumatic fever. His father was a terrible man, a notorious drunk. The mother Naomi Kavanaugh was a decent woman, but she was a listless, down-trodden mouse who had never once stood up for herself. Mrs. Broom felt Ray was a good companion for her son, who would otherwise be almost friendless. The only reason other kids even visited the motel was to see Ray. Ray was almost a brother to her boy.

The Nazi also wanted Ray to come back. He and his mom worked on Mr. Broom every chance they got.

The Nazi told his dad that Ray was experiencing psychological damage because he never grieved the murder of his father or even got visibly angry about it. He said inside himself Ray was a bubbling cauldron of grief and shame and frustrated anger, and no wonder. Ray had become self-damaging. His father had been murdered! Ray was punishing himself for not avenging his father's death. But how could Ray? Or anyone? No one knew who the murderer was. The Nazi said he was not fooled by how cool and cocky Ray acted. Deep down inside, Ray was a psychological wreck and needed help.

Mrs. Broom pointed out that Ray was not ALL bad, considering his disadvantages. She pointed out that, by staying with them, Ray was helping his mother, poor Mrs. Kavanaugh. Ray's widowed mother got the Social Security survivor benefit after Red was murdered, which included an allowance for her two dependent children. By living at the motel with the Brooms, Ray was in effect giving his mother his portion of the allowance and not taking a penny for himself. Besides, he was a much-needed maid, much more reliable about cleaning rooms than their son Wolfie, who as Mr. Broom knew all too well, tended to be lazy.

Mrs. Broom did not say it, but Ray always called her Ma.

The Nazi often referred to her as "that fat cow."

By Wednesday of that week, Mr. Broom reversed his decision. Ray was allowed to return.

25

Bees

A week later, my family of seven made our annual car trip to the South to get reacquainted with my mom's side of the family.

On the way down, my mom told us the story of how her dad got stuck in a dirt-poor county in Oklahoma. Her ancestors had immigrated to the east coast of the United States many years ago from Holland. The originator of the American branch of the family had carved out his farm in the American wilderness, demonstrating a capacity for hard work and stick-to-it-iveness. He was the first member of her family to actually own land. She felt in general everyone in her family was blessed with that same pioneer spirit; it had passed down the generations all the way to her, and it could be a blessing to us kids if we ever learned to work hard and appreciate our good fortune instead of whining and complaining all the time the way we did.

Mom said, every generation, her ancestors had moved westward. Each time, the oldest son inherited the family farm. That is how things were done in those days. The younger sons never once complained. Instead they loaded up a wagon and moved west. They had the pioneer spirit and did as their fathers had done. Again and again, they found

188

virgin land and transformed it from wilderness into farmland. That was the kind of people our ancestors were. Pioneers. Honest, god-fearing, hard-working farmers who never complained.

Her grandfather had attempted to do what his ancestors had done. Since he was a second son, he left the farm where he grew up. He and his young wife, who was pregnant at the time with my mom's dad, had loaded everything they owned into a wagon pulled by a mule and an ox. They had walked all the way to Oklahoma, where the United States government was giving away land. On that long, long walk, my great-grandfather demonstrated the same fearless, can-do spirit his ancestors had demonstrated. Unfortunately, once he got to Oklahoma, my great-grandfather fell victim to a landshark.

"A what?" I said. "There's no such thing."

My mother explained that a landshark is a man. A silver-tongued liar. A no-good swindler. This wolf in sheep's clothing had convinced my great-grandfather to trade away his land grant. At that point, my great-grandfather had not yet seen the plot of land he was to receive. The landshark looked at the map and told my great-grandfather he was unlucky. That there forty acres of land was worthless. No water. Thin rocky soil. Not to mention, it was located smackdab in the middle of Tornado Alley. Probably my great-grandfather and his little family would starve to death on that land or blow away. The landshark could help them, though. He too had a land grant. And it was for a much better piece of property. Thank the Lord, he already had more land than he needed, and it broke his heart to think of another man suffering like this, especially a man who had a wife and a baby on the way. He said he was willing to swap his grant for my great-grandfather's. It was the Christian thing to do. He didn't even want to be thanked.

My great-grandfather made a fateful decision. He agreed to the swap and signed over his contract to the landshark.

As winter approached, my great-grandfather and his pregnant bride walked the rest of the way to the property he had traded for, only to find out it was a worthless piece of land, not worth a can of spit. The land he should have had was in fact much better, a good piece of land with plenty of topsoil and running water.

To survive that winter, to keep from starving to death, my great-grandfather had been forced to sell his ox and his mule. My grandfather was born in the wagon. No matter how hard they worked, it was impossible to farm that property and eventually my great-grandfather lost it in a card game. The young family had never recovered. My great-grandfather and his wife and kids (eventually there were eight) descended into poverty.

My grandfather grew up poor as poor can be. Grandpa never made it past the eighth grade. That was why he never managed to own anything and had to be a tenant farmer, working for others all his life; a renter but never an owner. He married my grandmother – she was only 16 years old at the time — and they had seven kids of their own, including my mom.

Then, when my mom was just a girl, the Great Depression arrived. Mom said modern kids like us, spoiled and well fed, could not possibly understand what her life was like when she was a kid. Despite all that, Mom said she managed to graduate from high school and go to a little college and graduate with a teaching certificate, the first one in her family ever to get a college degree. She met my dad and made a life for us, a good life. As a result, we were homeowners, not renters. My mom said we kids had no idea how lucky we were.

You might imagine that I learned to be grateful and hard-working by listening to this story but in fact I just got bored and wished my dad would turn on the car radio.

When we got to Oklahoma, we found out Tony one of my cousins was planning to enlist in the Army as soon as he graduated from high school next fall. The women in the family praised him to the skies. They told him girls cannot resist a man in uniform, and my girl cousins acted as if this was in fact true. I got envious and then disgraced myself by saying the war was a bloody disaster and Tony was an idiot to join up. He would probably get himself killed. And for what? Every week, the generals were demanding more troops. *We need more troops. Two thousand more! Ten thousand more!* Every day, B-52s dropped half-ton bombs on villages. We were murdering poor people, peasants! But what good did it do?

We need more guns! More bombs! More bombers! More troops!

I further disgraced myself by praising the March on Washington that occurred that spring. Thousands of college kids and war protestors descended on Washington DC demanding peace.

Peace now!

In the opinion of most of my relatives, my cousin Tony, the boy who was planning to enlist, was a brave patriot. Jack DeWitt, on the other hand, was a coward and an idiot.

It had long been the opinion of my Oklahoma relatives that I was an idiot. I came to visit them almost every summer. On almost every trip, I managed to do something stupid. Sometimes I did a half dozen stupid things.

There was the time when, at age nine, I tried to flirt with the little farm girl who was riding on a Shetland pony. I had demonstrated idiocy by standing behind her pony and switching its butt with a thin branch. The pony had kicked me so fast I had not even seen the hoof moving through the air. I flew six feet and landed on the ground, miraculously unharmed.

There was the time I jumped off a culvert onto the remains of an abandoned railroad track. When I landed, I landed on top of some old boards. I got a funny look on my face. One of my cousins could imitate the exact look I got on my face. I tried to take a step. A board came with me. I took another step, and the board came with me again. I looked down and saw the point of a ten-penny nail sticking up through the top of my tennis shoe. How stupid was that?! I had to be taken to a local doctor to get a tetanus shot.

After this story was told for about the tenth time, I said, "That was one of the few times in my life I felt close to Jesus." It took my cousins a minute to work out the joke, and then two of them ran to my mom and said I had just mocked Jesus. My cousin Tony, the one who had enlisted, challenged me to a boxing match. I said no way. He was a foot taller than me. My cousins said that proved I was nothing but a coward.

It was decided by my parents that perhaps it would be a good idea to separate me from my cousins for a day so tempers could cool. I was sent to spend the night with my grandparents.

The story of how I had once managed to drop my grandfather's flashlight into the pile of poop underneath his outhouse was still fresh in everyone's mind. Perhaps this time I could redeem myself.

I got through the night with my grandparents and nothing painful happened. My grandpa showed me his box full of geodes, and I thought they were impressive. He found an old photo of himself holding a giant catfish in his arms, and I was thrilled.

"Tell me the story, Grandpa!"

Wearing nothing but his underwear, he waded into Catfish Creek. He used his bare feet to "feel up" the creekbank until he found a hole big enough to conceal a giant catfish. He pushed a bare foot into that hole and, sure enough, his toes touched the side of a catfish. The side of a catfish that size is unmistakable. It feels totally different to one's toes than mud and roots and rocks. Once he was certain the hole contained a catfish, my grandfather took a deep breath, closed his eyes, and went underwater. It was pretty near impossible to see anything down there because of the muddiness of the water. He felt his way into the hole.

When his fingers bumped into the sides of the fish, he felt around until he found its gills. He plunged his hands right into those gaping gills! He got his feet under him and stood up, bringing the catfish with him, bear-hugging it, holding on no matter how desperately the monster squirmed. He never let go. He stood up in the waist-high creek water, with the fish in his arms. One of his boys, my uncle Johnny, snapped the photo. "There's enough meat on a fish that there size to feed a family reunion," Grandpa told me.

I went to sleep thinking I had misjudged my grandfather. Maybe he had been poor his entire life. A renter, not a homeowner. Maybe he was missing so many teeth people said if he tried to eat a steak, he had to gum the meat to death. Maybe he never wore anything except overalls and never read anything except his bible, but he was the finder of geodes. He was the conqueror of giant catfish.

The next morning, my grandpa woke me up and told me we were going to "do the bees." My grandfather had a half dozen wooden boxes of the dangerous insects. He made the boxes himself and set them on a big stretch of grass that sloped down to his garden. I was terrified of bees. When I visited, I never spent one moment in his back yard, not if I could help it.

When he tended his bees, my grandfather did not wear a hazmat suit or a helmet. He wore his usual clothes, bib overalls and a long-sleeved shirt. Sometimes he wore gloves. If he felt the bees were agitated, he had the smoker. It looked like Aladdin's magic lamp; a thin stream of smoke issued out one end of it. He would cause the smoke to drift into the box, and the bees would fall asleep. When he collected honey, bees would land on his hands and arms. My grandfather would calmly shake them off. So far as I could tell, he never once got stung. I never got close to the operation though. If I watched, it was from inside his little house. At all times, I wanted a wall or window glass between me and the bees.

"Doing the bees" meant I was supposed to follow behind Grandpa carrying a plastic bucket. He would cautiously approach one of the boxes. Each box contained drawers. He could pull out a drawer. It would be full of honeycomb. And bees. Bees would be crawling all over the honeycomb. He could shake the drawer and make the honeycomb fall into my bucket. We were going to harvest an entire bucketful of delicious honey that morning.

I was terrified.

I had not brought any special clothes. I was dressed in t-shirt and shorts. Shorts! My arms were bare! My legs were bare! My face was protected by nothing!

I felt I had to do the bees. I could not demonstrate cowardice again.

I followed behind Grandpa. We entered the World of Bees. In the air all around us, they were flying in straight lines to and from flowers. I tried to ignore them but as we approached the first box, the air got ever fuller of bees. Bees here, bees there, bees everywhere. Even if I closed my eyes, I could hear the buzzing.

I stood behind my grandfather while he extracted a drawer and dumped honeycomb into my bucket. I got stung on my left elbow.

I had been told by my cousins that if you demonstrate fear around bees, they will attack you. If you scream or flail your arms or run, they will chase you and sting you. When bees attack, they do it together. A bee attack, how many bees is that? A lot. Bees are like kamikazes. When they sting you, it kills them. Do they care? Not when they are in attack-mode. They can't help themselves. A kid who has triggered a bee attack by demonstrating fear may get stung a hundred times. Maybe two hundred. My cousins told me that boys they knew, boys who had screamed and flailed their arms and run, were now dead.

My grandpa extracted honeycomb from four boxes before he felt we had plenty. My bucket was two thirds full.

At the last box, I got stung again. On my right wrist.

When we got back to the house, my grandfather took the bucket from me and showed its contents to my grandmother.

"How'd he do?" she asked.

Grandpa said, "Boy got stung twice. Didn't even flinch."

To this day, that is the best compliment I have ever received.

26

Lady Lush

The way our school system worked was that elementary school ended after sixth grade. Junior high consisted of grades seven through nine. Then you went to high school for ten through twelve. For the two semesters of our ninth-grade year, Calvin and Michael and I were the lords of the school. At least, we were in our imaginations. The ninth graders who were jocks or hoods were the true lords of junior high. Brains like Calvin and I slunk quietly down the hallways and hoped not to get beat up. We gazed longingly at the pretty girls and worked on our sarcasm.

By ninth grade, which would turn out to be his last year of formal education, Ray had a cigarette habit. He preferred Marlboro Reds but, in a pinch, would smoke anything, even Kools. Previous to our night at the Bel-Air Ballroom, Ray had been allowed to help himself to the cigarettes that were stacked behind the counter at the motel and sold to guests. When he was allowed to return from exile, one of the conditions of his return was that he submit to extra discipline. He could continue to help himself to pop from the pop machine. He could help himself to anything in the fridge, but he was no longer allowed to grab himself a pack of cigarettes. To make sure this policy remained in force, Mrs. Broom kept track of how many packs she had in the motel office. If even one pack disappeared, she knew about it.

For a while, Ray obtained his cigarettes from a grocery store that was between my house and Poe Junior High. Every day on the way to school and on the way home, we walked past it. When he needed cigs, Ray entered the store, stole a pack, and walked out without paying. Never once did he get caught. Unfortunately, he soon became an object of suspicion. When he entered the store, someone who worked there would follow him at a discreet distance, keeping an eye on him until he left.

To cope with the surveillance, Ray tried out various strategies. Sometimes he would take my little brother Dean with him. Ray would enter the store by himself. Soon, the manager would be trailing him. Dean would enter a couple minutes later. Dean would locate the manager and approach him. He needed a bottle of mustard. Did they have any mustard?

"Aisle 9," the manager would say, keeping his eye on Ray.

Dean would say he didn't want any of that brown paste that pretends to be mustard. "If it ain't yellow, it ain't mustard. Which way is Aisle 9? Did you say Aisle 9 or 6? This way or that way?" Dean would start walking in the wrong direction. "Is it this way?"

"For god's sake, kid," the manager would say. "It's that way!"

"Could you please help me, mister? My mom says I gotta get the right kind."

While this was going on, Ray would pocket two packs of Marlboro Reds and exit without anyone noticing him.

Lately however, the mustard ploy did not work. On one disturbing occasion, after stealing a pack of Marlboros, Ray had been stopped and patted down. Fortunately, he had thought to push the cigs into his sock, so even when he was asked to turn out his pockets, there was nothing there.

In the end, Ray was reduced to paying for his cigs like everyone else. He obtained them from the machine at the bowling alley, in the bar. A pack cost four quarters. There was a sign on the machine that said NO MINORS. Ray paid no attention to this sign.

I followed behind him into the cool gloom of the bowling alley bar. While he was pushing coins into the cigarette machine, I noticed someone familiar was sitting in a booth reading a book.

"Is it any good?" I asked.

Mrs. Ryan was reading a novel called *Herzog* by Saul Bellow. All I knew about it was that it got a great review in *Time Magazine*.

She marked her place with her finger, stopped reading, and gazed up at me for a moment as if unsure she recognized me. I did not take offense. She had not seen me since the previous spring when she quit giving me rides, but that was not why she was slow to figure out who I was. I recognized the symptoms. Like me, Mrs. Ryan was a true bookworm. She dived deep into whatever she was reading. Reading for us was like swimming at the bottom of a deep pool. We were happy down there. If suddenly made to emerge from the pool into the bright light of day, we were momentarily discombobulated.

Finally, her eyes focused on me and she smiled and said, "Jack DeWitt."

I loved the way Mrs. Ryan said my name. I loved the smile that appeared on her face when she recognized me. That smile made me feel as if I was a movie star.

"That book," I said, pointing at it, "pretty good?"

She looked thoughtfully down at *Herzog* and tapped the page she had been reading with her index finger. "Do you know any Jews, Jack? It's about Jews."

I admitted I did not know any Jews except the college kid Jimmy Levine who worked at the record store. His younger sister, a super-brain somewhat lacking in social skills, was in some of my classes. She wore glasses and people called her Four Point because that was her grade point average.

Mrs. Ryan said, "I think you would like Jews."

"Sure," I said.

"This book is … challenging. When it is too much for me, I put it aside and read this one." She tapped a second book lying on the table in front of her, *Up the Down Staircase* by Bel Kaufman. "It is also by a Jewish writer. This seems to be the season for Jewish writers. This one is about a high school teacher and her students. It's funny and I think you would love it."

"It's great to see you," I said. "How've you been?"

Five minutes later, I was walking out with Ray. He unwrapped his pack of cigs in the parking lot, shook one out, and lit it with a match from a book of bowling alley matches.

"How come you were talking to Lady Lush?"

"What?"

"You ever meet her daughter, the Artist? Goes to Catholic school. I call her Lady Lush Junior."

"What?"

Ray said Lush Ladies are ladies who drink. Alone. "Know what I mean?"

Sometimes, when someone tells me something, it is as if too many thoughts and memories swarm into my head all at once, leaving me speechless.

"She just drinks tea," I said. "Iced tea."

"London iced tea," Ray said, blowing out a smoke ring. Ray could blow a smoke ring, a big one, and then blow a series of smaller rings right through it. "Look it up in the Bartenders Guide. She has two or three of those bad boys every afternoon."

That weekend, I looked up London iced tea in the encyclopedia at the library. A London iced tea does not contain any actual tea. It is three kinds of liquor in a tall glass with a little Coke and lemon juice to give it extra flavor.

The cloud of memories that flew into my head when Ray called her Lady Lush had to do with her driving. Mrs. Ryan was at times a scary driver. Until that afternoon in the bowling alley parking lot with Ray, I had blamed myself for her bad driving. I had assumed that, when she was giving me a ride home from school, I was so darn interesting, gabbing about stuff, that she quit paying attention to the road.

That semester Michael and I began to focus on girls. I think for our friend Calvin girls existed but only in the abstract. They were interesting to him the way that clouds were interesting or birds. He had theories about them. He told me he had studied the topic of menstruation. He said when girls were menstruating, they developed a puffy, bloated appearance, and became moody. He said at such times, they were best avoided. If they said anything crazy-sounding while bloated, just ignore it. They cannot help it and will soon return to normal. He said there was a time – two weeks before a girl had her period – when she was fertile to the max. At such times, girls found boys irresistible. That was when you wanted to make your move.

Since Calvin never to my knowledge made any moves on girls, I concluded this was entirely theoretical advice. So far as I could tell, it was not really possible to be sure if a girl was temporarily bloated or not. At least I couldn't tell. In any case, whether a girl was two weeks ahead of her bloated zone or not, it made little difference; girls found me resistible a hundred percent of the time.

Michael focused his attentions on a quiet girl named Jenny who was in our English and history classes but not our geometry class. Apparently, she sucked at math, but she was pretty and had very good handwriting. The reason I was aware of her handwriting was because she wrote me notes in English class. These notes mainly focused on

Michael. Did I think he liked her? Did he ever talk about her? At a certain point, she stopped writing me notes.

I asked Calvin what he thought it meant. "Why would she quit writing me notes?"

He said probably Michael and Jenny were dating but didn't want everyone to know it. "If they're dating, what does she need you for?"

"Why keep it a secret though?"

Calvin said if I had not yet noticed it, our buddy Michal was as secretive as a spy.

When I asked Michael point-blank if Jenny was his girlfriend, he said, "We just like talking to each other. What's wrong with that?"

I inspected his neck for signs of a hickey but could not find any. Come to think of it, Michael was secretive. It seemed impossible to get him to do anything. One time, our eighth grade English teacher tried to get him and me to sign up for the school play. She was going to direct. She said there were these two great parts for non-singers, the Nutt Brothers, comical villains. Michael and I were born to play these roles. I got excited and Michael did too. We started brain-storming all the funny stuff we could do if we got cast. I signed up and pretty soon I got picked. But Michael's name was not on the cast list. The other Nutt Brother was going to be this dorky seventh grader named Gordon. I went to the teacher and demanded to know why she didn't cast Michael. She told me she did offer him the part, but he said no. I went to Michael and said, "We were going to do it together!" He wouldn't say why he pulled out of the show. That sort of thing was typical. You thought he was going to do something with you, and then he called you up and said his plans had changed. Never did he tell you why.

In 9th grade, I got interested in Four Point Levine. Her real name was Janet, but no one except teachers called her that. It seemed to me she had a several good points. For one thing, she was smart. She was the little sister of Jimmy Levine at the record store, a person whose opinions about music I considered reliable. In study hall, she was often reading a book, often something not assigned by our English teacher. Also, she was OK in the looks department – at least a B plus.

Maybe I should ask her out.

I discussed Four Point with Michael. Possibly if I asked her, she would go with me to a basketball game or a wrestling match or something like that. The wrestling season had just begun. What did he think? Michael said, "Go for it."

"How exactly do you do it, ask a girl out? Can you just write her a note?" I thought it would be easier to write Four Point a note than to stand in front of her and ask her a direct question.

"Does she like talking to you?"

"It's possible she doesn't even know I'm alive."

"First step: Try talking to her. Girls like that."

I also consulted Ray. Ray's view of girls was simple. He divided them into two categories: girls who like sex and girls who don't. A girl who likes sex is great. Girls who won't go all the way but will go three fourths of the way are pretty good. If she has large breasts, extra points. Girls who will not do anything except kiss are hardly worth bothering with. Ray figured Four Point was in this last category. But who knows? "Maybe a female Brain like Four Point naturally has feelings for a male Brain like you."

Ray admitted he had scant experience with intelligent girls. He thought since Four Point was super smart, she was obviously a virgin and probably scared of sex. It would be hard to know if she would turn into a tiger the moment she was kissed, all that repressed sexual need just exploding like you lit a fuse, or would she be repelled and feel sick to her stomach and then maybe report you to the police? Hard to say. He suggested I get Four Point alone and try to kiss her, see what happens. He amused himself by imagining the consequences of two super brains having sex. He figured if I got Four Point pregnant, she would produce a Super Genius Baby that would grow up and become Emperor of Earth and cure cancer.

"Real funny," I said.

I also got advice from her brother Jimmy. I went to see him at the record store. As usual, he tried to get me to buy something weird, a record called "Minnie the Moocher" by an old jazz cat named Cab Calloway. "It's a collector's item." Before I could ask him about Four Point, two college girls came in and he had to wait on them. He predicted they would want to buy "Woolly Bully" by Sam the Sham and the Pharaohs. "Girls love that song to death." When they left, he tried to get me to buy *Highway 61 Revisited*, a new album by Bob Dylan. I couldn't afford it but did buy the single, "Like a Rolling Stone," which Jimmy said was the Song of the Year, probably the Song of the Decade. After I bought it, I asked him about his sister, did he think she would go out with me if I asked her to the wrestling meet? He said, "Are you talking about professional wrestling? She'd probably go for that, knowing her." I said no, junior high wrestling. We could go for nothing because we were students. I was not exactly flush with cash.

Before I could stop him, Jimmy went to the store phone and called his sister. I was so nervous, I started sweating. He came back after five minutes and said, "She'll meet you there."

27

Wrestling

When I arrived at the wrestling match, Four Point was nowhere in sight. I probably should have called her after supper before I walked over to the school, just to make sure she understood when the match started. There were not a lot of people in the stands. Wrestling was not that popular. My friend Calvin was there sitting by himself in the middle of the stands, but I ducked out of his sight and sat five rows behind him because I didn't want him to overhear my conversation with Four Point.

The match got going. Still no Four Point. I should have called her.

Our wrestlers sat in a row of folding chairs on one side of a large square mat. They wore orange onesies and were arranged by weight, with the lightweights on the right and the heavyweights on the left. I noticed our heavyweight was the Hulk. The other team was sitting on the other side of the mat. They wore blue onesies. Their heavyweight looked at least fifty pounds smaller than the Hulk.

The match started with the lightweights. Two child-sized wrestlers met in the middle of the mat, supervised by a referee. They shook hands and then grabbed one another and attempted to fling each other to the mat. A bit later, the ref made them start over. One of the wrestlers got on his hands and knees. The other one knelt beside him, holding him. The referee got in front of them and blew his whistle. The little guys wrestled like mad. Every now and then, the referee stuck up one or two fingers, which meant he was awarding points to one of the wrestlers. This sort of thing continued until finally the match was over and the referee grabbed the hand of the victor (the kid on the other team) and held it up. Most of the audience clapped politely, but two adults cheered like they were at the World Series. I figured they were the winner's parents.

I noticed the Hulk was staring at the other team's heavyweight. The Hulk never moved; he just sat there staring at his rival.

After two matches went by and Four Point still did not show, I went down and sat beside Calvin. I took my glasses out of my pocket and put them on. If I was going to spend the evening with just Calvin, I didn't care if my glasses made me look like a dork. Calvin wouldn't even notice and at least I would be able to see the wrestlers clearly.

With my glasses on, I could see the Hulk was making his rival nervous.

Calvin was surprised to see me. "I thought you hated stuff like this."

"Like I had anything better to do." I did not tell him my date had gone south. I figured he could at least explain the rules of wrestling to me. Calvin was a born explainer.

Even with Calvin explaining the point system to me, I could not keep it straight. Was it one point for an escape or two? Does a reversal get three points or just two? What is riding time again?

The lower weights were skinny boys, seventh graders, some of whom appeared not yet to have experienced puberty. Then you got the tall beanpoles who had very long arms and very long legs and resembled spider monkeys.

About halfway through the match – by then the wrestlers were getting big and had well developed muscles – someone poked the back of my neck. I twisted around and saw Four Point. She poked Calvin too, and he happily scooted over so she could sit between us.

Four Point apologized for being late; she had to get a ride from her brother Jimmy and he got confused about the time and did not even come home to get her till half past seven.

"Hey," she said, looking at me. It was the kind of look I found hard to interpret because it did not involve a smile. Four Point was not a smiler. Most girls are. If they like you, even a little bit, they treat you to a big toothy smile. Girls pride themselves on their smiles. Not Four Point. She looked you straight in the eye as if she was peering directly into your brain and reading your thoughts.

"Hey," I said.

"You ever seen wrestling before?" Calvin asked her.

Four Point said only pro wrestling on TV. Her favorite pro wrestler was Big Moose Jolack, a huge hairy man who wore an enormous moose head, a real one with antlers and everything.

Calvin said this kind of wrestling was different. This was a true authentic sport, not just a fake sport designed to entertain stupid people. He started explaining the rules, and Four Point listened.

I experienced irritation because I did not want to have to share Four Point with Calvin. Now, for the rest of the match, he would be explaining things to her, while I would have to sit there and say nothing. I had no doubt in my mind if I tried to help him explain the rules, I would almost immediately say the wrong thing, which would give Calvin all the excuse he needed. He would hold up his hand and interrupt me and correct my mistake. I thought about asking Four Point if she would like to sit somewhere else, but I could see that would be awkward.

By then, Calvin was telling her about Binge and Puke, which is a wrestling thing. The wrestlers choose to wrestle at a specific weight – like 135 pounds. During the week, if they eat too much, pretty soon they weigh five pounds too much. Then they have to do crazy things to get rid of that excess weight before the weigh-in. He said the wrestling practice room is always hot as hell, like a sauna, just to make the wrestlers sweat and lose weight. If at the weigh-in, they weigh 137 pounds, that means they do not get to wrestle, not at 135. Sometimes the wrestlers get so hungry trying to make weight they can't stand it. That is when they Binge and Puke. They scarf down three cheeseburgers. Oh, yeah! They gobble three orders of French fries with plenty of ketchup. Hell, yes! They wash all that food down with two chocolate shakes! Oh, my God! Then they run to the restroom, enter a stall, stick two fingers down their throats, bend over fast, and puke the whole disgusting mess into the porcelain bowl.

Four Point seemed to find all this information fascinating.

I thought about removing my glasses and attempting to look at least a little less like a dork, and then decided it was too late to bother. I noticed the heavyweight on the other team was trying to make light of the fact the Hulk was staring at him. He made faces at the Hulk, and finally stuck out his tongue at him. The Hulk never responded, just kept staring.

The rival heavyweight poked the wrestler beside him and nodded at the Hulk. The two of them stared at the Hulk. The Hulk just kept staring at his rival. He seemed unaware of the other guy. It was as if so far as he was concerned, no one even existed except the other heavyweight.

The teammate lost interest in the stare-down and went back to watching the match. The rival heavyweight started acting as if he no longer noticed the Hulk was staring at him. He looked at his hands or his feet or at people in the stands, anything except the Hulk.

The Hulk just kept staring.

I thought about telling Four Point the story of The Fight. Ray vs. the Hulk. The Fight That Did Not Involve Hands. But I could not find an opening. By then, she was asking questions, and of course Calvin was answering the questions. He was like a Professor of Wrestling.

I conducted an imaginary conversation in my head with Four Point. I told her the story of The Fight. I did a really fantastic job explaining how Ray kicked the Hulk right in the crotch. Four Point loved my story. Her eyes bugged out with excitement. When Calvin tried to interrupt and change the subject, Four Point shushed him. She grabbed my hand and asked me to tell her more stories. I told her kicking in the crotch is not permitted in junior high wrestling so there was no doubt the Hulk was going to win this match. He would pin the other guy, no problem. What is a pin exactly, Four Point asked, touching my hand again. I explained. She said I was way better at explanation than Calvin. She wondered if wrestlers are self-absorbed sociopaths. I had recently learned the term sociopath, a person who has no conscience and believes the rules never apply to him. I said one might imagine wrestlers are like that but in fact they take rules very seriously. They love the heck out of rules. Wow, you really know a lot, Four Point would say. Then maybe I would ask her if she had read the novel *Herzog* yet. "It's about Jews like you." "Wow," she would say, "that is so fascinating! I wondered what it was about!" She would probably tell me I should be a writer, since I was such a good storyteller and so smart that I was already reading challenging books about Jews even when I was only in the ninth grade.

When the next-to-last match came to an end (their guy won), the Hulk walked onto the mat and shook his rival's hand. The two heavyweights faced each other, and the ref blew his whistle. The Hulk grabbed the other guy. They struggled for a few moments, and then, bam bam bam, it was over. The entire match took all of two minutes. It was as if, the whole time he had been staring at the guy, the Hulk had figured out how exactly to do it, how to grab the guy and twist and take him down and flip him onto his back and pin his shoulders to the mat. The referee hopped around the Hulk and the other guy and finally slapped the mat. Pin!

Everyone cheered.

"Well, that was pretty cool," Four Point said.

I realized, since she had sat down between Calvin and me, I had hardly said one word to her. "Glad you came," I said.

Calvin told her he too was glad she came to the match. Very glad. Delighted in fact. He said he went to all the matches, so if she came again, he would love it if she sat beside him – "since you like wrestling so much."

I wanted to push him over the side of the bleachers.

Four Point walked out of the gym beside me. Calvin looked unhappy to see her do that. It was finally dawning on him that Four Point and I were in a dating situation.

Four Point used a school phone to call her brother Jimmy. He was going to come pick her up. She said I could wait with her if I wanted. "You need a ride home? Jimmy will give you one."

I told her I had to get home. "I like to walk." By then, I was avoiding eye contact with her. I had this crazy idea that if I did not look directly into her eyes, she would not be able to read my mind.

"Hey," she said. She reached out and touched my arm. Surprised, I looked up at her. Eye contact. "Sorry about this," she said. "But – you know – I never watched a wrestling match before. It was sort of fascinating. I mean in an anthropological sort of way."

I realized I would have to look up the word "anthropological" in order to find out what she meant.

"Catch you later," I said and started to turn away from her.

She grabbed my arm and pulled me back to her.

Walking home by myself fifteen minutes later, I was amazingly happy. Before I left her, when we were out in the parking lot, and Jimmy was pulling up in his old car, a junker with lots of rust and dents, Four Point told me she was sorry we hardly got a chance to talk. "Hey, I know what. Why don't you come to the protest rally with us this weekend?" It was news to me, but there was going to be a rally. She said protests were going to be held that night all over the country. If I wanted to come, Jimmy would swing around my house and pick me up. No problem.

"That sounds really cool," I said.

Before she jumped into Jimmy's car, she leaned forward and kissed me, just a little peck, on the cheek.

28

The Rally

Friday night, Jimmy picked me up. There was a black guy in the front with him and a white guy in the back with Four Point. I had to squeeze into the back seat. Four Point was wedged between me and the white guy. Jimmy introduced me to his friends. The black guy in the front was Billy and the white guy in the back was Nathan.

I wondered if Nathan was Jewish. He didn't look Jewish. My mom said Jews have hook noses. That's the main way you can tell they are Jewish. Billy did not have a nose like that. Jimmy and Four Point didn't either, so I suspected my mom's information was unreliable.

Was it possible the black guy Billy was also Jewish? Could black people be Jewish? I was pretty sure my former friend Rose White was Baptist. Four Point told me Billy was a history major and Nathan was a double major, political science and anthropology.

I remembered that, after the wrestling meet, Four Point used the word "anthropologically." Was it possible she had lots of conversations with Nathan? Maybe she had a crush on him! How could someone like me, a mere ninth grader, compete with a cool Jewish guy who is a double major?

From the moment Jimmy backed out of my driveway, he and Billy never stopped talking. I listened, but every other thing they said meant little or nothing to me. Billy was talking about Lyndon Baines Johnson, our president. He said LBJ was a tragic figure.

What did that even mean?

Jimmy said. "He can't let go, right? Viet Nam is like the Tar Baby."

The Tar Baby? The more they talked, the more ignorant I felt.

I put on my glasses. In this group, it seemed OK to look like a dork. Four Point noticed me doing this and told me I looked better in glasses. I felt flattered, but then I feared she was just being nice. *Maybe she thinks I'm a phony?* Jimmy wore glasses, Four Point did, and so did Nathan. Billy was the only one in the car who was not wearing glasses. I wondered if black people have superior eyes to white people, but then I remembered that Rose White wore glasses.

Nathan said something I couldn't hear to Four Point and she laughed, which made me wonder if she liked Nathan. I decided I hated him.

I thought about trying to hold Four Point's hand. It was right there on top of her knee. She was wearing a black skirt and a zipper sweatshirt and sensible shoes. No socks. It was a lovely knee and I wanted to touch it.

If Calvin had been with us and knew what I was thinking, he would have said, "But that would be wrong."

I sort of wished Calvin was with us.

We parked in a university parking lot. Jimmy said he did not have a parking permit and would probably get a ticket, but he didn't care. This lot was the only one close to the library. Billy said probably we wouldn't get a ticket because all the campus cops would be at the rally.

I was impressed and a little disturbed that this university was so big it had its own cops. You could fit my entire school into one little corner of this place.

Other college kids were getting out of cars. Like us, they were on their way to the protest. You could tell because lots of them were carrying homemade signs. *Stop the War NOW! Vietnam for the Vietnamese! Bring the Troops HOME! No More DRAFT!* One sign said: *Respect Geneva Accords.* It was the only sign without an exclamation point.

I had no idea what the Geneva Accords were, or why I should respect them. Nathan pointed at the girl carrying this sign and said, "She's the daughter of the provost." The black guy said, "Of course she is." I had no idea what a provost was. Four Point made a little nod as if to say, *That explains it.*

The college students seemed much older than me. They were only – what? – five years older, but already they were adults. Each one of them was obviously way cooler than I would ever be. What was a dopey ninth grader like me doing here? What if one of those campus cops saw me and told me I had to leave?

I stayed close to Four Point and wished I could hold her hand. We trailed behind Jimmy and Nathan and Billy. All three of them seemed like nerds, a fact I found comforting, but they seemed better than typical nerds. They were at the high end of nerdiness — cool, sophisticated nerds. I doubted if even my friend Calvin could keep up with them. They knew about all kinds of important stuff like the Geneva Accords that punks like me and Calvin and Michael had never even heard of.

At some point, I realized I was holding Four Point's hand, but did not know how that had happened. She squeezed my fingers and said, "You nervous? Don't be."

How did she know I was nervous? Did I look nervous? Was my hand sweating? Jimmy and his friends did not seem nervous. Why wasn't Four Point nervous? She was cool as cool can be. She let go of my hand so she could ask Nathan something.

Jimmy and Billy were talking about LBJ again, how much they hated

213

him. Billy said, "Give the man his due. He signed the Voting Rights Act." I sort of vaguely remembered that was something about black people, but I couldn't remember what exactly.

Billy said the war was overshadowing the Civil Rights movement. "That's not necessarily a good thing."

Jimmy said, "Because of the draft."

The draft was something I knew about. Even in my junior high, kids talked about it. When you turned eighteen, if you were male, you were required by law to register for the draft, but if you went to college like Jimmy and his friends, you could get a deferment. But what happens when they graduate? Was it possible, in just another year or two, Jimmy and his friends could be in Vietnam? Already, the older brothers of kids I knew were getting drafted.

I thought about Micky, Big's boyfriend. He had enlisted in the Marines. A lot of the fighting in Vietnam was led by the Marines. They were the "tip of the spear." Right this very second, halfway around the world, Micky could be in a jungle, killing Vietnamese. Or he could be dead. I decided not to mention him.

When we got to the library, we found a mob of college students, hundreds of them. Pretty soon our little group was right in the middle of the mob. I realized we were trapped, couldn't go forward or backward. I started worrying about a stampede. What if the campus cops used tear gas like the cops did on that bridge in Selma, Alabama, on Bloody Sunday?

The crowd was mostly white kids, as many girls as guys, lots of signs. *End the War NOW!* I noticed some old people in front of us. Professors? I saw four nuns in habits, clustered together near the front. They didn't have any signs. I wondered if there was such a thing as a Jewish nun. I really needed to read that book *Herzog*.

The stage was two long tables pushed together. A college kid with big frizzy hair was standing on top of the stage talking into a microphone.

He seemed to be running the event. Jimmy said his name was – Abner Allen Stein? I wasn't sure if Allen Stein was two words, or just one.

Four Point said, "He's the student body president."

I wondered, *How does she even know this stuff?*

Abner Allen Stein introduced two folk singers, a guy with long dark hair and a girl with long blonde hair. The guy was strumming a guitar, and she was banging on a tambourine. Jimmy said they were a brother and sister act.

"Masters of War," I said before Jimmy could say it. "That song. It's a Bob Dylan." I was proud I recognized the lyrics. Unfortunately, no one was paying any attention to me. Four Point was talking to Nathan again. I noticed the nuns in front of us had been joined by a young priest.

After the folksingers finished the song, Abner Allen Stein introduced Professor Somebody. He was pretty cool-looking for a professor. If he was at teacher at my junior high school, they would never let him have hair that long. The rule at Poe Junior was your hair cannot touch your collar. The cool professor was talking about Gandhi and non-violent protest.

Jimmy said he wasn't sold on non-violence, but Billy said violent protest is stupid when sixty percent still support the war.

Nathan said, "Sixty percent is a conservative estimate. Probably eighty percent."

Abner Allen Stein led us in a chant. *Stop the War NOW! Stop the War NOW!*

The folk duo returned and led us in a sing-along of "Blowin' in the Wind." I realized it too was a Dylan song. Maybe college students, at least the radicals preferred Dylan to the Beatles?

I noticed Four Point was talking to Billy. She said something and he laughed.

I couldn't imagine being cool enough to make Billy laugh.

The crowd noise was loud. Billy's head was practically touching Four Point's head. I decided I hated Billy. In fact, I hated all these cool college guys. College students have no business flirting with a ninth-grade girl. There should be a law against it. Her brother Jimmy should step in and make Billy and Nathan stay away from Four Point – at least six feet away.

Four Point returned to my side, and I regained a little bit of sanity. I brushed the back of my hand against the back of her hand, but she pulled away from me and moved closer to the stage.

By then the young priest I had seen earlier with the nuns was on the stage. He was talking about conscientious Americans who burned themselves up to protest the war. I got confused. Was he talking about protestors actually burning themselves up, or just burning up their draft cards? I remembered hearing about Buddhist monks setting themselves on fire in Vietnam, but Americans? He told us about a member of the Catholic Worker movement who was photographed burning his draft card in Manhattan in front of the Armed Forces Induction Center.

I sort of remembered seeing this photo in my grandpa's *Life Magazine*.

The priest said the draft card burner was an American hero. People were applauding everything he said.

When the priest got off the stage, Abner Allen Stein told us that the Movement had gone International. He said rallies were going on tonight in DC, New York, San Francisco. In Rome and Brussels. In Copenhagen and even in Stockholm *Fucking* Sweden.

I couldn't believe he said the word fucking.

I decided swear words were thrilling, especially if you said them into a microphone to a big crowd. I wondered what Calvin and Michael would say if I started using the word fucking, like at lunch.

The folkies returned and sang a sad song called "I Ain't Marching

Anymore." I had never heard this song and was pretty sure it was never played on the radio.

Abner Allen Stein led us in a thrilling and shocking new chant: *FUCK the war NOW!*

Jimmy pointed out that there were real cops in attendance. Ten of them, wearing helmets, standing in a line not far from the stage. I wondered if Abner Allen Stein could get arrested, just for swearing in public. Now, the entire crowd was yelling it.

FUCK the War – NOW!

I wanted to grab Four Point's hand and pull her out of here.

I was suffering from sensory overload, too much new stuff all at once. I needed to go to the restroom, but we were trapped in the middle of the crowd. I tried to make myself calm down.

Abner started a new chant: *LBJ, how many kids did you kill today?*

"We're just about done," Abner said, when the chant ran out of gas. "Calm down. Everybody calm the fuck down. I hope you're ready for this. Are you ready?"

Everyone yelled, "We're ready!"

Abner said, "Tonight, boys and girls, we are going to make history. Are you ready?" He introduced someone, the final speaker. People around me were still yelling that they were ready, so I didn't catch the name. A young skinny guy climbed up on the stage. There was nothing special about him. He looked scared. "I have to do this," he said.

Girls were shouting, "You can do it!"

Do what? I wondered.

The skinny guy pulled out his wallet, removed something out of the wallet and held it up so we could see it, a piece of paper. "You guys know what this is?"

People were shouting, "Do it! Do it!"

Abner Allen Stein held up his hands like he was blessing us, and everyone got quiet.

"It's his card," Four Point told me. "His goddamn draft card."

Abner Allen Stein had a lighter. He flicked it on. A flame squirted up.

The skinny guy said, "A light against the darkness." He held the little card in the flame until it caught fire and then turned to face us. He held up his flaming card. For a second, everyone was silent and shocked and thrilled, as if he was burning up a bible right in front of us. He dropped the flaming card, and a huge cheer went up. I looked sideways at Four Point and saw she had tears in her eyes.

"The cops are just standing there," Jimmy said, as if we were witnesses to a miracle. "The fuckers don't know what the fuck to do."

29

Naomi

After the rally, when Jimmy dropped me off, Four Point got out of the car, walked me to the door, and kissed me good night. Then I went inside and got yelled at by Mom.

I lay in my bed that night and thought about the beautiful college girls staring up at the pale young man with love lights in their eyes. Was it possible the Dylan song was right? "The times they are a-changing." From now on, the radicals and hippies were going to get the girls, not the jocks?

Monday morning, at school, Four Point was waiting for me at my locker. She informed me she didn't want to lead me on. She said all day Sunday she gave our relationship a lot of serious thought and concluded she didn't want a boyfriend. "That's not what I want to focus on right now. It's not personal."

I thought if Four Point did not want a boyfriend, then she was the only girl in our entire school who felt that way. Boys! That is all girls ever talked about. Obviously, there was another guy. She was in love with someone, just not with me. "Is it that goddamn Nathan? He's too old for you! Is it because I'm not Jewish? Billy? You're in love with Billy? It's Billy, isn't it? Because of anthropology and he's black."

Four Point gave me a look and said, "Wow. You need to calm down. You're starting to sound like a stupid person."

Before I could think of a response, she turned on her heel and left me standing there.

I wondered if I was a bad kisser. That was probably when I blew it, but at the time I was nervous. I didn't have a whole lot of kissing experience. Besides, my mom was right on the other side of the front door, glaring at us through the little window. How can you kiss a girl properly when your mom is on the verge of insanity, staring at you, inches away? I had been forced to turn Four Point away from the door so she couldn't see my mom.

At some level, however, I was not that disappointed. I'd had a feeling Four Point was going to dump me. I wasn't advanced enough for her.

At lunch, I told Calvin and Michael about the anti-war rally and how cool it was. Calvin said he already knew about the rally because, on the front page of the morning paper, there was a big picture of the skinny kid burning his draft card. The article said he and Abner Allenstein got arrested later that night. (It turned out Allenstein was one word, not two.)

Michael said, "So… you and Four Point, huh?"

I did what he always did, looked surprised and said, "We're just friends."

Michael appreciated my imitation and grinned.

Calvin said, "Yeah, right. Tell us another lie."

Ray had dinner with his mom and sister once a week, usually on Thursday because Ray didn't want to give up even a moment of his weekend. His mom told him to bring a friend. She kept nagging him about it. For a while he took the Nazi with him. Unfortunately, even for a guest, the Nazi talked too much. One time, at Naomi's dinner table, he revealed he was an admirer of Hitler. Then, another time, he talked about the stock market for a solid hour. That year, stocks and bonds had become the Nazi's new obsession. Every morning, he studied the stock market page in the newspaper. He said he was going to talk his dad into staking him. He would invest wisely, make a fortune by the time he was 21, and never have to work a day in his life.

I asked Ray, "Your mom doesn't like the stock market?"

Ray said he might have been able to go on bringing the Nazi over to his mom's house despite his unattractive fondness for Hitler and capitalism, but on his last visit, the Nazi had revealed he was an atheist. That did it good and proper. The Nazi was banned from the house. "You're the only half-decent friend I have left."

I said, "But I don't believe in God either."

"Just don't say nothing about it. Nothing about religion period. When we say grace, bow your head. Can you do that, or is that against your atheist religion?"

"Do I have to say Amen?"

"Do this one thing for me, OK?"

The Nazi told me to be prepared for a shock if I went over there. He said since Red's death, Ray's ma had changed.

"Changed how?"

"She's... queer."

"Queer?"

"Not queer like that, the other kind of queer. "

"Like what?"

"She says weird things. Act like you don't notice."

"What do you mean? I need examples. What kind of things?"

"If she says something weird, just nod your head."

I asked my mom if she ever went to visit Naomi Kavanaugh after Red got killed.

"I went over there twice with Betty." Betty was a friend of my mom's and lived on our street.

"What happened?"

"Naomi's let her hair go white."

I looked surprised. Ray's mom was not that old.

According to my mom, Naomi's hair went white prematurely after she gave birth to Julie Ann, but Red didn't like it that way. He didn't want a wife who looked like she was his ma, so he made her dye it. After his death, Naomi let it go white. She did it in a weird do-it-yourself way. She just quit using the dye. After a time, you could see her white roots. Then, for a while, she was half and half. The hair near her scalp, the new hair, was white, and the hair farther away was still dyed. Finally, the white got long enough, and Naomi cut off all the dyed ends. "It was disconcerting to see."

"People say she's odd. She says things."

While we were having this conversation, my mom was ironing one of my dad's shirts. For half a minute, she ironed that shirt as if she wanted to kill it. Then she said, "Red kept that woman locked up. Not allowed to speak in her own house. No friends. People said he beat her. And now."

"What?"

"She's trying to be normal. But she isn't. She went too many years like that, and now…. You just remember who you are, Jack. You hear? When you go over there, remember you are a DeWitt."

I had never seen the inside of Ray's house, except for the one time, Red's wake, when it was full of people. The Nazi said Naomi now acted as if Red had been a saint. "She plans to join up with him in heaven when she dies."

We both had our doubts that Red was in heaven.

When Ray and I went over there, I had to take off my shoes. At my house, that was not necessary, and I didn't like it. There was something about being in somebody else's house, walking around in my sock feet, that felt wrong. It didn't help that there was a hole in one of my socks.

Naomi was wearing black. Since Red died, she was in permanent mourning and never wore any other color. Ray's little sister Julie Ann was in the living room slumped on the sofa watching TV.

"How you doing, Ugly?" Ray said. "Got a boyfriend yet?"

Without taking her eyes off the TV, she flew him the bird.

"Julie Ann, Julie Ann!"

"Hey, Ugly, Ma's calling you."

Julie Ann switched off the TV and departed for the kitchen.

"The table's already set. You sit there." Ray pointed to a chair by itself on one side of the table.

The table was set for five. "You guys expecting somebody else? I hope your mom didn't invite a priest or a nun or something."

"No one sits at the head of the table. That's where Red sat."

I noticed Ray called his dad Red. Not Dad. I wanted to comment on the fact that Naomi was still setting a place at the table for her dead husband, but I kept my mouth shut.

Julie Ann came out of the kitchen, carrying a platter. "I hope you like meatloaf," Ray said.

When all the food was on the table, Naomi came in still wearing her apron. When she saw me sitting there, she looked surprised. Didn't Ray tell her about me?

"I'm Jack," I said. I wasn't sure what to do. Should I stand up?

Ray said, "Wolfgang can't come today, Ma, so I invited Jack."

I thought, *Wow, they call the Nazi Wolfgang.*

"You're more than welcome to dine with us, Jack," Naomi said. She did not make eye contact with me. "Raymond, will you say grace?"

Ray was going to pray?

Ray crossed himself – Naomi and Julie Ann did too — and said, "Bless us, O Lord, and these, Thy gifts, which we are about to receive from Thy bounty. Through Christ, our Lord. Amen." The three of them crossed themselves again. I did it too but clumsily, not being used to it. At my house all we had to do after grace was open our eyes. At least, here, we didn't have to hold hands. One time I had dinner with Calvin's family and his mom made us hold hands. I had even heard of families that make you sing the grace.

I loaded my plate with mashed potatoes, meatloaf, and sliced carrots, but passed on the green beans because no one in his right mind likes green beans.

We started eating. Nobody said a word, which was fine with me. Maybe if we ate fast, Ray and I could get out of here quick too.

Then Naomi started asking me questions, no eye contact, no context. It was as if she had a list of questions in front of her and was working her way down the list, not paying much attention to my answers.

"How are your classes, Jack?"

"Are you in any of Raymond's classes?"

"How is the football team doing? Do you like football? My husband always loved the St. Louis Cardinals."

"Do you participate in a sport? I always hoped Ray would participate in school athletics, but of course he has his bowling."

"Did you see the article in the paper about the draft card burners? I expect they will be sent to prison. They were Jews. Do you have any in your classes? They are smart, the Jews are, but they are still Jews."

"When boys become men, they go off to war. Unless they are unfit. I am certain Raymond will not be drafted because of his heart."

Ray rolled his eyes to indicate there was not a damn thing wrong with his heart.

"Have you noticed the leaves have changed? I predict a hard winter."

"What do you want to become when you graduate from high school, Jack? I imagine you will go to college. Raymond says you are smart. Intelligence is a gift from God."

"I go to mass every morning. My life revolves around the church."

"Did you know my husband passed away a few years ago? I am a widow now. I will never remarry. My husband was the love of my life."

Naomi sometimes drifted off and looked vacant. I had the impression her body continued to sit there in the chair at her end of the table with its eyes unfocused while her soul left her body and wandered elsewhere, perhaps in outer space.

Julie Ann brought in the apple crisp.

Naomi said, "I thank the Lord you and Raymond are able to attend a school that does not allow Negroes. Their women are sexually voracious, you know."

Ray ate rapidly and kept his eyes fixed on his plate.

"Jack, I know a way to get rid of pimples. You must rub your face with holy water while saying the Hail Mary. Say it three times. You may obtain holy water at the church. There is always plenty for everyone."

"Ma!" Ray said.

I thought: *Dear God, even though I don't believe in You, will You please prevent this woman from talking any more about my pimples?*

"I have filled this house with pictures of the Virgin. Did you notice them? The Virgin protects our home. I also have a picture of John Fitzgerald Kennedy, our greatest president."

When we were finished eating, I offered to help clear the table, but Naomi said, "That is women's work. Julie Ann will do it."

"Can we be excused, Ma?"

"Raymond, if you boys are going to smoke, please do it in the garage. Thank you for coming, Jack. You are a credit to your mother. I hope you will give her my regards. Raymond, you boys may leave the table now. It was a pleasure to meet you, Jack."

Ray took me out to the garage. "She won't let me smoke in the house. Don't worry, we don't have to go back in. You did your duty. You can go home now if you want."

"I don't mind hanging around for a bit." I got the strong impression that Ray did not want me to say one word about his ma.

While he smoked his cig, I looked around the garage, thinking about the murder. "Hey, what happened to your dad's truck?"

"She sold it. To my uncle. But it's OK because he has a line on this old Harley. It's in pieces, but he's gonna buy it for me and help me put it back together."

He noticed me looking at the empty hook on the garage wall where the murder weapon used to hang. "You thinking about the missing hammer? The cops have it."

"Right. Sorry. Didn't mean to bring up bad memories."

"The cops aren't doing a damn thing. If you're wondering." He flicked away his cigarette butt. "They know who did it. Of course, they do, the fuckers. Everybody knows."

"I don't."

"It was Tommy White, or his dad, or someone else they know. But the cops won't arrest them."

"I don't get it. Why would they kill your dad? Did Red burn down their house? I thought it was Big and Middle."

Ray did not like me asking these questions. "You better split," he said. "Thanks for coming."

The next morning, when I was still in bed, half awake, my mom came into my room with the front part of the newspaper.

She sat down on the foot of my bed, which was strange, and looked at me.

"Hey," I said, sitting up, "I'm in my underwear! Leave me alone! Why are you looking at me like that?"

"You're not going to like this, Jack," she said. "It's on the front page."

30

Closure

Ricky Fox took me to the junkyard to see what was left of the white Cadillac. It didn't make me cry. Mrs. Ryan's funeral didn't make me cry either. Nothing made me cry. From the time I saw the headline in the paper, *Wife of Prominent Businessman Dies in Crash*, I had not felt anything except numb.

I told myself my emotions existed somewhere, not inside me, but nearby. A little dark cloud of emotions floating over my head.

Probably that was not true.

By the time Mrs. Ryan died, Ricky Fox and I were friends. I am not entirely sure how this happened. He was two years older than me, and I hated his guts. There was the time I destroyed his Cross of Jesus (made of matchsticks) and the time he threw pepper into my eyes. We went to the same church though, so it was impossible not to see him on a regular basis.

One time, he came up to me after Sunday School and said, "You're smart. I can respect that." I assumed he meant that my brain was the ONLY thing about me he respected.

After a while, he was talking to me on a regular basis. I got the impression Ricky did not have a lot of friends his own age.

Ricky knew stuff about me. He had known me since I was a baby. Also, his mom knew my mom. According to Ricky, my mom often bragged about me. Ricky said his mom got a little irritated having to listen to how smart I was, the high scores I got on tests, that sort of thing. He was one of the few people who knew about me and Mrs. Ryan, how last winter she gave me rides home after school. I never mentioned it, so I figure my mom told his mom, and his mom told him.

After the story of Mrs. Ryan's car accident was in the paper, Ricky came up to me at church and asked me if I was going to her funeral.

"Don't know," I said. I didn't want to talk about it, not to him, not to anyone else. I tried to radiate bad vibrations but, if Ricky was aware of my vibrations, he ignored them.

"You were close to her, am I right? You should go to the funeral. I'll even take you." Ricky had his own car, a used Plymouth his parents got for him for his sixteenth birthday.

My parents might have taken me to the funeral. They probably would have if I had asked them to. My mom offered, but first she said she didn't really know Mrs. Ryan that well. It was going to be a Catholic funeral at a Catholic church. But if it was important to me, she'd take me.

I said, "No thanks."

I did in fact want to go to the funeral, I just didn't want to go with my mom. At this point in my life, I often had difficulty expressing my needs. Instead, I just got angry. Anger seemed to be the one emotion I was still feeling capable of feeling.

Ricky said, "You need closure." His dad was a florist, the owner and proprietor of Fox's Flowers, so he knew all about closure. He said, "You ought to send some flowers." I wondered where he thought I was going to get the money to buy flowers. "Flowers help us get through the big moments of life. Whether it's a funeral or an anniversary,

Valentine's Day, whatever. We like to have beauty around us on special occasions. That's where flowers come in. Nothing says 'I care' better than flowers."

"Right," I said, wishing he would shut up.

"You won't be able to see her, not in the coffin, because this funeral is a closed casket. That's what my dad said. You get better closure if it's open casket. You want me to take you? Because I will be glad to do it for you."

"Why do you care? Leave me alone!"

He jumped back as if I had poked him with a stick. A hurt look in his eyes. I turned on my heel and stalked away from him. Like I wanted to go to her funeral. What was it with Ricky? Did he have a thing for funerals or something? After a while, I felt sort of bad about rejecting his offer. He had been trying to do a nice thing for me. It was probably in the Boy Scout Code. Maybe the Scouts have a Funeral Merit Badge. You have to go to six funerals and comfort the grieved. Or something. I was glad to hear it was going to be closed casket. No way did I want to see Mrs. Ryan lying dead in a coffin. Ricky probably was trying to be a good person when he made the offer. I wondered if his mom might have put him up to it. He wanted to be my friend. Ricky didn't have a lot of friends. Did he have even one good friend? I felt sorry for him. He couldn't help being a jerk. It was probably genetic.

Finally, I repented and told Ricky I'd changed my mind. I apologized for being rude. "If the offer is still open, I would like to go. And if you still want to drive me –"

Ricky said, "The service is at 3 PM. I'll pick you up at 2. I can come get you at your school. Tell your mom she has to write you an excuse." Like a lot of other people, Ricky often talked to me as if he believed I needed careful instructions to do anything at all. "I'll meet you at the back door by the gym. Wear a dress shirt to school, so you won't have to change. Bring a tie. You can put it on in my car. I wanna get there early because everyone in town will be there, all the important people I mean. The movers and shakers will be well represented. You can take my word for that."

On the way to the funeral, Ricky talked about himself. He said he was a junior and would a be a senior next year, so he was thinking about his career path. His mom and dad wanted him to go to college, or he could follow in his dad's footsteps and become a florist. Neither one of these options was his dream. His dream was to become a police officer.

Ricky said he was not like me. Sure, he did fine at school, got good grades, but he had to work at it. Why? Because he did not care that much about history and math and the other school subjects. Guys like me, possessing my type of school-oriented brain, could just breeze through their classes. Didn't even have to study. Not him. He had to grind away at it. On the other hand, he loved cops. Always had. There was a Scout Badge devoted to law enforcement. To earn it, he had to go on three ride-alongs. On one of these, he saw an arrest. That moment – it was a domestic dispute – when he saw the husband getting put in cuffs, it changed his life. It was like – well, he did not even know what he could compare it to. He didn't have the words.

I said, "Do you have to get a degree for that?"

Ricky said, to be a cop, all you have to do is take four semesters at the community college.

We drove toward the cathedral in silence for a minute, and then he wanted to know if I had seen Little Grimm lately.

"Just in school," I said.

"I guess you know about her sister."

"Which one?"

He said kids like the Grimms are unable to plan for the future. He said ability to plan for the future, to understand that actions have consequences, is one of the main features that distinguish the

Successful from the Unsuccessful.

"OK," I said.

He said Middle and Big were now high school dropouts. Did I know that?

"I heard rumors."

"Know what people like that are called, dropouts, who never plan for the future?"

"What are they called?"

"White Trash."

"OK."

Ricky wondered if I knew that someone knocked up Middle. "She went somewhere, probably to one of those Homes for Unwed Mothers, and had a baby. Gave away the baby. Her own child. Just gave it away."

"I heard something about that, I guess."

"What kind of guy would do that? Get a girl pregnant and then abandon her. I'll tell you. An irresponsible guy. A guy who is working day and night on his White Trash degree."

I didn't say anything.

Ricky said he "did the deed" with Little one time. He said, even at the time, even in the heat of the moment, he had known it was wrong, but he had been overcome by the overpowering tide of lust. By the grace of God, Little did not wind up pregnant like her sister. Ricky said after he and Little were saved by the Gospel Brothers, after they gave their hearts to Jesus, he had offered to marry Little. Because if you are going to do it, you must step up and do the right thing.

"Wow," I said.

Unfortunately, since then, Little Grimm had drifted from the Lord. She had had two boyfriends since her return to sin, two that he knew about, but it could be more. He said Little was obviously boy crazy, which happens all too often when girls do not have fathers.

"That's too bad," I said.

When we got into the packed cathedral, I noticed Ricky looking all over the place, and I wondered if he was nursing a hope that Little might be attending the funeral. She was nowhere in sight, of course. The Grimm sisters and their mother were not what our town considered to be important people. Ricky said lots of country club types were here. The Chamber of Commerce was here in force. He said the mayor was here and the chief of police.

There was a large portrait of Mrs. Ryan on an easel up near the altar. Ricky said Big Bill had commissioned a famous artist to paint it and gave it to her last Christmas.

"There's Big Bill. See him? That girl beside him with the long hair, that's his daughter."

I found it impossible to focus on the funeral. There was music, singing. Someone played a violin. A priest talked to us.

At the end of the service, six men carried the coffin out of the cathedral. A hearse was parked right in front beside the curb. Ricky said the coffin bearers were local businessmen. Friends of Bill.

After the funeral, we did not follow the parade of cars to the cemetery. Instead, Ricky drove us to the junkyard so we could look at the white Cadillac.

She had sideswiped a parked car in her own neighborhood, bounced across the street into someone's yard, straight into a big tree.

Ricky kept telling me it was OK if I wanted to cry.

I didn't feel like it.

After a minute, I said, "Let's go."

"I just hope you got what you needed," Ricky said. "People need closure."

31

Bubbles

Over the course of the rest of ninth grade, Calvin grew to the height of six feet. He looked like a beanpole with a big head on top of it. Michael also grew but not as much as Calvin. As usual, he grew more attractive. I grew too, but not as much as Calvin or Michael. I remained at about the same level of dorkiness. My pimple situation continued as usual, and I continued to walk around in a fog, only wearing my glasses when absolutely necessary.

That spring, I got into a fight with my dad. One Wednesday evening, when it was time to go to church, I decided I would not go. Everyone else was out in the car, but I stayed in the house. My brother Dean ran in and told me to hurry up. "Dad sent me!"

I said, "Tell them I'm not going."

Dean looked happy and interested and ran out to the car to tell my parents that I had been possessed by the spirit of rock and roll rebellion. Again. My dad had to get out of the car and come into the house. He made Dean wait in the car with the rest of our family.

I don't think my father was angry. When I grew rebellious, his tendency was to deal with me the way he might handle a disobedient dog. He looked me in the eye and talked to me in a serious, calm voice. "Come on, Jack," he said, "we have to go."

"Maybe you do. I'm not going."

"You are coming with us," my dad said.

I lost control of myself. I was never any good at arguing with my father. Anger and fear always leapt into me and turned me into a raving maniac. I started yelling at him. "I'm not going, I'm not, you can't make me, I don't even believe in God, why should I go, I won't go." That sort of thing at high volume.

Instead of arguing with me, my dad slapped me in the face.

That shut me up.

"Let's go," he said. "We don't want to be late."

I followed him back to the car.

My brother Dean was delighted to see me.

The next Wednesday, when it came time to go to church, I was not in the house. My family had to go without me.

I never went to Wednesday evening church again.

Not much else of interest happened to me for the rest of my ninth-grade year except I got caught cheating.

Normally I did not cheat. Hoods cheated. Jocks cheated. Dumb kids cheated. I was a brain and did not need to bother. I was vain about my ability to ace tests. Test-taking was my one skill. I was no good at sports. I was not good looking. I was not popular. But at least I could score high on tests. My goal usually was to be one of the first to finish the test, to wind up with the highest grade in the class, and to accomplish these goals without a lot of studying. If someone like Four Point got a higher score than me, that was acceptable.

Calvin and Michael were also in my biology class. Ninth Grade Biology was a smart-kid class taught by Mr. Jones, the hottest teacher in our school. He was 35 years old and looked like someone so cool he might hang out in Las Vegas with Frank Sinatra. He wore cool suits

234

and narrow ties and expensive shoes. He could play the piano by ear. People said he had a gorgeous wife and two or three girlfriends on the side. He once gave two of the jocks a lesson in dancing. He said if the song is slow, you hold the girl real close, you hardly move, you let the music do all the work. The jocks believed if they could just dance like Mr. Jones, any girl would become their bedroom dream for the rest of the night. Who could doubt it?

Calvin said the three of us should study together for Mr. Jones's exam. We needed to study because this test was going to be an important one, worth one third of our entire grade. We could meet at Calvin's house on Saturday and study in his kitchen. His mom would make snacks for us. To my surprise, Michael agreed to this plan, so I felt obliged to agree too.

When Saturday arrived, Michael and I walked over to Calvin's house. We sat in Calvin's kitchen and ate snacks and studied by asking each other questions having to do with biology. I soon got bored to death. After an hour, I refused to study any more. It was Saturday, for god's sake. We should not spend the entire afternoon indoors studying.

Calvin said we only had one more important thing to study, a detailed diagram of a cell. I looked at the picture in our textbook. It was amazing how many little squiggly things are swimming around inside a cell. All of these little things have names.

I said no way was Mr. Jones going to put that cell diagram on the test. "See you around, nerds!"

On Monday, we were in class, hunched over at our tables taking Mr. Jones's exam. I sailed through all the questions on the first page. I turned the page and there, on page two, was the drawing of the cell that Calvin had said was going to be on the test. The little squiggly things inside the cell had lines that led to the spaces where we were supposed to write the names of the little things.

With total confidence, I wrote down the names of three of the little things. There was one other little thing I was ninety percent sure about and another thing I was sixty percent sure of. I had no clue what the other little things were called.

Michael was sitting directly across the table from me. I looked up and saw he was busily filling out the labels for the cell diagram. He and Calvin had remained in Calvin's kitchen when I left; they had studied that diagram to death, and now Michael was reaping his reward. His hand was moving confidently from one answer to the next.

I leaned forward and started reading his answers (upside down) and then writing them on my exam. When I was about three fourths done with this chore, Mr. Jones said in a loud voice, "Someone in this room is cheating. It better stop!"

I stopped cheating and turned red. I kept my eyes fixed on my test and answered all the rest of the questions. At the end of the class, we filed past Mr. Jones who collected our exams. I made sure not to make eye contact.

The next day, Mr. Jones returned our exams. I was astonished and thrilled to see I got a B. Maybe he had been talking about some other cheater? I flipped to the second page and right beside the cell diagram Mr. Jones had written CHEATING. He had given me zero points for that section of the exam but full credit for all my other correct answers. At the end of the exam, where he totaled up the final score, he had written: SEE ME AFTER CLASS.

After class, Mr. Jones told me he was disappointed in me.

"I am disappointed in myself," I said.

"I don't like to do it, but I'm going to have to assign you detention."

"Right," I said.

I figured I got off easy. I had been terrified he was going to tell my mom.

The next day, when I was in Study Hall, Michael arrived and talked to the Study Hall supervisor. She stood up and called my name. I walked to the front of the room, wondering why Michael was there.

"Jack, you have to go see Mr. G. Take your books."

It turned out Michael worked for Mr. G, the school guidance counselor. This was one of the many things about Michael I did not know, despite the fact he was one of my best friends. It was his job to carry messages for Mr. G, like the one he had carried to my Study Hall. He would give the message to the Study Hall supervisor and then escort the kid who needed guidance to Mr. G.

Mr. G was a pudgy bald man who was also known as Bubbles because of his habit of blowing spit bubbles when he talked.

"What does Bubbles want with me?" I said.

"Probably the cheating thing," Michael said. "You got detention, didn't you? Bubbles always finds out about that. He gets notified."

"Right," I said. We walked toward the guidance office. "You think he will call my mom?"

According to Michael, Bubbles had a big concern about his weight. He always wore white short-sleeved shirts and a black tie. Despite his constant dieting, he always looked a size too big for the white shirts.

Michael said he hardly ever called anyone's parents.

Bubbles welcomed me to his office. He said we had not met before, but he knew I was a good student.

"OK," I said.

Bubbles was looking at a folder with my name on it.

He said he noticed that my detention for cheating in Mr. Jones's class was the second time I got assigned to detention. The first offense had occurred way back at the start of my seventh-grade year, the gum incident. "A lot of kids find that first year tough, a time of adjustment," he said.

"Right," I said.

"No incidents since then."

"No," I said.

"Some of your teachers, not just Mr. Jones, inform me your grades are starting to slip."

"Maybe," I said.

"We don't want you to go into a slump, do we? We don't want you to go into a tailspin."

"Nope," I said.

"What we want to do is turn this situation around, nip it in the bud. Otherwise, when I make my recommendations for high school, who should be in the classes for gifted and talented students, I will have to leave your name off the list. We don't want that, do we? We want to keep you in those challenging classes with the other college-bound kids. Do you agree? We're on the same page?"

"Absolutely," I said.

Bubbles said he had noticed me in the hall, and he had noticed I had two kinds of friends. I was pals with his student aide Michael, for example, a good kid from a good family. A smart kid who kept his nose clean. Just a good decent kid all around.

Michael was sitting at a little desk outside the room Bubbles and I were in. The door wasn't even closed, and I wondered if Michael was hearing every word of this.

Bubbles said he had also noticed I was pals with a few other boys, boys of a different type than Michael. Boys who were perhaps leading me down the wrong path.

I didn't say anything.

Bubbles said he thought he could help me make better choices in the future if I would keep seeing him. He said, the next time I had Study Hall, he wanted me to come straight here to his office. He would make the arrangements with the Study Hall supervisor. Would I do that? Would I cooperate in my own improvement?

"OK," I said.

Bubbles said he would give me a test. It wasn't a perfect test.

Personality tests are not the perfect instrument we wish they were, but this test would be a good indicator, a useful tool that would help us understand what was going on with me. "How's that sound? Not too painful, I hope."

"OK," I stood up to leave.

"Anything unusual going on at home?" Bubbles said.

"Nope," I said.

When I arrived the next day to take Bubbles' test, he told me not to worry about it. "There's no such thing as a wrong answer."

The test asked me a bunch of yes or no questions like: *You are almost never late for your appointments. Yes or No.* I circled No. *You enjoy having a wide range of friends. Yes or No.* I didn't have many friends, so I circled No. *You feel involved watching TV soap operas.* We didn't have a TV at my house, and I had never seen a soap opera in my life, so I circled No.

The test went on like that for a couple pages.

Bubbles analyzed my answers in his office while I waited outside his door with Michael, who kept making funny faces at me and trying to make me laugh.

On a piece of notebook paper, Michael wrote: *Do you enjoy masturbating? Yes or No.*

I turned red.

When he finished analyzing my test, Bubbles had me come back into his office.

He said I was a somewhat unusual person. Unusual in a good way. Only three or four percent of the general population were like me. My same type. I thought this was probably true. He said I was the sort of person who could talk about nearly any topic. I thought this too was somewhat true. The sort of person who did well on tests. Definitely true. The sort of person who felt superior to others and sometimes felt the rules did not apply to him. I squirmed in my chair but did not disagree. The sort of person who sometimes seemed a bit distant and unemotional to others.

I said, "If you say so."

Bubbles said I needed to get more involved with school activities. He suggested I join the chess club. I thought I would rather lie down in the street and let a bus roll over me than hang out with chess club nerds but did not say anything.

After three more meetings, Bubbles said he felt we had made good progress and we would not need to have any more chats. Not unless there was more trouble.

"Great," I said.

That spring, Rose White covered herself in glory.

32

No Biracial Dating

When I was coming to the end of my ninth-grade year at Poe Junior High, Rose White was coming to the end of her junior year at East High. We had been incommunicado since the Bloody Sunday phone call, which had ended with her hanging up on me. I missed her. I realized she was two years older than me. That fact alone meant friendship between us was pretty much impossible. She was also better read. More mature. She lived on the wrong side of town. And she was Black. Despite all those barriers, there were certain topics – of all the people I knew in our town, only Rose White could properly appreciate those certain topics.

I wanted to talk to her about the Stevie Wonder song "Uptight (Everything's Alright)." Did she consider Stevie a genius? Did she think Stevie's genius was connected to his blindness? And then we could talk about "When a Man Loves a Woman" by Percy Sledge. I believed it to be a perfect song, right up there with "Yesterday" by the Beatles. I wondered if she thought Percy Sledge should change his name because it was maybe the worst name ever. How had Percy Sledge survived childhood with a name like that? How had he survived playground? And yet, somehow, against all odds, he had created one of the most perfect love songs of all time. That fact seemed to me a great topic for me and Rose to discuss. I wanted to ask her if she believed genius is directly connected to misfortunes like Stevie's blindness and Percy's horrifying first name.

My interest in this topic was – well, let's face it — I was trying to find some useful aspect of my pimple situation. Acne was obviously ruining my life, my entire adolescence. If at the end of my years of suffering, I got to write a song like "When a Man Loves a Woman," wouldn't it all be worth it? OK, I had zero musical aptitude. No argument. I was never going to write a great song. But maybe I could write something great, a book or something.

A book!

Possibly polio played a similar role in Rose's life.

She might appreciate my idea because basically I would be telling her I suspected she was a genius. Probably someday (I would tell her), because of her leg situation, she too would write a masterpiece.

Since she would no longer accept my phone calls, my conversations with Rose about important topics like Percy Sledge and Stevie Wonder had to be conducted entirely inside my own head.

Rose White covered herself in glory that spring by leading a school-wide protest against the no biracial dating policy at her high school. First, she got every single member of her class – including the white kids — to sign a petition demanding an end to the policy. The principal accepted the petition and said he would take it under advisement. When pressed a week later by Rose and her team of rebels — in public, at an assembly that was supposed to be about school spirit — he declared the policy could not be changed. It was necessary because if mixed race dating was permitted, fights between whites and blacks would occur. The policy might seem harsh, but it protected the health and safety of the students at East High School, and protecting students was his number one priority.

Was Rose daunted by this set-back?

One week before junior prom, Rose led the entire junior class in a walk out. They had signs and everything. They stood out there on the school lawn chanting "Black Power! Black Power!"

The principal said he had no choice. He cancelled the junior prom.

Rose responded with a "Monday sick out." She did not get one hundred percent cooperation but 40% of the entire school – grades 10 through 12 – called in sick that day.

All of these events were reported in the newspaper. A photo of Rose White in her wheelchair with her fists in the air was on the front page.

I felt that Rose White had ascended far above me. She was now a great civil rights hero like Martin Luther King, Jr. or Stokely Carmichael.

I heard rumors that Rose's brother Tommy White called up the East High School football coach and said he would not be participating in football next year unless the dating policy was changed.

For whatever reason, the principal of East High School announced he had consulted with many members of the community and reconsidered his position. The no interracial dating policy was rescinded.

The junior prom occurred as scheduled. Rose White was elected Prom Queen. Once again, her photo was in the paper – on page four. On page one there was a large photo of a black boy dancing with a white girl.

At Poe Junior, we had a Ninth Grade Dance, but it was a ho-hum event compared to the junior prom at East. I went to the dance with Calvin. The DJ played a lot of sappy music – Herman's Hermits, Tom Jones, the Dave Clark Five, crap like that. Calvin and I drank non-alcoholic punch and watched the jocks dance with the cheerleaders. When the slow songs played, the jocks did their best to dance in the sexy way Mr. Jones recommended.

I bragged to Calvin about my friendship with Rose White, the liberator of biracial love at East High. I did not mention the fact that Rose and I were no longer speaking to one another, even on the phone.

Calvin said desegregating a prom is all very well, but real civil rights is all about jobs, jobs, jobs. For example, Rose's dad had a job at the factory, but only as a custodian. "No way is a black guy ever going to get into management."

Sometimes I felt that Calvin had a gift for raining on other people's parades.

Stuff That Happened That Summer.

Michael invited me to his house (first time ever) and attempted to teach me how to box. Apparently, on a regular basis, his dad took him and his brothers down into the basement, put gloves on them, and smacked them around. This was their idea of family fun.

Michael toyed with me for a few minutes, and then I managed to hit him in the face. That poke irritated him, and he decked me. From the mat (they actually had a mat down there, just for boxing), I declared I was done. No more boxing for me, thank you very much.

I made more visits to Michael's house that summer but never again descended into the basement. I was allowed to visit only when no one in his family was home. Michael would call me up and tell me the coast was clear. I could come over if I wanted. Usually we just shot baskets in his driveway. I rarely made a shot. He would work on his tan and his muscles by dribbling and shooting and so on. I would keep my t-shirt on because I did not want him to notice the pimples on my shoulders.

That summer, Calvin and Michael took Drivers Training at the high school. By the end of the summer, they obtained their drivers' licenses.

I continued to walk all over town and take buses when I had any money. My favorite destinations: the public library downtown, the record store where Jimmy Levine worked, and the paperback book racks in the mezzanine of Brown's Department Store.

I developed a nasty habit of stealing paperbacks from the department store. Hoping to reduce my ignorance about the topic of sex, I looked for books with covers that said UNEXPURGATED EDITION. These novels included detailed descriptions of the hero locked in a steamy embrace with a beautiful but dangerous woman. I studied these descriptions carefully.

Besides unexpurgated editions, what did I read that summer?

Canticle for Leibowitz by Walter M. Miller. After nuclear war destroys modern civilization, scientific knowledge has to be preserved by monks. By the end of the novel, you realize every few millennia civilization destroys itself and has to start over. It's a tragic cycle. At the time I read this book, I thought it pretty obvious we were in the phase of the cycle when everyone is gearing up to destroy the world. It was comforting to think that, when practically everyone was dead and our cities in ashes, a few monks would be crawling around in the rubble preserving Science.

Silent Spring by Rachel Carson. Pesticides are destroying the natural world. Humans try to save the elm trees from Dutch Elm Disease by dosing the trees with pesticides. Farmers dose their crops with other kinds of pesticides, trying to increase food production. The poison of the pesticides gets into the water and then into the fish. Eagles swoop down, seize the fish in their talons, and eat them. That is how the poison gets into the birds. The shells of their eggs get thin and collapse when the mama eagle tries to sit on them. No more bald eagles, that is what we will get if we keep using pesticide. Also, no more flying insects – which is why Springs will soon be Silent. Also, people will get cancer. This book made me wonder about my mom. Every summer, the school park across from our house got dosed with pesticides. Maybe that was why my mom got cancer. I also wondered if there might be a connection between pesticides and acne.

That summer, Ray's uncle got him a construction job, so I saw him only occasionally – in the evenings or on weekends.

Ray was recruited by a friend of his to be the drummer for a rock band named What? The name was a tribute to the British group The Who. Ray loved their hits: "I Can't Explain" and "M-M-M-My Generation." He said their drummer Keith Moon was a genius. I think he said Moon was a *fucking* genius, which in Ray's mind was an entire step higher than an ordinary genius. That summer, he decided the Rolling Stones were better than the Beatles. The Beatles, in his opinion, were starting to get fancy. Rock and Roll should never be fancy. The Beatles song "Paperback Writer" was an example of the mop tops getting overly fancy. That summer, the Stones put out a string of dark masterpieces, and Ray loved them all. "(I Can't Get No) Satisfaction" was in his view the greatest rock song of all time. "Paint It Black" and "Get Off My Cloud" and "Under My Thumb" were tied for second place on his list.

After he got invited to be in the band, Ray got Mrs. Broom to rent him a set of used drums from a music store downtown. He and his band buddies were allowed to practice in the motel basement, but only in the afternoons, when there were no guests in the rooms. They worked on what Ray called The Basics, simple but hard-driving songs like "Louie, Louie" by the Kingsmen and "All of the Day, All of the Night" by the Kinks.

33

Ouija Board

That summer, the summer before I got into high school, I spent a lot of time with a kid my age named Bobby Hinson. He had been in a bunch of my classes, so we knew each other. He was already friends with Calvin and Michael, so I decided he could be my friend too. He and Michael convinced me one day to buy a t-shirt with the cartoon of a Viking on it. The Viking was fat and looked as if he had drunk five too many beers; he was wearing one of those metal caps with horns coming out of it. I was wonderfully ignorant about sports and had no idea the Viking was the symbol of a famous professional football team. Bobby and Michael thought it hilarious that I loved that t-shirt, wore it almost every day, and never had the slightest idea I was advertising the Minnesota Vikings.

Bobby and Michael also attempted to convince me I should bleach my hair blonde, but when I suggested this to my mom, she threatened to murder me. Calvin took the same view as my mom.

"You think I should bleach my hair?" I asked him.

"Only if you want everyone in town to know you are an idiot."

That summer, my neighborhood got super excited when a nice old couple that lived down the road from where Bobby lived got murdered.

I knew the old couple because sometimes they hired kids to do chores – mow their yard, help the old lady with her flower garden, that sort of thing. The story of their murder was on the front page of the paper. The killer cut their throats and left bloody footprints all over their house.

I heard my mom on the phone talking to a friend of hers. "Why can't the police catch him? Who will get killed next? All I'm saying is – LOCK YOUR DOORS!" My mom noted that the killer of Red Kavanaugh was still not caught. "Maybe it's the same killer!"

One of the neighbors, a mailman, came over to talk to my dad. He said he was thinking about moving. "What's gonna happen to our property values if this neighborhood turns into a violent crime zone?"

While the investigation was on-going, Bobby Hinson suggested we try to contact the spirits of the victims using a Ouija board. Bobby had received one of these boards for Christmas and he figured the double murder provided a perfect opportunity to put it to use. Bobby said it is possible ghosts are real. In fact, it's probable. Why would there be so many ghost stories if spirits are not real?

I wondered if he believed in vampires as well. Or leprechauns. There are lots of stories about them too.

Bobby said when people are murdered, their souls stay in the neighborhood. They linger. Why? Because, if they got murdered real quick — for example, if their necks got slashed — the dead do not realize they're dead. Their confused spirits linger here wondering what the heck just happened. Bobby said, if you read ghost stories, you learn (once they figure out they got killed) the spirits of murdered people want justice. They refuse to proceed to the afterworld until their killers are captured and made to pay.

"Think about it!" Bobby said. "The spirits of the old couple could still be here! We can contact them!"

"Right," I said. Calvin was with us, and I winked at him. We were in

Bobby's bedroom.

A Ouija board is covered with alphabet letters and numbers. The words YES and NO are prominently displayed at the top. To use the board to contact the dead, you put your fingertips on this little triangle thing with plastic legs. Bobby explained that the board works best if two people put their fingertips on the triangle. If a spirit is nearby, pretty soon the triangle will start to glide around the board. The spirit is moving it. That's when you can ask the triangle Yes and No questions. If you are respectful, the spirit will respond to your questions. But you have to be respectful. You have to believe. Spirits hate doubters. Sometimes the spirit will spell out whole sentences using the letters on the board.

"Let's do it," I said.

In Bobby's bedroom, Bobby and I knelt on the floor over the Ouija board. We put our fingertips on the triangle thing. Calvin stood above us with his arms folded. On his face was the expression he always had when he was forced to endure the stupidity of normal people.

I could not help myself. I made the little triangle go where I wanted.

Bobby said, "Spirit, are you there?"

I gently nudged the triangle to the word YES.

"Oh, my God!" Bobby said.

I made the triangle spell out M – E – R – D – R.

"Murder!" Bobby yelled. "It's him! It's the spirit of the old man!"

I made the triangle spell out A – V – N—G and M – E.

"Avenge me!" Bobby cried.

"Looks like our spirit isn't a good speller," I suggested. "Probably illiterate."

Calvin snorted.

"Spirit!" Bobby cried. "Who killed you? Tell us *how* to avenge you!"

I amused myself by making Bobby believe he was in touch with the dead old man until Calvin got fed up and pointed out he could see my eyes moving around as I searched for the letters of the words I wanted to spell.

"You're not funny," Bobby said. "You shouldn't make fun of people, especially friends."

"Right," I said.

The next day, the cops arrested the kid who murdered the old couple. He was a dorky 19-year-old that Bobby and I knew. The old couple had hired him a few times to mow their yard. He had heard a rumor that they had money hidden in their house. That was a popular rumor in our neighborhood. Supposedly, the old couple did not trust in banks because they had been in the Great Depression. They hid all their extra money in a suitcase somewhere in the house. A lot of money. Thousands! Cash money! The dorky kid believed in the existence of that suitcase. He could not stop thinking about it.

One afternoon, when it was hot and humid, he went to see the old couple. The old lady answered her door. The kid asked her for a drink, something cool. The old lady took pity on him. She invited him into her house and gave him a glass of lemonade. There was a knife lying on the corner beside the sink. When she had her back turned, he picked it up and used it to kill her. He found the old man in a different room of the house and killed him too. Blood was all over the place. He searched the house but never found a suitcase full of money. All he found was a coin collection.

The dorky kid called a taxi. The driver arrived at a house where he never normally went. A teenaged kid ran out of the house carrying a sack and jumped into the taxi. He gave the driver the address where he wanted to go. The driver wrote down the address in his ride book. When they got to that address, the kid opened the sack and started pulling out coins. He paid the fare using quarters and dimes. Old quarters and old dimes. The driver noticed the kid's tennis shoes had what looked like red paint on the toes.

When the story of the murder appeared in the paper, the taxi driver read it. Since it was on the front page, it was hard to miss. He called the police.

The cops went to the kid's house. He was in his bedroom, playing with his new coin collection. In his closet, the cops found the bloody tennis shoes.

The story of the arrest was all over the front page the next day. The paper even had a photo of the kid's shoes.

My friends and I talked about the crime and the capture of the killer. Bobby said, "I can't believe he killed them. Nice old people like that."

I said, "I can't believe how stupid he was. He could at least have hosed off his shoes."

Calvin said, "Murderers are not known for having high IQs."

That night, I couldn't fall asleep, so I got out my flashlight and wrote a story in my notebook while my brothers were sleeping in their bunkbeds. A ghost story.

A boy woke up in the middle of the night. He sat up in bed, feeling something was wrong. The curtains were open, and his room was full of moonlight. A spirit was standing by the window. "Mrs. Ryan?" the boy whispered. The spirit looked at him but did not seem to recognize the boy. She seemed confused. Did she even know she was dead? Maybe she died real quick, in a car accident, and did not even know she was no longer alive. She looked around the boy's bedroom as if she was trying to figure out where she was. And then the boy guessed what she was thinking. She was trying to figure out if she was in heaven.

Or hell.

The next day, I let Calvin read my story. He handed it back to me and said, "It's too short."

"You know what?" I said. "We ought to be able to figure out who killed Red Kavanaugh. And you know why? Because killers are stupid."

34

The Yellow Beetle

It was easy to find the grave of Mrs. Ryan because it was marked with the statue of an angel. The angel was the largest statue in the entire cemetery. The cemetery was in a fenced in area behind a church. To be buried there, you had to be Catholic. It was an old cemetery, so there weren't that many vacancies. Probably Big Bill made a pretty big donation to get his wife in there.

I put the book at the foot of the angel and just stood there for a minute feeling sad and lonesome.

"What do you think you're doing?" someone said.

I turned around and found a long-haired girl. And when I say long hair, I mean super long hair. It was so long it fell below her waist. She could probably sit on that hair. That's how long it was. Thick brown beautiful hair. Her eyes were beautiful too – large blue eyes.

"Nothing," I said. "Not doing nothing."

This sort of thing often happened to me if anyone confronted me. My ability to talk nearly disappeared. Instead of talking in sentences, I would talk in monosyllables, as if I had become a stupid person with a fifty-word vocabulary.

I knew who the girl was.

"That's my mother's grave."

"Right."

"What is that?" She pointed at the book I had placed at the foot of the statue.

"Don't know."

"Of course, you know. You put it there. I saw you."

"Right."

The book was *The Autobiography of Malcolm X*.

"You've been putting books on my mother's grave." She reached into this big purse she had with her and pulled out *The Source* by James Michener. She opened the cover of the book and read, "Property of Verle DeWitt."

"He's my dad."

"You *stole* this book from your father?"

"Michener is his favorite author."

She made me take the Michener, reached back into her purse, and pulled out *In Cold Blood* by Truman Capote. "This is a library book. You stole this book from the public library."

"Maybe."

"Did you steal that one too?" She pointed at *The Autobiography of Malcolm X*.

I had just stolen it that day from the mezzanine at Brown's Department Store.

"She liked to read," I said. "Your mom. She liked to read all the bestsellers."

"Can't you leave flowers — like a normal person?"

She made me take back the Truman Capote book, so now I was holding two books.

"Your mom and me, we were sort of like... friends."

"Pick up that other one. You can't leave it there."

I picked up *The Autobiography of Malcolm X* without dropping the other two books.

She was staring at me. "You're Baritone Boy!"

"Your mom called me that?!" I was shocked.

"My mother never said anything bad about anyone. She was a kind person. You did not know a thing about her if you think she ever called you that. I called you Baritone Boy because she talked about you all the time — incessantly — which was irritating."

I blushed, very pleased that Mrs. Ryan had often talked about me. "You're her daughter. You're Cathy Ryan."

"I am ordering you to take the Truman Capote book back to the library. What is wrong with you? It's bad — very bad — to steal books from a library."

I juggled the books. The Capote book appeared to be rain-damaged. "Right," I said. No way was I going to return it to the library.

I noticed she was wearing a flower in her hair and wondered if she had stolen it from the bouquet at the base of the statue. Every morning, more flowers arrived. Her dad must have a standing order with a florist to leave flowers at the grave every day. Maybe it was not really stealing in her case if her dad paid for the flowers.

"Do you need a ride home?"

"What?"

"I'm going home. I'm willing to give you a ride. Do you want one?"

I noticed she was now talking to me in that one way, as if I was a stupid boy who had to have everything spelled out for him. This often happened to me. I had an unusual brain, a good brain that often turned into a brain that hardly worked at all. When people realized they were talking to a person with a defective brain, that is how they talked to me.

I followed behind her to her car. It was not a brand-new Cadillac.

She saw me looking at her car, hesitating to climb into it. "You thought it was going to be a Caddy, didn't you? What sort of girl wants

254

to drive around in a Caddy? It would be ridiculous. Are you getting in, or are you just going to stand there?"

Her car was a bright yellow Volkswagen Beetle.

I got into the front seat. It was nothing like getting into her mother's Cadillac. Compared to the Cadillac, it hardly even seemed a real car. It seemed more like a toy. Even compared to my dad's car, it was small.

She pulled out into the street without looking. This other driver had to slam on his brakes to keep from hitting us. She asked me where I went to school. She said she was going to a new school in the fall. She didn't seem to care if I answered her questions. She said we were probably going to the same school in the fall, West High School.

"Aren't you going to St. Joe's?" St. Joseph's was where all the rich Catholic kids went.

She said she was finished with schools run by Catholic clergy. She said the nuns at her previous school, St. Mary's, made her retake the ninth grade.

This shocked me because she seemed intelligent.

She said the main issue was not stupidity but truancy. She did not like school, did not see the necessity of daily attendance. "If I can pass all the tests, why do I have to bother going to all the classes?"

"Right," I said.

She said, "The nuns blackballed me after I refused the eucharist. I was in a condition of unbelief, so how could I accept the eucharist?"

By then I had met a few nuns. When my mom got her teaching certificate, she signed up to be a substitute teacher. The school that called her the most was a Catholic School, Sacred Heart. One time she invited home a couple nuns. They were nice ladies and I could not imagine why they would blackball anyone.

She said the nuns told Father Tony she was trouble, so she had to go see Father Anthony with her father.

"Wow," I said. "Who's Father Anthony?"

"He's headmaster at St. Joe's."

I found it difficult to believe that any school would deny admission to the daughter of Big Bill Ryan no matter what she did.

Father Anthony said she could be admitted to St. Joe's even if she was in a condition of doubt, but she would have to agree to make the attempt to regain her faith.

"And did you?"

"Of course not. I told him, 'I renounce Jesus and all his pomps!'"

"You said that?!"

"Don't be gullible. I'm not a theatrical person. You shouldn't believe everything you hear. But it is enjoyable to freak out a priest. It's very pleasant. You should try it sometime."

I thought I would gladly freak out a priest if I knew one.

She asked me if I knew that Emily Dickinson was thrown out of her high school for refusing to profess her belief in Christ.

I told her at Poe Junior we did not study a lot of poetry.

"Perhaps if you studied poetry, you would not be so gullible."

I liked it that she used the word "perhaps" instead of the word "maybe." I noticed in the back seat of her car she had the new Beatles album, *Revolver*. I considered one song on this album, "Eleanor Rigby," to be a work of genius.

She saw me looking at the album and said, "I am in love with George Harrison. Madly in love with him. Go ahead; make fun of me. Everyone has a favorite Beatle. Mine is George, the soulful Beatle. I can see you are the John Lennon type. It's obvious."

She seemed able to read my mind. It was unnerving. In fact, John was my favorite Beatle.

"The sitar arrangements in that album, that's all George. Who else would think of putting a sitar on a pop record? No one except George because he's brilliant."

I did not know what a sitar was but decided not to reveal my ignorance.

She said on every Beatles album, George was permitted to include two songs, only two. She thought that was a shocking miscarriage of justice because George was every bit the songwriter that Lennon and McCartney were. "John Lennon and Paul McCartney are selfish and over-rated. They are glory hogs. George is more musically adventurous than they are. Spiritually, he is the most evolved Beatle. They resent that."

Her voice sounded like her mother's voice. I could close my eyes, and it was as if Mrs. Ryan was talking to me.

"Are you all right?" she said. "You had your eyes closed."

I told her I sometimes dreamed about her mother. "I dream I am in a blizzard, struggling with my baritone case, and then your mother appears in her white Cadillac like an angel and saves me."

"Baritone boy!" she yelled. And swerved right in front of a pickup truck. The driver honked at us.

She said she had dreams about her mother too. "My therapist says such dreams are common. If we miss them so badly we can't stand it, our dreams attempt to reduce our pain. We should be grateful to our dreams. We should thank them."

She dropped me off at my house. I felt embarrassed because my house was a low-end house in a low-end neighborhood. Her house was probably an enormous mansion, maybe even a palace surrounded by a moat.

I started to climb out of the car. She reached out and stopped me by touching my bare arm. "I do not normally talk this much. I am ordinarily a shy person."

I found this hard to believe.

"You must not imagine you are going to see me again."

"Right," I said.

"We're not friends. If I see you in high school, do not expect me to talk to you. We don't have a relationship of any kind, is that clear?

"Right," I said.

"I could never be friends with a person who steals books from a library."

"OK," I said. I had three books in my hands and one foot out of the car.

"Don't leave any more books at my mother's grave, especially ones stolen from the library. I want your word. It's just plain stupid."

"I promise I won't do it anymore."

"I appreciate your devotion to my mother. I really do, but there's no need to be ridiculous. Goodbye, Baritone Boy."

She drove away in the yellow Beetle.

The next day, I took the Truman Capote book back to the library and handed it to the librarian. She looked at its condition and frowned.

"It didn't get checked out," I said. I wanted to tell her I was not the person who had stolen this book. I wanted to tell her I had just found it on a park bench. Someone else must have stolen it. I was just bringing it back. I resisted this impulse to lie.

I apologized for the water damage. I told her it accidentally got wet. "I can pay for the damages."

"I hope you didn't drop it into a toilet," she said.

"I'll pay for the damages, if you want me to." I pulled a dollar out of my pocket. It was wrinkled, so I smoothed it out and laid it on the counter beside the Truman Capote book.

"This book cost more than a dollar," the librarian said.

I was terrified she was going to say I would no longer be allowed to check out books.

"Thank you for bringing it back," the librarian said. She pushed my dollar back to me.

35

Firebugs

I defended the honor of George Harrison to Ray and the Nazi. I said only someone as brilliant as George would think of putting a sitar on a Beatles song. I said they were probably ignorant and did not even know what a sitar was. "It's like a guitar, like a giant mandolin. It has like 18 strings. You have to be a genius to even play it. You know their new album *Revolver*? Those weird sounds on the song 'Tomorrow Never Knows'? That's all George. Or that song, 'Love You To.' George wrote that one too. John and Paul only let him put two songs on every album, but the George songs are always the far-out ones, the deep weird ones, know what I mean? He's so underappreciated."

Ray looked bored and said he preferred the early Beatles, the "Twist and Shout" Beatles.

I thought about attacking "Twist and Shout" because it is not even an original Beatles song; it's a mere cover. But the Beatles version of "Twist and Shout" is a work of genius. If you played it at a party, kids went nuts dancing. I considered it the greatest of the early Beatles songs, greater even than "I Want to Hold Your Hand."

I could see Ray had already lost interest in this topic, and the Nazi had not been paying any attention to me since I started talking.

Ray was looking at the Nazi, who had a squeeze bottle of rubbing alcohol in his hands.

The Nazi said we were going to do something spectacular with fire. We were in the motel basement.

The Nazi and Ray loved fire. I did not hate fire, but I was afraid of it. The frightening quality of fire simply added to its thrilling beauty so far as the Nazi and Ray were concerned. Fire seems alive. It is almost a living thing like wind, but it is also bright. It twists and blazes, and it can grow. It can spread. In less than a minute, a tiny flame can become a roaring inferno and burn down your entire house.

The Nazi had been on a binge of fire-making. "Step back!" he said. When the Nazi was in the mood for fire, he was scary – like a wizard in a fairytale. He got this wild look in his eyes.

The Nazi upended the bottle and dumped out most of the rubbing alcohol. It formed a large puddle on the cement floor of the basement. He pulled out a cigarette lighter and ignited the alcohol still left in the squeeze bottle. He squeezed the bottle, turning it into a flamethrower.

All this looked super dangerous to me. "Be careful," I said.

"Watch this!" The Nazi bent over and squeezed the bottle. Flames spurted out and hit the spreading pool of alcohol on the floor. Just like that, blue flames danced over the surface of the pool.

"Jesus Christ," Ray said.

I retreated two more steps and located the exits in case I had to run for my life.

The pool of alcohol was now a lake of fire.

In a minute, the fire consumed every drop of the rubbing alcohol and went out. There wasn't even a smudge on the cement floor.

Ray said, "Your old man is going to be pissed if he finds out you wasted that whole bottle of rubbing alcohol."

"Time for a Zorch!" the Nazi said.

"A what?" I said.

"Wait till you see this," Ray said.

To make a Zorch, the Nazi needed a plastic bag, a cigarette lighter, and a bowl of water. To create the Zorch Experience, he also needed a room in a basement, a room with no windows. The Nazi tied the plastic bag into knots, so it resembled a string of pearls. Then he tied the string of knots to a pipe in the ceiling, so it hung down. He maneuvered the bowl of water underneath the Zorch. He used his lighter to ignite the end of the chain of knots. Once the Zorch caught fire, he didn't have to do anything else except yell to Ray to turn off the lights.

The sudden darkness fixated our attention on the burning chain of plastic. A weird blue flame began to crawl up the chain until it engulfed the first knot. Molten plastic began to fall through the air. It made a sound. *Zorch! Zorch!* Pretty soon, the thing produced a steady stream of flaming droplets.

Zorch! Zorch! Zorch!

When the last flaming remains of the Zorch fell into the bowl of water, the Nazi wanted to make another one, but Ray said he was bored with Zorches. He did not have a long attention span. "See you losers later," he said.

That night after it got dark, the Nazi invented the Fountain of Fire.

Mr. Broom did a lot of things by himself. He had grown up on a farm. One of the things he did for himself was change the oil in his car. He crawled under the car and removed a bolt or a plug or something. He put a metal dishpan under the car and got out of the way. Pretty soon, dirty oil began to drip down into the dishpan. When he finished, Mr. Broom had a dishpan full of oil. He put the bolt or plug or whatever it was back where it belonged and poured cans of clean oil into his car.

When it got dark that night, the Nazi pointed out that we had a dishpan full of oil.

Ray had not returned. It was just me and him and a little neighbor kid named Jeff. The kid lived not far from the motel. Like the Nazi, he was an only child. Jeff was usually accompanied by his dog, a mutt. The dog had a tendency to bark for no reason, and when that happened, the Nazi ordered the kid to remove the dog before he killed it. I am fairly sure the Nazi was never going to kill the kid's dog, but Jeff got worried enough to take his dog home and chain him to a doghouse.

The Nazi had trouble trying to light the oil in the dishpan. It would not catch fire. He tried to get it going with the lighter. That didn't work. He tried throwing matches into the oil. When he threw in paper matches, they would hit the oil and go out. He tried wooden matches. Same thing happened.

I noticed the kid Jeff was back, but he was staying at the edge of the motel property, just watching us.

I thought the Nazi was going to have to give up on getting any excitement out of the crankcase oil, when he had a flash of genius. "A wick!"

"Right," I said, not really understanding.

The Nazi got a rag and dipped it into the oil. When the rag soaked up some oil, he let it loll over the edge of the pan. One end of the rag was still sopping up more oil. "This is gonna be beautiful!"

I stepped back.

The Nazi used his lighter to ignite the end of the rag. It caught right away. Flame moved rapidly up the wick and lit the oil in the pan.

"OK," I said. I retreated another step.

We gazed at the oil in the pan for a minute. All it did was burn in an unspectacular fashion. It was like looking at the flames of a burner on a gas stove.

"Zorches are way better," I said.

The Nazi looked around the yard. We were behind the motel. The dishpan of flaming oil was sitting on the ground. A garden hose was coiled up, hanging on a hook on the back of the motel. The Nazi looked at it for a while.

When it came to fire, the Nazi's mind never stopped working. He uncoiled the hose and turned on the water. Water spurted out the end of the hose. He amused himself by squirting me with water.

"Hey!"

I thought he was going to use the water to put out the little fire in the pan, but the Nazi had a better idea. He made the water shoot straight up into the air. He held his thumb partially over the end of the hose, so the water squirted out with considerable force. The stream of water shot up into the air and fell back down. "Will you look at that?" The Nazi jerked his wrist, so water splashed down close to me.

I yelled, "Hey!"

The Nazi took his thumb off the end of the hose. Now the water came out in a civilized way. He turned to face the oil pan.

"What're you thinking?" I said.

The Nazi made the water squirt straight up and fall back down. He began to jerk his hand, so the water dropped closer and closer to the fire in the pan. The water fell in sheets.

When the water finally hit the burning oil, a miracle happened.

A Tower of Flame rose out of the pan. It was like a genie emerging from a bottle. Twenty feet, thirty feet into the darkness, a Tower of Flame higher than the motel!

And then it was gone, as if it had never existed.

"I'm gonna tell!" the little kid Jeff said and took off.

The Nazi did it again. He made the water shoot up into the air and fall back down until a sheet of H2O fell directly into the bowl of flames.

Once again, the Tower of Flame rose into the night sky, tall and proud, a cobra made of flames. An evil spirit straight from Hell. And then it was gone.

The Nazi made the Tower of Flame appear and disappear again and again. We probably would have used up all the dirty oil in the dishpan except that we heard his dad stomping down the back steps inside the motel.

It turned out the little kid had told his dad we were burning down the motel. His dad ran out and saw it, our Tower of Flame! He ran back into his house and called the motel.

By the time Mr. Broom came out of the backdoor of the motel to see what the trouble was, the hose was lying harmlessly in the grass, and the fire in the dishpan was only an inch high.

"What you kids doing back here?"

The Nazi and I acted innocent. "It's nothing, Dad. It's just this little bitty fire. It's harmless."

Mr. Broom made us smother the fire in the pan. He carried the oil away and disposed of it before we could get into any more trouble with it.

The Nazi got revenge on the kid the next day. He burned down his doghouse.

36

It's Only Rock and Roll

What if they did it?

Ray and the Nazi. Fire.

I had always imagined the Grimm sisters did it. Big did it and probably Middle too. Big fell hard for Tommy, and Tommy spurned her. Big flattened the tires on Tommy's dad's car. Then she set the clothes on Mrs. White's clothesline on fire. Because thwarted love is a 200-mph wind that flattens everything in its path. And then she burned down Tommy's house. Probably Middle helped her.

There had always been problems with that theory because Mrs. Grimm and her girls were out of town the night the fire occurred.

Ray and the Nazi were not out of town.

Another thing. That same summer, the summer of the fire, the motel got robbed. When the welcome desk in the lobby was being manned by Mrs. Broom, a black man with a gun came in and told her to lie down on the floor while he robbed the register. Mrs. Broom, a big lady, did as instructed, laid full-length on the floor, praying to Jesus that the guy would not kill her. The black guy scooped up the money in the register – not that much – and ran out of the motel. Mrs. Broom had trouble getting back on her feet, so she yelled for help. Mr. Broom was nearby. He came running and was shocked to find his wife on her hands and knees on the floor. She told him she had just been robbed by a black guy. Mr. Broom got so upset, he forgot to help his wife to her feet and instead ran out into the parking lot. Who knows what was in his mind? Did he think he might be able to run down the black guy, tackle him? In any case, the black guy was long gone.

The Nazi told me he hated black people as a result. I told him don't be stupid. He said he hated it when I got on my moral high horse and acted superior to everyone else. I said it's stupid to hate people just because of the color of their skin. He said I too would hate blacks if my mom got robbed by one. He teared up telling me this. I let him wipe the moisture out of his eyes and then said, "So, if it was a white guy who robbed your mom, would you hate all white people?"

He told me not to be stupid.

So, there was that. Plus, the Nazi was a talented firebug.

Ray was different. He just liked to raise hell. If the Nazi took it into his head to burn down the house of the only black family in our neighborhood, Ray would gladly carry the can of gasoline just for the sheer joy of it.

Maybe in the middle of the night, when Mr. and Mrs. Broom were asleep, the Nazi and Ray left the motel carrying cans of gasoline, made their way to the Marsh, to the street containing the Whites' house. Ray's family also lived on that street. Ray had plenty of friends on that street. One of them might have told Ray that the Whites' house was going to be empty.

Maybe Ray and the Nazi broke a window, let themselves in, entered the dark house, kicked over chairs and tables, splashed gasoline all over the place, probably laughing, feeling some kind of giddy wicked depraved hilarious feeling, stood in the open door, looking back into the house, smelling the gasoline, and flung a match, probably a wooden match, saw the gas ignite, saw fire explode every which way, and ran all the way back to the motel, sometimes halting to turn around and look back and see it: the glow, the flames rising up into the dark night.

I told my friend Michael my theory and he said, "What I can't figure out, why do you hang out with those jerks?"

"But what do you think? Maybe they did it! Don't you think it's possible?"

"What about the murder of Red Kavanaugh?"

I squirmed. I had forgotten to think about that aspect of the story.

Michael said, "Some people think it was Red who burned down their house."

"Why would he?"

"Because he had a thing for Tommy White's mom."

"That's ridiculous."

"What I heard, Red Kavanaugh was always chasing women. And his son's just like him."

"Red and Tommy's mom? That's just plain nuts!"

"It's something people say. They say Red made a pass at her. And then, Tommy's dad supposedly went over to Red's house when he found out and had a talk with Red, right in front of Naomi. A week later, the Whites' house gets burned down."

"You never met Tommy's mom, or you wouldn't even think that." Tommy's mom was a tall, smart, sensible, no-nonsense sort of woman. His dad was the same sort of human being, but the male version. If Red Kavanaugh was ever rude to Mrs. White, she wouldn't need her husband to protect her.

Michael said, "The police have probably explored all these rumors twelve times. If they haven't figured it out, you're never going to solve this case either."

I pouted.

"Did I hurt your feelings? You think you're a boy detective, don't you?"

"Shut up."

"Jack DeWitt, also known as Sherlock Holmes!"

One Saturday evening in late August, Ray and his rock band put on a show in the backyard of the motel. The Nazi helped the band get their amplifiers and microphones set up. Ray told him he would make an excellent roadie. All you had to do was tell the Nazi something like that, and he would work like the devil to help.

Mr. and Mrs. Broom were absent that evening, attending a Chamber of Commerce Dinner followed by a dance. Ray and the Nazi were supposed to run the motel. Instead, they turned on the No Vacancy sign and started setting up the equipment behind the motel. The little kid Jeff whose doghouse got burned down had forgiven the Nazi, so he was running around helping. Rock and Roll was like that. A Holy Cause. Teenagers were eager to assist that Big Beat in any way possible. Even little kids.

The band was no longer called The What? They had a new guitarist. He said he would not join a band with a name that sounded so obviously similar to The Who, one of the most famous bands in the world. They were now The Brain Damage.

Brain Damage consisted of a drummer (Ray), a bass player, the guitarist, and the singer. The singer was a rich kid whose parents financed his rock and roll obsession and paid for all the equipment. The singer felt he sounded like Alex Chilton, the singer of the Box Tops. He had that soulful, sex machine thing going on in his voice. At least he hoped he did.

Brain Damage spent an hour figuring out their playlist. You would not think it would take them that long because they could only play five songs. The chore that took all the time was the order in which they were going to play them.

Brain Damage would open the show with the garage band classic "Louie Louie." That song would get the crowd in the mood. Then they would launch into "Land of a Thousand Dances" by Wilson Pickett. That number would create pandemonium. Then they would unleash their killer version of "Kicks" by Paul Revere and the Raiders, followed by "Wild Thing, You Make My Heart Sing" by the Troggs. And then something special, something mind-blowingly awesome, an original song composed by the singer called "Dance Till You Puke, Baby." "Puke" was going to be the climax of the show. It contained a guitar solo AND a drum solo. If by popular demand they had to play an encore, they would play "Land of a Thousand Dances" again, an elongated, psychedelic version that took 12 minutes and was guaranteed to make every kid within a radius of a mile dance until he collapsed.

Kids started arriving by 7 PM when the band was still arguing about the playlist, a dozen kids. More kids arrived during the soundcheck.

Rock and Roll! In our neighborhood! Tonight!

Brain Damage was going to play loud. The hell with the neighbors. "We're gonna make your ears bleed, baby!"

By the time the guitar and the bass player played the opening chords of "Louie Louie," a hundred kids were packed together in front of the band.

I don't know any way to recreate the power that rock and roll had that evening. Primitive wonderful rock and roll! It was good for what ailed us. It made our toes tap. It made us shake our booties. It made us feel glad all over.

Someone called the cops. Probably the neighbors. Adults feared rock and roll. It was too powerful, too loud, too anarchic, too beautiful. It hurt your ears!

Brain Damage never did get to play "Dance Till You Puke."

Before the cops arrived, before the crowd dispersed, I noticed Big Grimm was there, standing beside her boyfriend Micky, the one who had joined the Marines. He had enlisted but for some reason he was home, people said for good. Was it possible to drop out of the Marines the way you could drop out of high school? He looked sort of lost, still had short hair. Big Grimm was ignoring him. She was swaying to the beat and looking at Ray as if he was a teenaged god.

Despite his service to our country in Vietnam, Micky went home alone that night. Big Grimm spent the night in one of the spare motel rooms with Ray.

In one more week, I was going to start high school, and I could hardly wait. Because everything was going to change. You better believe it. West High was going to be so much better than Poe Junior. A million times better! Probably my skin would clear up. Probably my eyes would heal themselves. I wouldn't even need my glasses, and I wouldn't have to walk around in a fog. Not anymore. Probably cool girls, rich girls like Cathy Ryan, would start talking to me, asking me my opinions about books and rock and roll records. The world was changing. Probably the doctors and scientists were going to cure cancer. I wouldn't have to worry about my mom anymore. Not to mention Motown. Not to mention The Beatles. Music was going to change everything and everybody, even old people. Martin Luther King Jr. was going to cure the United States of America of racism. He would probably figure out how to end the war in Vietnam too. And if he didn't end the war, the college kids would, the protestors would. The government would end the draft. Kids my age would not have to worry about getting sent to Vietnam. We wouldn't have to kill anyone. Peace would descend like rain. World Peace was just around the corner. Why not? And I would learn how to drive a car. I would get an after-school job. People were going to start respecting me. And you know what? I would figure out who set the Whites' house on fire. I would expose that person. Who killed Red? I was going to find that out too. Because I was smart, not stupid! Oh, yeah! Dance till you puke, baby!